LEISA EBERE

Crows and Angels

novum pro

www.novum-publishing.co.uk

All rights of distribution, including via film, radio, and television, photomechanical reproduction, audio storage media, electronic data storage media, and the reprinting of portions of text, are reserved

Printed in the European Union on environmentally friendly, chlorine- and acid-free paper.

© 2016 novum publishing

ISBN 978-3-99048-502-6
Editing: Nicola Ratcliff, BA
Cover photos: Anagram1, Konradbak | Dreamstime.com
Cover design, layout & typesetting: novum publishing

www.novum-publishing.co.uk

Chapter 1

Hannah sat on the hill overlooking the meadow and her family's farm and contemplated the turn of events that had happened in the last few days. She breathed in the fresh spring air, taking in the lush green grass, yellow daisies, and blue sky of her beloved home and wondered how she could ever bear to leave such a place. At the tender age of 14, she understood her father had dreams he wished to fulfil; yet she was frightened, as she had heard stories of bloodthirsty savages and dangerous sea journeys from her papa and brother that had thoroughly put her off of any idea of adventuring.

The birds sang merrily overhead and the sun still shone brightly in the Norwegian sky; but nevertheless, Hannah's life had changed forever; when her papa had arrived home from town a few days ago, and announced to his family, in no uncertain terms "I have decided we are moving to the Americas." He then proceeded to show a newspaper clipping to his wife, which read *"Farmer adventurers required for the Dakota Territory, 100 acre land tracts allocated to settlers."*

Hannah's family had just sat down to their evening meal around the kitchen table, when the news had broken. The kitchen was normally a cheerful place, the floors tidy and swept and bright curtains on the windows. Her mama always made sure the broom was placed behind the kitchen door, as she said: "It was bad luck to keep it anywhere else." Yet Hannah always thought the practice was a silly one, because everyone always knocked it over, coming through the door anyway. But today, the usually cheerful family kitchen was filled with tension, as the Nelson family members tried to digest the news of immigration, in their own way.

Anya, Hannah's mama, who was a small frail woman with silver blonde hair and refined features, appeared the most shocked at the news, and said nothing at first; but then tears welled up in her eyes, and she lowered her head in her hands in dismay, weeping quietly. After a few moments, she lifted her head saying, "No Eric, you can't do this to us, this is our home." Peter, Hannah's brother, a big brawny 16 year old youth, with a shock of yellow hair and the beginnings of a beard showing on his face, in contrast, leapt to his feet, smiling broadly, and shook his father's hand saying: "Papa that is grand, I can't believe we are going to the Americas" and whooped in glee, clapping his hands in excitement. Hannah's two younger brothers, Otto and Lars, ages 3 and 5, both appeared baffled, at the sight of their mama crying and brother whooping; and started crying themselves; sensing unrest and tension in the family. Hannah, an auburn haired, petite girl with a razor sharp wit and intelligent green eyes, took in the scene, in dismay. She could not be called a beauty, yet she had a distinctive look that made her stand out from a crowd, and was a natural born leader. She quickly assessed the situation and went across to try to calm Anya and placed her small hand in the hand of her mama's; and looked with condemning eyes at her papa, for in her mind, he had caused this mess.

Anya looked at her daughter with her lip trembling, and shook her head helplessly, not daring to challenge her husband directly; because she knew he would not tolerate disobedience from his wife. In fact, in the past, Eric had manhandled her to prove his point; and Anya did not want to spark his temper off, in front of the children. Hannah had never seen the physical abuse her papa had rained down on her mama, yet she had heard it happening whilst lying in the farmhouse loft as a small child. During these times she had stayed in her bed, terrified. She remembered being curled up in a ball, under the blankets, with her hands over her ears, trying to block out her mama's screams. Hannah had also seen bruises on her mama's back and legs, from time to time, when they had bathed, as the only females in the house. But, oddly there were never any bruises on her mama's beautiful face. Hannah guessed, as she got older, her papa didn't want the outside world to know what he had done. Hannah's brother, Peter seemed oblivious to what had been transpiring between their parents though, as he slept heavily through the night and had never mentioned it, which seemed very strange to Hannah indeed.

Gathering her thoughts, Hannah stood up from her perch on the hillside and dusted the grass off her skirt and headed off down the narrow path to the thatched cottage she had grown up in. She had promised herself that she would be brave for her mama's sake; but almost lost her resolve when she approached the farmhouse door and heard loud weeping coming from inside. She squared her shoulders and turned the knob, finding her mama weeping with her head resting on her folded arms at the kitchen table. Her two younger brothers were sitting at her feet, also crying and looked very tired and hungry. Hannah rushed to pick up the youngest child, Otto; holding him close, to comfort him. She then spoke softly to her mama and stroked her arm, treating her like a small child, which seemed to appease her. Hannah had seen her mama in depressed moods before, but it seemed she had been on the edge for days, and she knew this would never do. Determined to encourage her mama, she said matter of factly: "Mama you can fuss and cry all you want to; but you know Papa always gets his way, so we must somehow reconcile ourselves that we are going to the Americas, do you understand? Whether we like it or not, we are going to that place; do you hear me Mama? But don't worry, I promise I will help you every step of the way, and we will come through alright, I just know it in my heart." Several minutes passed and nothing further was said. Then Anya shook herself, as if a light switched on in her head, and sat up straight in her chair, looking blankly at Hannah and said: "Och, I must make your papa's supper, you know he does not take kindly to having to wait for his meal; Hannah I need you to go quickly and get coal from the shed outside please?" And then, as if nothing was wrong, she wiped her nose with a handkerchief, from her apron and rose to start cooking, without giving her two sons, or even Hannah, a second glance.

Hannah was well used to her mama's changing moods, and continued to sit at the table, while the two young boys sidled up to her, seeking comfort. She sighed; admitting to herself her mama had never been strong; and grimly thought to herself, that once again, she would have to act as surrogate mother to her brothers. But not just yet, for she was determined to tell Anya of what she had been shown whilst sitting on the hilltop, just a few moments earlier, and shook her head sharply, saying: "Mama, listen, Papa can wait a minute. I need to tell you about the vision I had on the hilltop today… please, hear me out." Anya stopped and turned, supporting herself with her arms on the table, and tiredly sat back down. As Hannah's mama, she was in great awe of her daughter's gifting, because she knew that everything that Hannah had ever seen in these visions; generally had significance or had indeed come to pass, in times past. Anya waited patiently; not speaking a word, and Hannah seized on her opportunity and began, saying: "I saw Papa standing like a giant in a flowing yellow field and all around him for miles and miles, all you could see were people that were dressed in leather looking clothes and feathers. I guess they were Indians," she added, "but they were friendly and smiling and we were there too, and all of us were so happy, Mama. I think my gifting is trying to show us in this vision, that we will be fine," she explained, "and that even though everything will be very different, we will be happy, can't you see?" Finally, out of breath, Hannah waited for her mama's response and hoped that somehow her vision had comforted her.

A look of resignation passed across her mama's lovely face, and she closed her eyes tightly for a moment, sitting quietly, and at last, said: "Och, then let God's will be done, my daughter, and may he have mercy on us all; and now my child, will you please go and get the coal?" Hannah half smiled and hurriedly put on her apron and scurried out to the shed for coal. Hannah didn't find much though, because she had noticed, that although her papa didn't like to admit it, the farm she loved so much, had been failing for some time. This decline of the farm had come about due to several years of poor and diseased potato crops, which had wreaked havoc upon the potato farmers, across Norway during the last few lean years. As a result, Hannah remembered that her own family, like many others, had barely etched out a living with the few farm animals and the vegetable garden they cared for. She found what coal she could, however; and returned to help her mama prepare the family meal, because there was scarcely an hour before the men returned from the fields.

Chapter 2

Even though his family had fallen on hard times, Eric Nelson was an ambitious man and determined to be rich, despite the fact it would be especially hard on his fragile wife. The rest of his brood were strong however, and he knew they would prosper in the new life he had planned for them. He also rationalised that, although Anya relied greatly on her own mother, who lived in a nearby village, she would have Hannah to help her. So, in his eyes, like it or not; his wife would have to adapt.

Anya had been plagued with dark moods throughout their marriage, and he grew weary of continually comforting and reassuring her, like she was a small child. He had sought the comfort of a strong drink and other women for solace, in the past, which he felt guilty about; but he felt most guilty about the drunken beatings he had given his wife, when the children were younger. He could scarcely remember them, because the drink had firmly taken hold on those occasions. In those days, he had returned home many a night, drunk from the town inn; and found Anya there with her sad face and he had just lost it with her; because he felt less of a man for failing to make her happy. Through the years, Eric had experienced flashbacks of the violence he had meted out to his wife; and had seen the evidence of the bruising he had inflicted on her body, and was repulsed by it. Yet, callously, he considered himself to be a good provider and father and he would push these thoughts to the back of his mind, feeling there was very little he could do, to change his wife's temperament or indeed the past.

Eric was aware his wife was frightened of him, and in his mind, he thought that maybe this was not such a bad thing. He loved her in his own way, but he admitted that he would never understand her. When Eric had first laid eyes on Anya, working as a seamstress's assistant in the nearby village over 17 years ago, her beauty had dazzled him, with her porcelain skin and pale blonde hair. He knew then and there that he had to possess her, as his wife. At the time, Anya's mother had warned him, when he announced his intentions to her; that her daughter was not strong. She had explained that Anya had lost her father in a terrible accident, saying: "He fell off a cliff and Anya witnessed the tragedy as a child, and she's never been right since."

Yet, Eric had arrogantly declared at the time: "I will make her happy and things will change once she is my wife." But things had not changed and Anya seemed even more mentally impaired since birthing Eric's two youngest sons. But believing in making the best of things, Eric had gritted his teeth when he told his family of his intention to move them to the Americas; and refused to be swayed by the emotional upheaval it caused in his household or indeed the mental state of his wife.

Eric was determined to make his mark in the world and wanted desperately to make a better life for his offspring. He stood in the rocky field of his farm, surveying his current property and decided he had struck a good deal with his cousin, Albert, for the sale of his farm. He finished feeding the donkey and sheep in the barn and mentally started preparing a list of the supplies he would need for the long journey on the ship to the Americas. In fact, he decided he would leave in two days' time to book passage on the next available ship to the new world, for Eric planned to have his family travelling within the month. He had done his homework and knew he needed to leave whilst the weather was still favourable or the seas could be more treacherous the longer they waited to make the journey; and so haste was needed to get to their destination safely and he was aching to begin a new life.

Eric had also decided that he must remove his daughter from the area, as soon as possible; because her gifting of second sight and healing was becoming a burden, for the entire family. More and more people showed up every day at the farmhouse; for her prayers of healing and visions of the future and he felt he could not protect his daughter anymore. Sometimes these people brought food or a piece of cloth to trade for her words or deeds; but Eric was very worried and felt it was getting out of hand and that he had to intervene or they would never have a normal life. He knew his daughter had a great gifting and was destined to help many, because she had proven herself again and again; but Hannah was only 14 years old and in his mind needed a chance for a normal life.

When Eric first read the advertisement about the fertile 160 acre land tracts available to settlers in the Dakota Territory, he thought perhaps he'd misunderstood the ad. Yet, when he had written to the shipping agent assigned to locate potential settlers for the offer, he was delighted to find it was a genuine offer. The agent had written back saying that the only stipulations were: *"that the settlers had to reach Fort Webster at their own expense and that they would be required to build a cabin and make improvements to the land, for a minimum of ten years; and that once those conditions were met, then the land would be deeded over to that settler."* Eric knew instinctively that this was an opportunity of a lifetime, and that he could not afford to miss out on it, no matter what the cost.

He walked through the door of his farmhouse one evening, and inhaled the succulent cooking smells of fresh Lefse, the soft potato flatbread he loved so much, and vegetable stew. Eric wondered if any meat had been found to put into the stew that night, for he was sick to the back teeth with the lack of meat in their meagre diets, due to their impoverished circumstances. Eric was a broad-shouldered, fair haired man, who had aged well, aside from his thinning hair and protruding belly acquired from his previous drinking binges in years past. But his usual expression was always solemn, which made it hard to read his thoughts at the best of times; and made him appear older, than his 35 years. He looked across to see his wife stirring the stew, over the hearth, in the big cast iron pot and asked brusquely, "Is supper ready wife?" She looked at him with a meek expression and responded, "Yes, husband, sit down and I will serve you." From her pained expression, Eric knew she was still very unhappy about his decision to immigrate; but he hardened his heart and stuck to his resolve, ignoring her. She placed the meal before him and he waited for her to sit down. In the Nelson household, the rest of the family did not start eating until their father took his first bite. Normally, they would have all bowed their heads to bless the food prior to eating it, but lately even that formality had gone by the wayside.

As Anya sat down with her family across from her husband, Hannah looked at her mama, and willed her not to say anything. She took in her mama's pouting lips and childlike expression, (and was) worried that Anya was on the brink of a nervous collapse. Yet, Hannah kept quiet, not wishing to make matters worse.

Eric broke the silence, looking directly at his wife, almost daring her to challenge him and said: "I leave the day after tomorrow to go to Oslo to book our passage to the Americas, have you anything to say for yourself?" Anya lifted her chin, and straightened her shoulders, as if to rally her strength, and all of the Nelson children held their breath, when she spoke and said, "As you know, I am not happy with this decision; but since you are the head of the household, I have very little choice husband, but to go along with this scheme. Och, let God's will be done," she added dejectedly. In a sigh of relief, all of the Nelson clan exhaled almost simultaneously and started eating their meals. Even the youngest child, Otto, usually a chatty child, remained quiet as he ate, sensing the thick atmosphere in the room. But, five year old Lars, who was surprisingly unaffected by the happenings of late and generally was always full of ridiculous questions, piped up and asked: "So Papa will there be any mean fish to swallow us up, when we ride in the big ship to the Americas? "Cos' Peter said there might be and that scares me." Eric looked sternly at his eldest son and said: "Have you been scaring your brothers again with your wild stories?" I will not have more upset in this house, do you hear me, Son?" Peter, looked across at Lars with a vengeful expression on his face, then changed his expression to an innocent one, when he met his father's gaze and responded, "No Pa, the little twerp has twisted what I said, why would I do that?"

Eric shook his finger at Peter saying: "Boy, I know you tease your little brothers to no good end, and this will have to stop; because I will need a man not a boy in the days ahead, do you understand?" Not meek by nature, Peter reluctantly held his tongue and nodded his head dutifully, letting the matter drop, whilst the family finished their supper. After the family had eaten their meal, they each started their bedtime activities for the night, without further comment on the uncertain events that were about to unfold. But the new life that lay at their doorstep weighed heavily on all of their minds. Shouting bouts from their papa and crying episodes from their mama was actually all the Nelson offspring had ever known, so in that sense, nothing much had changed; but each of the children feared for their mama greatly, and wondered if she would be strong enough to make the trip.

Chapter 3

Hannah's gifting of second sight had been discovered at the age of six years old, when she had dreamed of a rock slide and people being hurt in a nearby village, called Frogner, where her oma, Marguerite, lived, which was not very far from the Nelson farm. Hannah had told her vision to her oma a few days later, adding that in her dream, it happened on a Saturday and Marguerite in turn, had told the parish priest. Leaving nothing to chance, he warned his parishioners far and wide, about the dream, cautioning them to join him in the church on the approaching Saturday or risk their lives at their own peril.

Norwegians by nature, are a superstitious lot and so the people of Frogner flocked to the church, on the predicted and fateful day. Early in the morning, a fierce thunderstorm ensued with heavy rainfall, thunder and lightning. A lightning bolt then struck a rocky cliff face with a huge cracking noise, high above the village and in a matter of minutes, an avalanche of dirt and rock began dangerously hurling down, towards the sleepy village; leaving houses and streets covered with tons of dirt and debris, when the dust finally settled. Miraculously, the avalanche halted literally at the doors of the church, and all of the souls of Frogner were saved that day, except one elderly gentleman, who refused to believe the child's dream and had his untimely death.

This single event had catapulted Hannah to a new exalted standing within that part of Norway from that point onwards, as news spread of the remarkable little girl and her supernatural powers. Ongoing streams of people had in fact, come to the farm cottage in the last eight years, asking for her blessing, advice, healings, and visions, to help them overcome their day to day problems and to give them hope for the future. Healing powers had also been a significant part of Hannah's gifting, and one small child believed to be blind, had miraculously even had his sight restored. In fact, multitudes of people with broken limbs had been healed they claimed, as a result of her touch. Hannah always attributed these miracles to God, and stayed humble; and seemed in awe herself when these amazing things took place. She did notice though that her hands would become very hot, when she touched people that needed healing, which puzzled her greatly.

Hannah had a sincere and friendly face, and thick auburn braids; and her innocence and reverence captivated people in search of help. When she became older, her mercy and compassion became a constant trait that endeared her to all that came in contact with her. There were many times, when she would even escort her oma, Marguerite, to pray for the sick at neighbouring farms and nearby villages. Marguerite knew how drained and exhausted Hannah became after these sessions, and wondered, many times, if the responsibility was too much for her. But she would see the determined gleam in her granddaughter's eyes and would hold her tongue, not daring to tempt fate and deprive someone of a blessing.

Several days after Hannah and her family had been bluntly informed they were sailing to America, Marguerite came to the farmhouse to visit her daughter and grandchildren and Anya tearfully broke the news to her mother. The old woman was shocked at the news, but was traditional to the core and believed her daughter had a duty to obey her husband in all things. Her motherly heart knew well of her own daughter's weaknesses and she feared for her future; but having suffered both happiness and tragedy in her own life, she knew that with the right mindset, Anya could survive. Marguerite was determined to put on a happy face and encourage her daughter and her grandchildren; in spite of the deep sadness she felt, at the thought of parting from them. She would grieve on her own later, she thought; because she knew in her heart that once they left Norway, she would never see them again.

Time moved on very quickly, and it had been nearly two weeks since the news of the Nelson's impending departure to the new world. One day, Hannah visited her Oma's cottage and Marguerite, being happy to see the young girl, welcomed her by giving her a kiss on both cheeks and seated her at her small wooden kitchen table, and gave her a cup of milky tea. Once Hannah had finished her drink, Marguerite gently said: "My dear child, there is something I wish to give you, to help you remember me and your homeland, Norway." She then went into her small bedroom and brought out a beautiful multi-coloured quilt, with Norwegian people, foods, and events stitched into the fabric, in a beautiful handcrafted creation. Tears sprang to Hannah's eyes as she hugged her oma, and in a moment of weakness she said "I don't want to leave you, Oma, will you be alright?" Marguerite patted her on the hand and said, "Child, child, don't take on so, my life will be coming to an end one day, but yours is just beginning, with new adventures and beautiful sights for you to see; and you will continue to be a force for good, wherever you go, please remember that." "Now dry your tears and stay strong and remember, you must help your mama, as she is not as courageous as you are," she added.

Hannah took the handkerchief Marguerite offered her, dried her tears and blew her nose, looking closely at the dear face of her oma. The lovely green eyes, jolly expression, and slim physique reflected a woman much younger than her actual years. Hannah had seen her struggle at times with rheumatism in her joints and she seemed to tire more easily these days. After a time, Hannah realised she had been quiet far too long. She then shook off her concerns, smiled up at the beloved face of her Oma, and said "I will keep this beautiful quilt always, Oma, and thank you for your thoughtfulness and for believing in me, it means a lot." "Remember my child, your gift is something you must always use with wisdom and compassion, and remember to write to me and tell me about your travels, because I will always be here praying for you," Marguerite said solemnly. Then playfully she said to Hannah: "Now scoot, your mama will need you to help with supper." "I will bring the quilt over to your cottage before you leave, to give you a proper goodbye," she added encouragingly. Hannah kissed her oma goodbye and then left the little cottage never knowing the wrenching pain Marguerite felt at her leaving, for she had hidden it well.

Chapter 4

After Eric returned from Oslo, he walked into the farmhouse that evening and removed from his inside vest pocket, an envelope with six ship passage tickets, which would enable his family to travel to the new world. Smugly, he informed his family that the sale of the farm and its livestock had not only bought the family's ship passages; but also, there was enough for supplies, accommodation and transport to the Dakota Territory, once they arrived in New York City, which was their first destination, prior to travelling cross country by wagon train to Fort Webster. The boys all cheered, dancing around the small kitchen, whilst Hannah placed her arm around her mama's shoulders for support. Anya however, seemed calm and resigned to the news, and asked her husband simply: "So when do we leave for this strange new world, Eric?" Eric noticed the edge to his wife's voice, but chose to ignore it and said: "By the 26th of this month, we must be away on the ship, Anya, so you must start packing and say your goodbyes very soon."

Uncharacteristic pity for his wife and her weakness, entered Eric's heart at that moment, and he walked over to hug her, whispering against her hair, "We are a strong family, my wife, and we will help each other, let us not be in discord about this any longer." He placed one finger under her chin and lifted it, so that her inconsolable eyes could meet his, and willed her to be strong for her own sake, as well as for the family's wellbeing. He then kissed her long and hard on the lips. Hannah stood back to observe her parents; sensing at last, a genuine and tender moment between them; and was able to glimpse, if even for just a moment, the bond that must have brought them together all those years ago. Anya's shoulders shook noticeably, but she remained still, accepting her fate.

Ten more days passed, and it was time at last for the Nelson's life-changing journey to begin. The family had spent all day packing the wagon Eric had bought for the journey to Oslo. Several times, Eric had admonished his wife and offspring, declaring that certain belongings must be left behind, which caused upset and weeping especially from his wife and small boys; but Eric held firm to his resolve, not allowing their histrionics to sway him. Hannah and Peter were of two minds, understanding why it was necessary to pack light; but were also finding it hard to leave some things behind. They observed the emotionally charged exchanges between their brothers and Mama and Papa; but kept quiet, not wishing to contribute to the already tense atmosphere. By night-fall, however, all of the Nelson family including Anya, Otto and Lars, had succumbed to Eric's wishes and the wagon was finally packed, ready for departure the next morning.

At dawn, all the family stood sleepily in front of their farm-house, as Marguerite tearfully said goodbye to her son-in-law, daughter and grandchildren. She hugged each of them individually, trying to remain strong so she wouldn't upset the little ones and Anya. She then turned to Hannah and handed her the carefully constructed quilt saying: "Here is your quilt with all of my love to remember me by and never forget my sweet child, that God has blessed you with a great gift to be used for good, so guard yourself wisely, because there may be those that will try to use you up for their own ends." Marguerite kissed Hannah on both cheeks and hugged her tightly. Hannah's eyes widened as she listened to Marguerite's words, and she anxiously said "What do you mean Oma?" Marguerite saw Eric's impatient face, and quickly said: "Don't worry dear; you are already wise beyond your years; and a good girl. God will guide you, just listen to your father and take care of your mama please." And she backed away, watching with a grief stricken face, while Eric settled his family for the journey.

Anya sat stoically beside her husband on the buckboard of the wagon, her face betraying the emotions, she didn't voice. Han-nah climbed into the back of the wagon with her small broth-ers and Peter sat on the donkey and would be riding behind the wagon. Oxen were being used to pull the wagon to Oslo; which was a 30 mile journey and the trek would take at least two days, their father had said. Hannah felt both a mixture of sadness and excitement when she heard her father crack the whip urging the oxen onwards; and braced herself for the adventure ahead, whilst she waved an emotional goodbye to her oma.

Oslo, the Norse capital, was a teeming city, with a thriving shipbuilding and railroad industry. The city had been comprised of chiefly wooden buildings in its' early years and had suffered many serious fires in previous times, yet by the mid-1800s, it was an impressive city with its' brick and stone buildings standing tall throughout the city. It also boasted the Royal Palace which had been completed in the last few decades.

Due to turbulent political times of the day, in 1814; Norway was handed over by Denmark to Sweden and a constitution was passed. Norway was not happy with this arrangement and declared its' independence, but nevertheless, was occupied by Sweden, although the Parliament was allowed to continue to exist. Industrialisation began in a very big way, for the struggling country in the 1840s. However, due to political unrest and the failure of the potato crop for many years, it was not an easy place for many of its' people to make a life. Inevitably, the dreaded blight that invaded Norway's farmlands from the late 1850s caused large-scale emigration to North America and ongoing transportation to the New World took place for many years, thereafter.

The Nelson family had managed to make the two day trip to the capital and were camped about a mile outside of Oslo. Eric had seen and heard of the prostitution rings that were rampant in the city, and wanted to protect his women folk and children from such sordid sights. He went into the city to the dockyards to seek out when his family could join the ship, leaving Peter in charge on the morning of the third day. Lars and Otto had been irritable and tired during the two day trip, not being used to being cooped up in the back of a wagon; and Hannah had been at her wits end, trying to entertain her brothers. She was grateful, when at last, they halted the wagon and set up camp; and the carefree boys were allowed to run free, laughing and squealing in excitement, while the family all waited for Eric to return. Hannah shaded her eyes with one hand blocking the sun; and looked across at her mama, who sat on a blanket spread out on the grass. Anya looked at the campfire, blankly staring into space.

Hannah had been gathering firewood with Peter, and she quickly put the wood down and went across to check on her mama and said: "Mama, are you alright? Papa should be returning soon, and so we won't have to wait long." Anya looked at her daughter with a tired, broken expression and responded: "My head hurts a bit, so I was just resting, my daughter." Peter then came bounding up like an unrestrained puppy, and sat beside his mother, and hugged her, saying: "Snap out of it Mama, we are going on an exciting journey and you are lucky enough to be a part of all this." Hannah spoke sharply to her brother and said: "Peter, leave her be, she will come around in her own good time." Peter shrugged and jumped to his feet and said callously: "Well, it is always the same with Mama, she can never be happy, and by the way do you have anything cooked I could eat, because I'm starving?" Hannah walked angrily across to the wagon and handed Peter some crusty lefse and cheese, and said bluntly, "Here, this will have to do, now go crawl in a hole you big lout." She then returned to sit by her mama. The younger boys had stopped momentarily to watch the interaction with their older siblings; and spotting food, surrounded Hannah to get their share. She sighed and patiently went back to the wagon to get the same for her younger brothers; and felt relieved when she saw in the distance, her father walking back to the camp.

Upon entering the camp, Eric took in the state of his wife, and said to Hannah: "We join the ship in the morning, and I must take the cart and our supplies to the ship this afternoon. I will sell the wagon and the livestock in town, then we will walk in the morning, to the harbour as a family, to join the ship, and you must help your mama, Hannah, as this will be hard on her." Hannah noticed the hard set of her father's jaw and the grim look on his face, and nodded her head wordlessly. Eric Nelson was a hard man not to be deterred by a weak female and Hannah knew this to be the absolute truth.

Shortly thereafter, Eric dumped the bedrolls and removed the evenings' food parcels and water jugs out of the wagon, throwing them in a pile on the ground. He tied the donkey to the back of the wagon, and jumped up into the buckboard, calling out: "Daughter, have a good meal waiting for me tonight, I will be back with an appetite; and we sail to the Americas on the morning tide." Peter, Lars and Otto all cheered, whilst Anya looked despondently into the fire, pretending she hadn't heard. Hannah, looking frustrated, and said evenly: "Yes Papa, see you tonight." Without a backward glance at either his wife or children, Eric drove the wagon towards Oslo, leaving them to fend for themselves until his return, later that day. The weather was cold that day and even colder as nightfall fell; and the Nelson children and their mama huddled close together around the fire, whilst waiting for Eric to return on foot. Hannah had warmed the last of the lefse and wrapped it around cheese for her family's dinner. She knew they would be able to replenish their supplies on the ship, and she wanted them to eat well before their journey. Eric finally returned during the mid evening hours and was uncommonly jovial and had excitement written all over his face. He spoke little though, and when he finished his meal, he issued the order: "Now everyone, let's bed down early; because we will all have a long day tomorrow."

Hannah had a difficult time, settling the small boys, but drawing from her vivid imagination, in spite of her tiredness, she told them stories, until at last, they fell asleep. She was desperate for a few moments of solitude; and she sat quietly another half an hour, whilst her parents and brothers slept, and thought about her future. She shivered as a dark vision appeared before her eyes, of stormy seas spilling over into a ship, that she and many other people were travelling on. Hannah saw in the vision that crowds of people were screaming in terror, all around her and she saw a light suddenly shine down upon her in the ship. And then the vision suddenly ended. She shook herself out of the trancelike state she was in, and although frightened; she also felt a sense of wellbeing, that in spite of the vision she had just seen, that somehow, she and her family would be safe and make it to the new world in one piece.

Chapter 5

The next morning, the Nelson family rolled up their bedding and belongings and walked the one mile to Oslo to board the ship. As they reached the dockyards, a strong smell of rotten fish and unwashed human bodies assailed them, when they joined the queue to board the ship. Hannah looked across the crowds of people, and there were many farm families like theirs; but Hannah noticed there seemed to be a lot more men than women who would be going on the journey. She was not surprised by this, though, because her papa had told her that more and more young men were leaving Norway without their wives and families to go to work in the Americas. These men would be sending money back to their families, as best they could; and would be most likely working mainly in the steel and glass factories, in New York City. Most of them had been recruited by immigration officials as seasonal workers and had been dubbed "birds of passage". They later hoped to send passage to their families to join them in the Americas, her papa had told her.

The sheer size of the ship they were about to board, was daunting to Hannah and her family, when they first caught sight of it. The formidable steam ship, called Morpheus, was a huge metal mass which was equipped with both its' steam engine and a mast of sails. Hannah gathered her wits as she heard her father ordering the family to be careful, whilst they walked up the gang-plank of the ship. Hannah put her arm around her mama and held the hand of her youngest brother, Otto; whilst her papa carried Lars; and Peter trailed behind them taking in the sights and grinning from ear to ear. Anya nervously clung to Hannah, as she was very frightened; but each of them navigated the gang plank without incident. Because of her gifting, Hannah was sensing an onslaught of impressions and feelings, whilst the crowds milled around her; but she persevered entering the top deck of the ship; and held her feelings in check. Lars was chattering like a magpie and Otto had stuck his thumb in his mouth; while Peter stood beside his father trying to look grown-up. A ship bursar approached Eric and said in a no-nonsense voice: "I need to see your family's passage tickets, Sir?" Eric removed the tickets from his vest pocket and showed them to the bursar and the ship employee said: "That's fine Sir, now down the hatch you go, your cabin will be the second one on the right." Eric nodded and guided his family to the hatch, and instructed them to go one at a time, and then he handed the younger children down to their mother, with the help of Peter and Hannah.

Anya was dismayed, as she reached the lower deck cabin and opened the door. There were four bunk-like cots called berths and only a bucket in the corner for relieving themselves and no other fixtures or furniture in the room. In addition, the ship was already swaying terribly and waves of nausea assailed her nostrils. She sat down on one of the bunks wondering what her husband had done to them. Anya had heard stories of scurvy and horrible bouts of sea sickness during these lengthy sea voyages and feared for her family. She hastily pulled out the lye soap from her carpet bag, because she knew it was down to herself and Hannah to ensure the tiny space was as hygienic and habitable as possible and said: "Eric take the boys back upstairs to the deck and let Hannah and I clean this place first, I will rip up one of my petticoats and we can clean it using this lye soap." Eric somewhat heartened by his wife's show of strength, agreed backing out of the door. He had to duck his head going in and out of the small cabin, due to his height; and Anya and Hannah set about scrubbing the tiny space, deciding they had very little choice.

An hour later, the Nelson family was at last settled in the cabin, and although the women had made it as clean as they could, the smells of the lower deck and the sheer noise of crying babies, and people living their daily lives in the cramped dark spaces around the ship was deafening. But the Nelsons were luckier than some, because they had a cabin to themselves, in spite of its' small size. There were many poor souls, who had to settle for the dire conditions down in the hold; where only make shift blankets separated each family and the rats and filth was said to run rampant, throughout the cramped living space. Hannah looked at her fragile mama, with her eyes glassy with tears and her face so pale, and she wondered if the bout of cleaning had taken its' toll on her. She rallied herself, however; and began making the family a lunchtime meal and hoped that all would remain calm, in spite of the shaky start to their journey.

The first leg of the journey was to take three days to a place called Hull in England, where Eric had been told he must seek accommodation for his family for four to five days, as each of his family members would be required to undergo an extensive medical examination. During this examination, each of them would be required to take an antiseptic bath, be checked for lice, receive vaccinations and then be quarantined for several days before their departure. Eric had also been informed the family's luggage would be fumigated, before being allowed on the next steam ship. He had dreaded telling his wife about this part of the trip, so he pulled Hannah aside and described the next challenges the family would have to endure; advising her to: "Tell your mama; but break it to her gently." Hannah sighed, and reluctantly agreed and walked back to the cabin to tell Anya of the latest news. Otto and Lars were fast asleep when she returned, so Hannah asked her mama to join her in the small passageway outside the cabin, in hopes that she would not wake the children.

Hannah broke the news to her mama, and Anya started crying, placing her head on her daughter's shoulder, whilst Hannah patted her back, and said: "We are being treated like cattle, what a wretched journey this has already turned out to be." Hannah soothed Anya and reminded her: "It is not only our family, but all of the ship's passengers that will have to undergo these stringent examinations." and she also pointed out, "At least it will ensure that all the passengers we will be travelling with, will be clean and healthy."

Anya seemed cheered at her daughter's statement and dried her tears, sniffing now and again, and Hannah gently guided her back into the cabin and whispered: "Mama now lie down like the boys, because you need your rest." She was relieved that her mama agreed and laid down for a nap; because she was dying to go to the upper deck and have a look around, and breathe in some fresh air, and now at last she would have her chance.

Chapter 6

As the great steamship was navigated into the Hull Harbour, the weary Nelson family collectively breathed a sigh of relief. Even Peter had experienced sea sickness, as they had crossed the choppy waters of the North Sea, and he had lain in one of the berths moaning for most of the journey. Hannah had been annoyed with her older sibling, because her normally healthy and big mouthed brother had been reduced to a troublesome infant by the end of the journey. Only too glad to leave the cabin; when the family alighted with their belongings to the ship's top deck, Eric went to see one of the ship's crew to acquire several addresses for accommodations in the city, and then escorted them off the ship. The Nelson's other supplies would be offloaded and held in the dockyard and then loaded onto the next ship bound for the new world, once they were all cleared by the medical officials.

Eric became frustrated and irritable, as he went from boarding-house to boarding-house trying to find a suitable place for his family to stay, with the Nelson clan trailing behind him. The places in Hull either had no vacancies or were filthy; and by the fifth address; he was practically ready to give up, deciding they would have to camp outside the city again. Finally, at the last boarding house address, a kindly white-haired lady opened the door and said in a heavy British accent, when Eric asked for rooms: "Ok dearies, I can squeeze you in, but their 'haint much room. But me place is clean and I do feed my tenants vittles in the evenings, if you can pay me fees," she explained. Eric's budget was limited; but he hastily agreed, and the landlady led the way upstairs to the family's rented room. The room was little more than a dormitory with two other families taking up space. Yet there were six small cots placed at the far end of the room, which the landlady pointed to as theirs; and a privy in the back garden. The place seemed reasonably clean, though; and Eric paid half the money in advance to secure the room for his family.

The other families appeared to be Swedish with women and children, and they had a look of desperation and weariness about them. Anya having suffered tremendously with sea sickness during the Hull ship journey laid down on one of the cots wearily and turned her face to the wall without a word. Hannah shepherded her small brothers to the family's space and Peter, somewhat revived after leaving the ship, though still pale; agreed to go with his father and find food for the family. On the way out of the boarding house, Eric asked the landlady to bring a pitcher of water so his family could wash and she agreed. She shook her head when they turned to go and muttered to herself, "Poor dumb farmers, they don't know what they're letting themselves in for."

Vagabonds, pickpockets, and thieves were rife in Hull and it was a very different world to the simple farmlands of Norway. The father and son were amazed at the street vendors and dark atmosphere of the place; and hastened to buy fish, bread and cheese, and filling their water jugs, and they quickly returned to the women and children. It was clear the family and their possessions would have to be guarded night and day; so the dangers of the city would not overcome them. Eric had his money belt securely fastened around his torso and had no intention of being accosted whilst he stayed in Hull. He resolved to sleep very little whilst in the dark city and decided he would be very glad to enter the ship to the Americas, once and for all. Eric cautioned Peter and said: "My son, I am counting on you to help me keep watch over the family, this is a rough city and unlike one we have ever known, do you understand?" Peter nodded, his eyes wide with a solemn expression and responded: "Don't worry Papa you can depend on me."

In the next few days, the immigration medical officials had poked and prodded the members of the Nelson family; until they were satisfied they were healthy. The experience had not been a pleasant one, because they had been asked to strip off their clothes and had been spoken to harshly by the inspectors during the ordeal. Lars and Otto had cried with fright, throughout the entire experience, annoying the inspectors greatly. Yet the family had endured the examinations successfully and were finally declared fit to travel the six and a half week, 15,000 mile journey to New York, which rallied their spirits in spite of the immediate hardship.

At last, the day of the sea journey came and Eric ushered his family from the boarding house to the waiting ship called, White Star. He had great hopes that since the immigration officials had taken such pains to ensure the passengers were clean and healthy; that surely the White Star would have cleaner and roomier cabins, which would be in sharp contrast to the last steam ship they had boarded. Eric led the way, whilst Anya followed and shakily held the hands of her two young sons. Hannah and Peter brought up the rear, looking curiously, at the new sights of the waiting ship. Eric had been directed by the ship's crew to go below deck on the east side of the ship and he found the cabin easily for the instructions had been clear.

Upon first glance the cabin was small, perhaps a hair's breadth larger than the last time. However, it was better equipped because Eric this time, had paid for a family cabin. There were mugs and plates, two small chairs and five berths for the family, as well as two chamber pots rather than a bucket for toileting, like they had experienced before. Anya seemed marginally happier with the new cabin and sat down on one of the wooden chairs and began removing her sons' jackets to make them more comfortable. Eric placed the parcels of fresh food he had been carrying next to his wife and ruffled the hair of Lars and the little boy giggled. He had read accounts of food being stolen on the immigrant ships by other passengers; when the journeys had taken longer than planned, so he had bought a lockable trunk to place the food stuffs in. Eric looked at his wife wondering what she was thinking, because she said nothing to give her thoughts away. He left her alone though; because Anya seemed so engrossed in the task at hand and he soon shrugged his shoulders, telling Hannah, "We will see you in a bit," and left with Peter to explore the upper deck.

Hannah woke up with a start, the next morning; trying to focus, as she rubbed her eyes and looked around the small cabin. At first she didn't remember where she was, but as she looked at her sleeping family all crowded into the small space; she stretched and sat up, remembering the events of the past week. Hannah was determined to make the most of her day; and quickly pulled her dress over her head and donned her stockings. She quietly plaited her hair, and used the chamber pot, washing her face and hands. Afterwards, she crept to the door, carrying her boots and quickly slipped out into the hall and ran directly into Peter as he stood glowering down at her with accusing eyes. "Where do you think you are going Miss?" he hissed irritably, clearly tired from having kept watch all night. Hannah jumped back and whispered angrily, "Quiet you will wake the family, I am going to the upper deck to have a look around and you can't stop me cos' you are not my boss." Peter was clearly not impressed and responded: "I will tell Papa when he wakes up, you stupid girl and he won't be happy." Hannah shrugged her shoulders and haughtily said: "Let me worry about that, Pete, it is none of your business," and without another word, turning her back on him, she climbed up the ladder to the upper deck.

Hannah was hungry and her stomach was growling ferociously, but she had drunk a bit of water before leaving the cabin, and so breakfast would have to wait. She was rarely able to get any time to herself and was happy her escape plan had worked, for the moment, anyway. Hannah having carried her boots out of the cabin put them on tying the laces, and was shocked when she looked at the deep, green blue water surrounding the sturdy steam ship. She was also very surprised to see the masses of people standing against the rails of the ship. Hannah did not suffer from sea sickness like some of her family members; but she noticed that several of the ship's passengers were very ill; while they heaved, pitching their morning meal over the side of the ship, looking pale and weary. It was cold on the upper deck, and Hannah was thankful she had brought her shawl. She observed the other ship's passengers, huddled in groups around the upper deck; and realised that most of them were either Norwegians or Swedes. This was obvious when she caught snatches of their conversations and she noticed their fair skin and hair. Hannah was most shocked however, to notice that some were pointing at her, and the winds had carried their words to her ears, as they said: "See that special girl, she is well known in Norway for her second sight and special healing powers, and she is a good omen for our journey."

Embarrassed, Hannah blushed and turned, wanting to get away from the crowds and suddenly she heard a voice calling, which said: "Don't worry about them; they are just superstitious old fools." Hannah looked to her left and saw a plump girl with golden braids and a whimsical expression on her face. Hannah spoke up and said: "I'm not worried; I guess I just wanted some time to myself for a change." The girl, who was a year older than Hannah, gave her an encouraging smile and said: "My name is Ingrid Peterson and I'm fifteen and I don't have to stick around if you don't want me to; but I think you could use a friend right now." Hannah had to admit, that if the word had gotten out that she was on the ship, that it probably wouldn't be long before people would start knocking on her cabin door, and also, that Ingrid was likely right, she would need a friend. She was quiet for a time, and looked at Ingrid, smiled shyly and said: "Yes, I think you are right, thank you, it will be good to have a friend my own age on the ship."

In the next half hour, while the two girls began talking to get to know each other, Hannah learned that although Ingrid was friendly and full of fun, she also had her own problems and told Hannah: "I am also looking for a friend and will be trying to avoid my mama's matchmaking efforts throughout the voyage; because she is trying to barter me out like a prize heifer". "Would you believe it, she is trying to find me a husband in order to get rid of me, when we reach the Americas, cos' my mama and papa have too many mouths to feed?" "I have five other brothers and sisters," she declared. Ingrid was from the southern part of Norway and hadn't heard of Hannah or her gifting and took her hand saying: "Lets' make a pact then Hannah, I will protect you from the crowds and you will help me hide from my mama, is that a fair bargain?" Hannah smiled, touched at the older girl's plight and asked: "Don't you want to get married then, Ingrid?"

Ingrid became solemn, and with a mutinous expression on her face, said seriously: "Well yes, but I will do the choosing not my mama, and besides, I am not ready to get married yet." Hannah squeezed her hand and said: "If you ever need someone to talk to, I will be here for you; but right now I must go back down below to help my mama with the children and their breakfast, because I have been up here far too long already, but don't worry, you can count on me, I will help you." Ingrid, looking relieved, and merrily waved to her new friend, as she turned to go back to her cabin. Hannah also felt very glad she had found someone to share the long voyage with, other than her family. She dreaded having to tell her papa that people knew about her special gifting, on the ship. This task was daunting and made her anxious, because she knew how protective her papa was. Resolutely she straightened her shoulders not letting it spoil her day, and with a determined set to her jaw, climbed down the ladder to the lower deck to face her papa.

Chapter 7

The days crossed over into weeks, as the long ship journey continued on through the dark waters of the Atlantic Ocean and the inhabitants of the ship settled into a makeshift routine. Eric had not been happy when Hannah had shared the news that her fame had reached the ship, yet so far only a few women had knocked on their cabin door requesting Hannah's prayers for healing to help them with their sea sickness and nothing more.

Anya had rarely left the cabin during the journey, only being persuaded twice by Hannah to go to the upper deck to get some fresh air. Each time she had been severely frightened by the dark choppy seas that surrounded them and the crowds of people and had quickly asked to return to the cabin. Lars and Otto felt stifled in the cabin and it was Hannah's job to take them for walks around the upper deck each day, which was a real challenge. They were intelligent and curious children and would chatter away at the ship's crew members, who were less than enthused to answer their questions on a daily basis. Peter was still excited about the journey; but was struggling with the guard duties foisted on him by his father, every other night, and remained aloof to the rest of the family, except for meal times.

The seas although choppy had remained calm, and the skies had been clear for most of the journey in its' first two weeks. However, in the last few days, the skies had darkened with storm clouds and a cold and icy northerly blast of wind had started blowing, which alarmed both the ship's crew and passengers alike. The storm worsened as the night wore on, and the waves grew higher and higher, whilst the winds caused the waves to slam ferociously into the sturdy steamship, causing fear and anxiety amongst the inhabitants of the ship.

Inside the Nelson cabin, Eric warned his family to stay indoors and the small boys clung to Hannah and their mama, sobbing with fright, while the stormy waves battered the ship. Hannah was also frightened, but she felt a sort of peace in the core of her being; which she couldn't really explain, but it conveyed to her that in spite of the threat to their safety, her family would remain safe, and she encouraged them all, by saying: "My gifting has told me that all will be well."

Peter antagonistic as usual, said: "Little Miss know it all, says it is going to be fine, so let's just forget about the storm and pretend it is not destroying the ship, shall we?" Anya closed her eyes tightly and clamped her hands over her ears, and Otto and Lars cried even louder. Eric angrily rebuked his son saying: "Can you stop, you foolish boy, you are scaring your brothers and Mama? If Hannah says it is going to be alright, I believe her and you should too, now go out and stand guard at the door and I will go up on deck and check what is happening, do you hear me?" Peter nodded and trudged through the door, slamming it without a word. Eric followed him shouting, "And show more respect, young man." He then returned to the cabin to bid the women and children goodbye; and before he could leave again, he heard a commotion in the passageway outside the cabin and a large pounding on the door. As Eric opened the door a crack, he instructed the women to stay behind him, and said to his son: "Who is there with you, and what do they want?"

Before Peter could answer, an old woman with a high shrill voice cried out and said: "We need your daughter, the gifted child, to calm the seas or we shall all perish before we reach the new world." There were other voices that joined in chorus, shouting loudly in agreement, demanding that Hannah come out of the Nelson cabin. Eric opened the door wider to view the woman and the crowd of ten raucous people that were gathered in the passageway. The old woman had white hair and was virtually toothless, but seemed to be the ringleader in the group. He responded tersely to her, saying; "It is too dangerous for Hannah to go on deck by herself, for she is just a child." "She can only go if I go with her and you must all go back on the upper deck, and clear the passageway or we will be going nowhere, do you understand?" he declared. The old woman nodded but warned him, saying: "Bless you sir, but bring your daughter to save us, or our deaths will be on your hands."

Hannah had already begun to ready herself to go on deck, pulling her boots on and wrapping her shawl around about her, and Anya fearfully restrained her daughter, saying: "No, don't go daughter, something might happen to you." "Mama, Mama be still now, God will protect me, and I will return to you safely don't worry," Hannah assured her. Eric as usual, was of two minds, as he did not want Hannah exploited for her gift, yet he knew the crowds would not allow him to rest until he escorted her to the upper deck. He grudgingly waited for his daughter to prepare herself; and before leaving, he sternly told her: "We will go daughter to the upper deck; but you must stay beside me the entire time, so I can keep you safe, do you understand?" Hannah looked at her father and nodded solemnly and said: "Yes, I understand, Papa."

They both left the cabin and Eric climbed up the ladder first with Hannah following. They were amazed to see that even though there were high winds, pelting rain, and crashing waves, there were still masses of people on the upper deck huddled together, all appearing to be in a hysterical frenzied state. The crew were attempting futilely to keep control of the ship, but the vicious storm was causing water to overflow the ship and it was thought by all; that they would be dead and drowned before the night was done. Hannah stepped on to the upper deck and fear gripped her as the responsibility of what lay before her, hit her like a solid wall, making her feel sick.

Five minutes passed, and she and Eric moved to the centre of the deck. The crowds surrounded them, focussing all their attention on Hannah; and she waited silently, hoping desperately for some direction from her gifting. She sank to her knees, and closed her eyes tightly, and lifted her arms high to the heavens; and the crowd roared as a vast light shone over her from the sky, causing all those who looked upon her to be temporarily blinded. Then, miraculously and suddenly, quiet prevailed and the thunderous seas calmed, and the winds and rain stopped immediately. A great peace descended over the ship, and the crew and passengers cried out in astonishment, because it appeared as if there had never even been a storm in the first place. Unbelievably, even the deck appeared dry without the slightest hint of damp. The passengers put their hands down upon the deck and to their faces, not quite believing what had just happened, yet the reality was there for all to see.

Hannah opened her eyes, feeling calm and somewhat over-whelmed, yet perceiving that a true miraculous phenomenon had indeed taken place and just as quickly as it had come; the light had receded back into the heavens. The crowds suddenly started crying, laughing and cheering, and hugging each other. Eric was weeping as well, amazed and humbled at the miracle his daughter had managed to bring about, yet he stood in front of her protectively and shouted to the crowd saying: "Now you and the ship are safe, we shall return to our cabin; a true miracle has been seen today, so let us all be thankful."

Despite Eric's words, the crowds took little notice, whilst the frenzied celebration on the upper deck continued to escalate. Eric tried his best to protect Hannah from the reaching hands, because it seemed everyone wanted to touch their auburn-haired saviour. He was frantically jumping left and right shouting to Hannah to stay behind him, while they both tried desperately to edge to-wards the ladder, to escape to the safety of their cabin. But progress was slow due to the sea of people between them and the lower deck. Then suddenly, as if by magic; strong arms picked Hannah up unexpectedly, and hauled her to the entrance on the lower deck. Hannah screamed when she felt herself being picked up and looked into the face of her captor, and was surprised to see the most beautiful man she had ever seen. His golden hair, sea blue eyes, and cheeky grin kept her mesmerised, while she looked at him open-mouthed and spellbound. When he finally set her down, he unceremoniously said to her: "Now get down that ladder and be quick about it, little one." She choked out a quick "thank you" and scrambled down the ladder rushing to her cabin and slammed the door, behind her.

Hannah rested her back against the door, staring dreamily ahead, and thought it must have been an angel that rescued her, because she had not seen this young man on the ship before, for surely she would have noticed him. Anya looked up at her daughter and asked: "Are you alright daughter, because I was so worried about you?" Hannah nodded and said: "Yes Mama, the storm is gone and I met the most beautiful young man, and Papa should be back soon." Hannah didn't realize how much the events of the past hour had impacted her and she sat down hugely fatigued and a bit numb at the end of her bed. She thought to herself that this experience was probably just the beginning of extraordinary adventures she would have in the days to come; and the thought both intrigued and frightened her.

The next day Ingrid came searching for her at the cabin, and when Hannah cautiously opened the door, she said: "How are you Hannah?" "My parents say you are quite the little miracle worker, but between you and me, you are lucky the storm died down at the precise moment you came on deck, aren't you?" She grinned broadly and said: "And to top it all off, I have a message for you from a very handsome young man named, Christian; who is my cousin, and he was wondering if you were alright after last night's doin's ? So are you?" she asked cheekily. Hannah nodded, amused at the older girl's high spirits and said: "Yes, I am very well, thank you, and is Christian the golden haired man that rescued me last night then?" Ingrid nodded, still grinning, and said, "Yes, and he hasn't shut up about you since last night." "Shall I tell him you asked after him too?" Hannah shook her head, good naturedly and responded quickly: "Don't you dare, Ingrid, I don't want him thinking I am too forward; but you can thank him for me and tell him, I am grateful for his help last night." Ingrid agreed and said: "Don't worry, I will tell him what you said, I am only teasing. But I hope things will get back to normal soon; because I need my friend back on the upper deck with me, and you are far too famous now, for my liking." she declared. Hannah assured her friend everything would calm down soon, hugged her and bid her goodbye and again wondered dreamily about the young man named, Christian. She was pleased beyond words to learn, that not only was he a real flesh and blood man, but also Ingrid's cousin.

The remaining four weeks of the journey were difficult for Hannah, because she felt like she was under house arrest most of the time. Her every move was scrutinised by her father and any plans she had, to go to the upper deck by herself were quickly squashed by Eric. Her papa stuck to his resolve that she could only go above deck if her brother Peter accompanied her. Peter was somewhat malevolent with his newfound power, as well; and taunted her continually saying: "If you don't treat me nicely, I will not take you above deck." Hannah held her tongue, keeping her anger in check, however; and managed to talk him into escorting her to the upper deck at least twice a day, by giving him tidbits of food from the family's storage bin. It helped though, that Peter was also bored and wanted to go to the upper deck, because he had managed to befriend one or two boys his own age on the journey, and he was eager to discuss "tales of Indian fighting in the Americas" with his newfound friends. Hannah had found out more about Christian during these trips from Ingrid and Ingrid even introduced him to her friend on one occasion, which was the highlight of Hannah's week.

Both had seemed tongue tied in the beginning, but clearly there was an attraction, which Ingrid teased her about for days. Ingrid had also found a love interest that her parents seemed to approve of in recent weeks, as one of the ship's crew had taken a fancy to her, and he was a young seaman who lived in New York and was looking for a wife. His name was George, and he was originally from Wales, close to England, and owned a seaside cottage. In addition, he had a fair amount of money saved and so was considered a good prospect for a poor farm girl like Ingrid.

As the end of their journey drew near, Hannah learned that in spite of the fact that she would have to part from her friend, Ingrid, that Christian would be going on to the Dakota Territory by wagon train with Ingrid's family. Her heart leaped with joy at the thought of Christian remaining in her life; for she knew that already she had a special bond with him and she hoped with all her heart that it would grow stronger.

The great steam ship at last reached the harbour of Ellis Island on a sunny August day. Hannah had heard much gossip from her father and on the ship about the long immigration queues at Ellis Island and Eric had told her she would be kept out of sight and not allowed to disembark from the ship, until most of the crowds had left the ship for her own safety. Hannah looked at the tired face of her mama and the impatient countenance of her brother, Peter; and felt guilty for causing delays for her family members. Yet she knew they were all powerless to go against her father's wishes. Peter whittled a piece of wood he had found on the ship with his jack-knife to alleviate the boring wait, and Hannah did her best to help her mama tidy and pack the family's remaining belongings.

A few hours passed and finally Eric noisily opened the cabin door and said with a booming voice, his eyes wide with excitement: "Well family are you ready, the Americas await us?" Peter leapt to his feet grinning and clapped his father on the back and Hannah also stood up smiling, with mixed feelings of excitement and apprehension, as her stomach knotted in expectation. Anya quietly stood up, accepting the inevitable and spoke softly to her youngest boys to help them put their coats on. She then quickly gathered up all of the family's belongings and placed them together in a pile on one of the cots. She gazed finally at her husband and said: "Yes husband, I believe we are as ready as we will ever be."

Hannah was placed between her father and brother while the Nelson family made their way together with their belongings to the upper deck. She saw no excitement on her mama's face, only fear as her widened eyes and panic stricken face were tell-tale signs of the small woman's state of mind. Otto and Lars were like two escaped convicts, while they ran wildly beyond their family's reach on the deck. Eric shouted harshly at the two little boys, calling: "Boys, get back over here beside your mama, right this minute; this is no time for your wild antics." The young boys froze at the sound of their father's voice and scampered back to their mama's side, as soon as they were told, not wishing to be on the receiving end of their father's wrath. Anya wrinkled her nose, breathing in the rotten fish odour, whilst the family walked down the gangplank onto the docks, leaving the ship at last.

The gruelling afternoon had been an ordeal for the inhabitants who had left the ship, with all manner of poking and prodding foisted on the immigrants, wishing to make a new life in the new world. The inspectors appeared to all be beady eyed individuals with unkind and nondescript faces, who asked an astounding number of questions, which were both invasive and personal. Yet, the immigrants endured the endless questions and examinations admirably for the most part. However, there was one woman that became so distraught that she at one point, threw herself at Hannah's feet, pleading with her to lay hands on her and bless her because it was the only way she would be able to get through such an ordeal. Hannah looked at her father for assurance and he nodded his agreement, not wanting to draw attention to his family. Hannah swiftly laid her hands on the woman and whispered a silent prayer. The woman then seemingly calmer and duly appeased; promptly rose from the ground; nodding her thanks and returned to her family without another word.

After a week of relentless questioning and head to toe assessments, the immigration officials at last indicated they were indeed satisfied and the ship's human cargo were for the most part, fit enough to enter the New York port unhindered. As the Nelson family joined the crowded ferry, which was used to transporting the teeming masses across the short expanse of water between Ellis Island and their destination; Eric breathed a sigh of relief that all had gone well. He had been secretly very anxious that his wife would not pass the medical examinations; as her mental state was growing more precarious by the day. But Anya thankfully had remained quiet during their ordeal at Ellis Island and he was hugely relieved at the outcome. Finally he thought to himself, the next phase of my family's journey can begin.

The next morning, after a crowded and sleepless night in a dingy boarding house, Eric guided his family out the front door to the newly purchased wagon and four oxen he had purchased the day before. He mentally went over the list of supplies he intended to buy that day, so they could join the wagon train which was scheduled to leave the next day to the Dakota Territory. Eric patted his money belt which was firmly fixed around his waist; however, he had hidden the rest of his money, in a smaller money belt strapped around Hannah's waist, because she was the only family member, Eric trusted to keep the money safe. Hannah didn't really mind though and was proud that her papa had placed such trust in her. The family reached the wagon, which was located on the outskirts of the city, in a place called Long Island. Hannah and her brothers looked curiously at the inhabitants of the rough city and had been surprised at the unfriendly looks they had received. This strange new city was in stark contrast to the Norwegian countryside and the friendly upbeat environment they had all been used to; but at least the other families camping beside them with their own wagons were comforting, because many of them were of Scandinavian backgrounds and also headed for the Dakota Territory. Hannah, like her father, was concerned over Anya's health. Anya's increasingly vacant stares and diminished speech was a tell-tale sign that the journey had indeed unhinged her to no end. But all Hannah could do was to be reassuring to her mama and help her as best she could.

Otto and Lars chattered nonstop about the adventures ahead asking lively questions to anyone that would listen. Hannah smiled indulgently at them and did her best to entertain them, because her mama was clearly not able to give them the attention they needed. Peter was short tempered at both his younger brothers and mama and was often gruff and insensitive towards them. Nevertheless, when Eric returned with the food supplies, tools, and even a shotgun with powder, the family did their best to rally themselves for the gruelling journey ahead.

Ingrid, Hannah's friend, had married her seaman and had bid her farewell when they left Ellis Island, but Hannah was pleased to see that Christian was in the wagon train camp and was travelling with Ingrid's parents, ready to embark on the journey to the Dakota Territory, just like her family. Hannah had blushed and experienced a sharp intake of breath when she realized it was him, and surprised herself at how pleased she was that Christian would be continuing on the journey. She thought about how she was feeling and admitted that every time he was near her, that her heart would start beating fast and she felt all warm and lovely inside. Could this be love? Well time would tell, she thought excitedly.

Chapter 8

There is a legend amongst the Lakota Sioux people which tells of a revered figure called "White Buffalo Woman." The Sioux Indians are a warrior like tribe and their proverbs generally reflect that men dominate over women in this austere culture. Yet "White Buffalo Woman" is an exceptional example of an impressive female icon, who has been the guardian of the Sioux people, and has been honoured for generations. The legend goes like this: "One summer, a long time ago, the seven Chiefs of the seven council fires of the Lakota Sioux people came together and camped. The sun was strong and the people were starving for there was no game. So two young men went out to hunt and along the way, the two men met a beautiful young woman dressed in white, who floated as she walked. One man had bad desires for the woman and tried to touch her; but was consumed by a cloud of fire and then was turned into a pile of bones".

"The woman spoke to the second young man and said: 'Return to your people and tell them I am coming.' He did as he was told and not long afterwards the White Buffalo Woman appeared to the Lakota Sioux Indian people and brought a wrapped bundle. She unwrapped the bundle and gave to the Chiefs a sacred pipe and taught them how to use it. Whilst teaching them, she said: 'With this holy pipe, you will be sending continual prayers on your behalf and the gods will hear you.' The White Buffalo Woman also told the Lakota Sioux about the value of the buffalo and also of the Sioux Indian women and children, instructing the Chiefs to honour all three in equal measure. She told the Sioux Indian women, 'You are from Mother Earth and what you do each and every day is as great as what the warriors do.' Before she disappeared, she concluded by saying, 'I will return' and then she rolled over four times and suddenly transformed herself into a white buffalo calf and then faded away into the sunset."

"It is said that from that day forwards, the Lakota Sioux women and children have been greatly valued and the holy pipe is smoked daily to lift prayers on behalf of the Lakota Sioux people. Also, it is said that since the visit of the White Buffalo Woman, the Lakota Sioux people have no longer been hungry, as miraculously the buffalo herds have been plentiful across the land."

Little Crow lovingly watched his wife, Laughing Brook and his son, Wowinapa, as he sat on his blanket in his tepee leaning back and resting his head against one of his raised arms. The simple act of his slim and graceful wife preparing the family meal, while she playfully joked with their twelve year old son, made him feel happy to be alive. Even though lately, there had been hardships for his family, and indeed for the Lakota people; because war and famine threatened their very survival on a daily basis. He didn't want to think about the white settlers that flooded in stealing their sacred lands at the moment, he just wanted to savour the moment, as he drew strength and peace from his young family.

The middle aged Chief was named for the sacred crow, a bird revered amongst his people for its' wisdom and strength, and he wore in his headdress, its' feathers to signify his status. His braves also wore at least one crow feather to reflect they were under his leadership; and all of them had learned the hard way that the white man had no honour. Promises made to his people and other neighbouring tribes had been broken again and again. And although he did not agree with the violent retaliation that had been wielded upon the white settlers by other scattered and embittered Sioux tribes, he did understand the reasons why these uprisings occurred.

Yet, there was something inside of him that told him that not all white people were like the dishonourable government officials and soldiers that had dealt so unfairly with his people. And because of this, he held his own braves back from this type of violence, choosing instead to live free, outside the reservations on the run from the army soldiers. The great Chief was responsible for a large tribe of 2000 Lakota Sioux and he was not about to risk their lives because of his own pride. Nevertheless, he would also not allow them to live starving on the reservations, where there was no game and the promised supplies from the government officials never came.

Chapter 9

The wagon train had been on the trail for a few weeks and the travellers were feeling a mixture of weariness, excitement and trepidation, as they journeyed west to the Dakota Territory. The inhabitants of the wagon train had all heard of the ferocious Indians and wild animals that might waylay them during their journey; but also the stories of the harsh conditions during the Dakota winters had been a daunting aspect, as most of them knew they must get their homesteads built before winter came and time would soon be running out with the latter part of the summer months now upon them.

They would still have another three weeks on the trail and so the wagon master made a point of pushing his wagon train as hard as he could, so that fear and discouragement amongst the people entrusted to his care would not set in. Nevertheless, at last, after weeks of journeying and given the fact that the wagon train was now heading north, towards its' destination to Fort Webster, the wagon master decided they were making good time and allowed them to halt for a much needed respite, along the shores of the Lakota River.

Hannah poked her head out of the wagon, she had been riding in with her two small brothers and was in awe of the tall evergreen trees and sounds of the large flowing river just a few yards away. She breathed in the fresh scent of the lush green forest and promptly jumped out of the wagon, to stretch her legs. She then helped her younger siblings out of the wagon and cautioned them not to get too close to the water. Hannah looked up worriedly, watching her mama dismount the buckboard of the wagon, while Peter and her papa took care of the livestock and asked Anya: "Mama, can you watch the boys while I gather some wood for the fire?" Anya nodded and waved her daughter away, saying: "Yes daughter, go get some firewood, but stay close to the camp mind." Hannah grinned and turned to go. She loved the natural beauty of the region and could not wait to explore her new surroundings and get some time to herself; even if she was just gathering firewood. What was it about the wild beauty of the place that enticed her so? she wondered. It was as if her inner spirit communed with the whispers of the forest. Although Hannah's birthday had come and gone whilst journeying from Norway and she was now fifteen and was an adult in many people's eyes, she took off her shoes and splashed her feet in the shallow part of the river like a small child, delighting in the feel of the sand between her toes. She cleansed her face and hands and splashed Christian playfully when he joined her at the river. He smiled back at her, admiring her slim body and radiant face, and enjoyed the time they had together. Many of the other weary camp members, who watched the young people enjoying the river, went as well to wash and splash in the water. A few of the travel weary settlers, even dove fully clothed into the sparkling waters of the river and went for a swim; which made all who were watching laugh at the audacity of the sight.

Unbeknownst to them, the antics of the settlers had been observed by a young Indian girl named Little Deer and a small group of Indian women, who were hidden in the undergrowth of the trees and shrubs on the other side of the river. They had come to collect water for their village and were shocked at the sight of the settlers on their land. Little Deer was the younger sister of Laughing Brook, who was the wife of the great Sioux Chief, Little Crow. Little Deer crouched in the bush and trees that lined the river and watched, in fascination, at the splashing and laughing white people; never seeing such a spectacle in all her young life. She had heard stories around her village campfires about the terrible white settlers and soldiers stealing their land and cheating her tribe; but these people did not seem terrible at all to her. She focussed on the two young people nearest her, which were the copper haired young woman and the yellow haired man and promised herself; then and there, that despite the elder's warnings, that she would sneak back to find out more about these people in the coming days. The older women of the group began bird whistling to signal for the small group of women to return to their village, and Little Deer reluctantly obeyed; but vowed she would return the next day to learn more about the settlers.

The following morning a shriek sounded from the south end of the wagon train, followed by hysterical sobbing and a young mother ran across to the Nelson wagon, desperately calling out Hannah's name. Eric jumped up from the side of his wife, as they had bedded down underneath the wagon the night before; and gently shook the hysterical woman and asked: "What troubles you woman?" The woman tried to calm herself enough to speak, hiccupping between her phrases and said: "My baby is burning hot and has red welts all over his body." In all the commotion, a crowd had gathered at the Nelson family's wagon and several people gasped and shrieked, crying out: "It must be the small-pox we have heard about, we are all doomed." Eric tried to calm the crowd, whilst Hannah quickly dressed and hearing the up-roar, emerged from the wagon. She knew there was no doctor amongst the settlers, so for many, her gifting was their only hope. She said with a determined tone: "I must go Papa... there will be no peace until I do." Eric nodded to his daughter his approval; and she walked to the sick baby's wagon, with his mother at her heels and a crowd of settlers following closely behind them.

When Hannah reached the wagon, she climbed inside and spoke softly to the one year old infant wrapped in blankets, sitting on the lap of his distressed young father. She took the child and rocked and sang to him and unwrapped the blankets around him to help him cool down, whilst sponging his skin with cool water frequently. Hannah noticed the child did have a rash of some kind, but it soon faded when the child grew cooler. After a few hours, at last, the infant's fever broke and he was looking brighter and ready for his mother's breast milk. The young couple grateful for Hannah's efforts, hugged and thanked her profusely. and Hannah smiled and said to them as she left the wagon, "He is still weak and will need constant watching in the days ahead, but I believe he is over the worst of it."

After a few days it was clear that the affliction of the young baby had spread and it was now a full-fledged flu epidemic, that had struck the camp, and the wagon master, Will, knew this would delay their journey to Fort Webster, for at least a week if not more, and this worried him greatly. He was well aware that the threat of Indian attacks along the Lakota River was very real, and that rogue Indian braves roamed the forests looking for easy targets. He also knew of the reputation of Little Crow and his braves, who were known to be in this region and knew that they were normally no trouble; so if they were attacked it would be someone outside of his tribe. Yet, Will knew he would feel a lot safer when they were finally able to leave these forest lands and were inside the walls of Fort Webster. A reliable man with a heart for people, Will Ryder, the wagon master, was pleased to hear that although fevers, coughs, and colds appeared to be the worst of the influenza outbreak which affected mostly the children of the camp; that at least the dreaded smallpox scare had died down.

Little Deer had come secretly to observe Hannah and her family twice in the last few days. She was fascinated by the copper haired girl, who appeared to be around her own age. She had decided her best vantage point to remain undiscovered whilst observing Hannah and her family, was a large leafy elm tree standing on the outskirts of the camp. Fortunately, none of the Nelson family had been afflicted by the flu epidemic and Little Deer was repeatedly impressed by how much honour and respect Hannah received from adults and children alike in the wagon train. She herself received very little attention most days, except from her sister, Laughing Brook, who was always happy to give her a smile. This is why she guessed she hadn't really been missed by her village, when she went on her spying excursions to the white settler's camp.

Today, Hannah was spending time with another girl of the camp named Hilda, a big, vivacious golden haired girl, who seemed to never stop giggling. They walked out of the camp at one point and went further than they normally did into the forest; to gather firewood. The girls were quite engrossed in their conversation and didn't really notice how far they had actually walked; it seemed to Little Deer as she watched them. Growing concerned, Little Deer climbed out of the elm tree and crouched low, slowly following the girls, while they walked deeper and deeper into the forest.

Suddenly Hilda and Hannah let out terrified screams, and although the girls were too far away to be heard by the camp; Little Deer, who had been following closely behind was shocked to the core to see, a large six foot grizzly bear looming dangerously over Hilda and Hannah, as she came to the edge of the clearing. The female bear, who had two bear cubs behind her, was roaring viciously at the girls and rose on its' hind legs ready to swipe its' great claws into the faces and bodies of the horrified girls. Little Deer knew there was nothing she could do, but hide; yet she tried to distract the beast by making loud bird noises. Next, as if unsure what to do, the bear went back on all four legs and started swinging it's head right and left; whilst preparing to charge at the girls, while they stood clutching each other, frozen and terrified, awaiting their fate.

Then a great flash of light came down from the sky, blinding both the girls and the bear. Little Deer couldn't believe her eyes, as she saw the light radiate around Hannah's head and body, making her look like a heavenly being, Then suddenly the bear and her cubs ran quickly in the opposite direction from the girls; badly frightened by the cataclysmic event. After a few moments, the light receded into the heavens and Hilda and Hannah continued to hug each other with tears streaming down their faces, and turned quickly to return to camp, arm in arm. Still shocked beyond belief, Little Deer mumbled the words in her dialect, "White Buffalo Woman." She had heard stories from the elders about the White Buffalo Woman returning to help her people; but had never believed these stories until now. Little Deer knew she had witnessed some kind of miracle and that it had been her destiny to see such an event, and felt honoured that the gods had allowed her to see the mantle of the White Buffalo Woman, which seemed to rest upon the shoulders of the copper haired girl named, Hannah, from the white settler's camp. Yet she also knew that no one from her village would believe her when she revealed what she had seen; so she would have to save her revelation until the time was right.

Hannah and Hilda returned to camp feeling limp and traumatised, both crying and laughing at the same time, as they walked to the centre of the circle of wagons, and both sank to their knees in relief, whilst a crowd gathered round them. Eric fought his way through the crowd and asked: "What has happened Hannah?" "You both look as white as ghosts." Hannah swallowed hard and said: "Papa, God saved us from a vicious bear," and poured out her story. The crowd went quiet in awe, and Hilda's mother came weeping gratefully and hugged her daughter tightly, as the story unfolded.

The wagon master, however; being a practical man, admonished the girls and sternly said: "You were lucky today, but you must remember that a bear with cubs is a very real and dangerous threat in these here woods and you must never stray too far from camp ever again, let this be a lesson to you girls." Both girls nodded solemnly in agreement, declaring: "We will never stray so far by ourselves again." Christian walked up and gave Hannah a special hug with tears in his eyes and smiled emotionally saying: "I am just happy you are alive, God is truly watching over you." Hannah sank into his arms appreciative of his support and felt suddenly very tired and went to her wagon to rest, after the miraculous ordeal. Nevertheless, the event had spurred the men of the camp to form a shared round the clock guard, that day for the camp, to ensure no attacks from wild beasts or Indians beset them.

Will Ryder had led wagon trains for many years, but had never heard nor seen such tales as were being bandied about in regards to young Hannah Nelson. He found the Norwegian settlers to be a superstitious lot; which was sometimes a challenge in itself. But to make matters worse, he had also had to employ two half breed Indian scouts, to assist in tracking for hunting purposes and to get them through the Lakota forest lands. These men were uncouth and unscrupulous characters and often times leered open-ly at the golden haired, Norwegian women of the camp. The worst of the two was a surly looking and arrogant man named Black Feather and he seemed to be particularly partial to Anya, the slight blonde haired wife of Eric Nelson. And although Will did not really think that Anya noticed Black Feather's unabashed staring eyes, due to her mental state; he worried for her. He also worried because he did not feel she was properly protected, for to him, her husband seemed more preoccupied in protecting his daughter; rather than his own wife.

Chapter 10

Black Feather knew the Lakota Woodlands well, but as a half-breed he had encountered adversity from a young age. His mother had been a Lakota Sioux squaw ostracised by her tribe and his father a rough uncouth, white frontiersman, who trapped for fur pelts for a living. His father had abducted his mother whilst she was out gathering firewood one day for her village; and after being raped by the savage trapper, she had stayed with him feeling she had very little choice. The trapper's drunken rages had caused the death of his mother and Black Feather's embittered outlook on life had formed and shaped him into an angry man throughout the years, with very little conscience. He took pleasure at will and when the mood took him, he meted out violence in much the same way. He felt the world owed him something, because the way he figured it, the gods had abandoned him to a half-life; and he was determined that he would take by force if necessary, what should be rightfully his to make a life. His face reflected a scar from his left eye, down his cheek which he had received in a drunken brawl and his scar coupled with his angry expression; reflected a fierce persona to all who came in contact with him. Strangely, Black Feather also had one brown eye and one blue eye which many thought secretly, pretty much summed up his unstable character…

Little Deer quietly crept back into the Lakota village, arriving just before the evening meal. She was careful not to make eye contact or even conversation with anyone, for fear she might have to answer questions about where she had been for the last few hours. At first she didn't notice anything wrong when she surveyed the twenty four foot high tepees made of animal skins, which were scattered throughout the clearing of the trees and as she walked she saw the women of her village wearing their long deerskin dresses; and going about their daily tasks, which was normal for that time of day. She was hungry and breathed in the cooking smells of fish and root vegetables and clapped her hands in eager anticipation of a good meal. She also noticed that many of the men, due to the chill in the air, were wearing breechcloths with buckskin leggings and shirts, so it was clear the weather was changing and that northerly winds and snow would soon be on the way.

Little Deer approached her family's campfire and looked around, suddenly becoming aware that her sister was nowhere in sight and that some of the women of the camp were whispering in hushed tones and looking towards her sister's tent. Worried, Little Deer found her mother, Anpona, standing close to the tent and asked: "Mama, what is wrong, what has happened?" Anpona looked tiredly at her daughter wishing to reproach her for her recent disappearance, but instead hugged her close, enfolding her into her arms and whispered against her hair: "The Great Chief's son, your nephew, Wowinapa, is very ill, and we are worried the gods are about to take him to the spirit world." Little Deer's eyes widened and she extricated herself from her mother's arms, shaking her head in disbelief and backed away, as she rushed into her sister's tent. The young boy was very precious to Little Deer; and panicking; she looked to see the pained face of her sister and watched while she chanted prayers and wiped the feverish brow of her son. The twelve year old boy was covered with red blotches over his face, chest and arms, and to Little Deer his eyes seemed glazed. Feeling hopeless to the very depths of her soul, she feared the worst.

His father, Chief Little Crow was nowhere to be seen; yet knowing the ways of her people, Little Deer know he would be with the elders and the medicine man seeking advice and counsel for his son. As the hours wore on, no matter what she and her sister, Laughing Brook did, it seemed the young boy became sicker and sicker and with every passing hour, it looked as if death was looming ever closer to take his life. Yet, she just couldn't let that happen. "The gods can't take Wowinapa yet, it is not his time," she told herself. She looked at Laughing Brook and her normally joyful and serene sister was in anguish; with tears streaming down her face, and Little Deer, knew then and there, she had to do something. Without a word, she turned and ran out of the tent and not daring to think of the consequences, she headed to the tepee where the elders and the Great Chief were meeting.

She knew well the custom that women and children were normally forbidden to go inside the elder's teepee, except to serve food; but with a determined look, she straightened her shoulders and marched in, standing in front of her brother in law, boldly waiting for him to acknowledge her. Surprised, he looked at his young sister in law and fondness crossed his face. He kindly chided her, saying: "You must not be here little one, your place is by my wife at this dark time," and he bowed his head, the misery upon his countenance reflecting his black mood. Refusing to be swayed, Little Deer summoned all her courage and spoke quickly, feeling the disapproving eyes of the elders upon her, and said: "I know of a miracle worker that can heal Wowinapa." Not taking a breath, she pressed on and said: "She has pale skin and is honoured by her people for her great powers and I have seen these powers myself. She even faced a great bear and it bowed to her powers; and we must use her to save your son now, my brother in law, don't you see?" Little Crow spoke harshly in response to the young girl and said: "How do you expect me to believe such a tale child, surely such a person cannot have been raised up amongst the white people?"

Yet a seed of hope was planted in the heart of the Great Chief, as he remembered tales he had heard around the campfires of his people, as a child, which told of a White Buffalo Woman, who would be returning to save the Lakota people one day. He gestured for Little Deer to leave the teepee and then quickly followed her, anxious to discuss the girl's claims further. Little Crow knew his young sister in law's grasp of the English language was not good, so he thought, not wishing to question her honesty, that maybe she had just misinterpreted what she had seen. Yet, the more she described what she had observed, the more the seed of hope in his heart took hold and desperate to help his son and his village, he came to the conclusion that her words must be true. Little Crow was certain his son had smallpox, which he knew could only mean the eventual death of Wowinapa in a very short time; but also could be the cause of the destruction of the entire village, and he was stricken by the gravity of the situation.

Later that evening, the Chief checked on his son and listened to his laboured breathing and sadness weighed on his heart like a stone. He looked down at the dear face of his son and felt helpless to relieve his suffering and then made a conscious decision vowing to himself, that if there was no improvement by morning, he would capture the white woman to work her miracles upon his son, whatever the cost.

Morning light came and Wowinapa remained desperately ill, hovering at death's door. Little Crow went to his wife's side, and he felt deep pity for her; because he knew she hadn't slept the entire night and was deeply troubled. He kissed her on the cheek, hugging her close to him, almost crushing her in the intensity of his embrace. Then wishing to give her some shred of hope, he said with more confidence then he actually felt: "All will be well my wife, the gods have provided a healer that I will bring here shortly to save our son, do not lose hope." Then silently, he left his wife and son, intent on assembling his braves to plan the abduction of the white miracle worker.

Chapter 11

Hannah hadn't slept well during the night. The terrifying sight of the large bear she had faced down the day before; kept looming in her mind, and had invaded her dreams. Consequently, she didn't emerge from the family wagon until mid-morning. When she finally did crawl out of the wagon, she looked across at her family, and saw that her mama was cooking by the campfire and seemed calmer and more focussed then she had in weeks. In addition, her younger brothers were playing happily a few yards away. But in spite of the happy family scene, Hannah could not shake a deep foreboding that something was about to happen, which would deeply influence the course of their lives. She had been wide awake for hours with this feeling, and at first thought it was due to her frightening experience with the bear; but as the night wore on, she knew without a doubt that her gifting was telling her that this event was entirely different and would directly impact her family.

Black Feather watched and waited with his sights firmly fixed on Anya Nelson. His lust for her frail, blonde beauty burned in him daily; and he knew that it wouldn't be long that he would have to slake his lust and claim the woman as his own. The man that owns her doesn't protect her, so she is ripe for the taking, he thought to himself, "and I will take her."

Little Crow laid his plans carefully, and decided the best time to capture the "white miracle worker" would be to slip into the white settler's camp during the night. He had instructed his braves he did not want her hurt or interfered with under any circumstances; and he intended to ensure she was gagged and bound before she awakened, if possible. And even though it went against his better judgment to involve her, he knew he would have to include his young sister in law in the abduction plan; because he would need her to identify young Hannah Nelson, prior to her capture.

In spite of the urgency necessary to save his son's life, Little Crow was adamant that no white settlers were injured or killed when he captured the Nelson girl. He had refused to allow his tribe to go on the reservation and starve like many of his brothers and sisters from other tribes; and consequently, white soldiers were a daily threat to the Lakota tribes' survival and he didn't want to increase tensions even more, by injuring white settlers unnecessarily.

That night, Little Crow, five Indian braves and Little Deer surrounded the white settler's camp, communicating their positions via whistled bird calls. Little Crow knew he didn't have much time and the grave condition of his son drove him on to complete the task ahead. Little Deer was also driven with the same purpose and dutifully followed her brother in law, who had a knife clenched in his mouth, whilst they both crouched low and slowly crawled towards the Nelson wagon. Little Deer opened the canvas flap at the back of the wagon and pointed to the sleeping form of Hannah; and Little Crow with quiet precision, crept inside and carefully gagged and bound Hannah's hands without waking her. He was surprised at the appearance of the innocent young girl that lay before him, wondering if she could be all his sister in law had claimed; yet he stuck to his plan, because the life of his son depended on it.

Once Hannah was gagged and bound, he picked her up to carry her out of the wagon and she awoke with a start, terror clearly showing in her eyes, and made mewing noises at the back of her throat. Refusing to look at her frightened eyes; Little Crow lifted the knife to her face, motioning for her to keep quiet, which silenced her immediately. Little Deer felt sorry for the girl, but remained quiet, while she and Little Crow swiftly left the camp with Hannah bound and gagged. Little Crow motioned for Hannah to mount his horse and helped her to do so, due to her hands being bound, and then he mounted up, behind her. Little Deer did the same and turning their horses due north, and they both headed, without delay, to the Lakota village, which was a long ride ahead. Hannah could not imagine why she had been taken, and all sorts of frightening thoughts entered her head, whilst she was forced to ride uncomfortably through the long, dark night. Why was she the only one taken from the camp? Was she going to die? What was the purpose of all of this, God help me?" she desperately thought to herself.

Black Feather had been on watch and guarding the white settlers' camp, when Hannah had been taken. He watched, recognising the Great Chief's face and had no intention of stopping him. In fact, the more he thought about the activities of the night, the more he realised that this was the perfect opportunity for him to abduct, Anya Nelson, and blame it on Little Crow and his braves. It would make perfect sense to everyone that both the mother and daughter were taken at the same time; and as usual, Eric Nelson was off on a hunting expedition and was not guarding his wife. Even better, Black Feather thought, he took that hayseed son of his with him.

Recognizing his chance, the evil half-breed walked silently to Anya's pallet underneath the wagon and gazed down at her shapely form whilst she slept; and felt the lust rise in him like a burning cauldron. He ran his hand down her body stopping to pinch the nipples of her breasts and wanted to take her then and there, but she suddenly awoke with a start and opened her mouth to scream. To silence her, he reacted brutally and punched her in the face, knocking her unconscious. Her young sons remained fast asleep in the wagon, and so Black Feather left them alone, however; he had decided he would kill them if they tried to interfere with his plans.

He then picked Anya up and carried her outside of the camp, laying her by a tree and returned for his horse. Upon his return, he draped her unconscious body over his horse and mounted behind her and rode away into the night. He smiled darkly and thought, yes, sleep now woman, because your time is coming and you will see what a real man is like. "You will get it, good and proper very soon," he ground out to himself, chortling.

Little Crow's braves had witnessed Anya's capture, but decided not to intervene for fear of awakening the entire camp; but as soon as they caught up with Little Crow, they hastily reported what they had seen. Little Crow was surprised to hear of the assault and abduction of the miracle worker's mother, yet decided he must wait to help her, until he was able to get the miracle worker back to his son. The two hour journey seemed to take forever and Little Crow's heart was beating furiously in his chest. The fear of losing his son, caused him so much pain, he couldn't bear to think about it; but he refused to let his anxiety show, and rode on stoically, determined to get back to his son in time.

Hannah felt dazed and the gag in her mouth was beginning to make her feel sick whilst she was jarred up and down on the galloping horse. Nevertheless, she tried to keep her mind focused and did not let her fear show, keeping her back straight and emotions under control. In the early hours of the morning, the raiding party finally rode into the Lakota village, and Little Crow road his mount directly to his teepee and jumped down assisting Hannah to dismount, and removed her gag and untied her hands straightaway. He looked into her eyes and asked her in halting English: "What are you called?" Hannah gathered her wits and lifted her chin defiantly looking into his face, and retorted: "My name is Hannah and why am I here?" Little Crow admiring her courage spoke slowly and said: "I have brought you here to save my son. I have been told you are a miracle worker and that you have healing powers," he added, and beckoned her to enter his teepee, further saying: "come this way," and pointed to his son. Shocked at the Chief's revelation, she followed him inside his teepee and tried to adjust her eyes to the darkness and also to the smell of the smoking fire that assailed her nostrils. She started coughing, covering her mouth, and in the next moment, she looked across to see a beautiful, but weary Indian woman in a buckskin dress, sitting beside a young boy with red blotches over his face, lying very still. She whispered a silent prayer and walked across, nodding to the woman and knelt beside the boy removing the blanket to view his body better.

Hannah gasped to see the blotches that were spread across the young boy's entire body and found that his skin was burning hot, when she felt his brow. Laughing, Brook looked desperately at Hannah's face and choked out in English, "You must help my son, lady, please help him." Hannah's heart was filled with compassion at her words, and she spoke slowly, and tried to sound confident, when she declared: "Yes, I will do my best, so please try not to worry," and squeezed Laughing Brook's hand asking: "what is his name?" Laughing Brook answered and said quietly: "My child is known as Wowinapa, he is the son of the Great Chief, Little Crow and I am Laughing Brook." Hannah's eyes widened and she looked back at the Chief standing behind her with his arms folded. She had heard stories around the campfires of the wagon train of Little Crow and his exploits in the Dakota Territory; and she was truly astounded that she was now sitting in the infamous Chief's teepee and was expected to heal his son. Yet her gifting told her that this sequence of events was meant to be, so she tried to shake off her feelings of fear and uncertainty, and pressed on as best she could.

Hannah had guessed early on in her capture, that Little Crow was a Chief of some sort; because it was clear he was the leader of the raiding party. She had observed the way his braves obeyed his every word without question; but she had never imagined it was actually Little Crow that had captured her and that revelation had shocked her to the very core. He was not a tall man, perhaps only five feet eight, but his appearance was impressive nonetheless. Hannah was impressed by his muscular torso, and intelligent and authoritative face, which to her, reflected a leader who was not used to being challenged. His no-nonsense attitude was a part of who he was, she realised, and yet Hannah sensed there were many layers to this man and purposed in her heart at that moment, that somehow she would save his son.

Hannah was weary from the journey and it was still very early in the morning, yet she decided to cooperate with the circumstances she found herself in; and obey her gifting's direction. As a result, a vital energy engulfed her body in the next few minutes; and refreshed her for the task. Laughing Brook watched in fascination, and did not interfere in the young girl's ministrations to her son. She noticed in awe, that a light seemed to radiate around the girl, while she worked, which then proceeded to surround her son in the same way.

Hannah opened the flap of the teepee to let fresh air into the dark living space, and wiped the boy down with cool water to fight the fever. She then listened to the inner direction of her gifting and rose to ask the Chief's permission to take an action, which was different to what she had ever tried before. Hannah explained what she had been directed to do, and Little Crow, clearly shocked, nodded his agreement, determined not to question the little miracle worker's healing powers. She then returned to the child and knelt down stretching her body across his and covered him, palm to palm, and extremity to extremity; with her body pressing down on his and stayed throughout the early hours of the morning in that position, drifting in and out of sleep, for many hours.

Daylight finally came and Hannah slowly lifted herself off the boy, and feeling both stiff and tired she peered down at him. Relieved beyond measure, she gasped in amazement, as a broad smile stretched across her face. The young boy's skin had returned to the healthy tanned glow, it had once been, and there were no blotches remaining on his body, whatsoever. His eyes were open and shining, and his skin cool as he spoke for the first time in many days; looking up at his mother and asked: "Mama can I have something to eat, I want to go hunting?"

Laughing Brook looked incredulously at her son and clapped her hands with tears streaming down her face. She called out to Little Deer, who was equally joyful, with tears flowing and asked her to go to the elder's teepee to get Little Crow to see the wondrous healing of their son. The girl ran whooping and leaping with joy, and arrived at the elder's teepee, and did not stop at the entrance. She hurried straight inside and shouted "Great Chief, your son is healed; the gods have granted you great favour this day."

Little Crow leapt to his feet and trying to keep his emotions under control in front of the elders, he quickly followed the girl back to his teepee and hurried to his son's side. He was so amazed, when he first laid eyes on Wowinapa, he could scarcely take in the radical change in his son. The boy looked as if he had never been ill, and was sitting up and chatting to his mother and eating his breakfast without a care in the world. Little Crow thanked the gods for his son's miraculous recovery and hugged his wife and child excitedly. He then turned to thank the young girl that had been used as an instrument to bring about the miraculous healing of his son; and again was struck by the innocent countenance of the young fifteen year old white girl. She was sitting upright with her back leaning against the back of the teepee, with furs drawn up around her for warmth and in spite of the noise and excitement all around her, she had fallen sound asleep. He walked across and moved her gently to a lying down position on the fur blankets and covered her reverently, letting her sleep.

The Chief acknowledged there was greatness in this young white girl and felt humbled the gods had brought the "White Buffalo Woman" in the personage of this child to save his son and his people. Little Crow knew that he would be forever in her debt; and after this great victory for his family, the Great Chief felt compelled and honour bound to repay this debt, at least in part, by going to rescue the girl's mother, and he decided no more time could be wasted in bringing this about. Feeling relieved at his own good fortune and burning with this new conviction in mind, he left his teepee immediately, set on gathering his braves for the imminent rescue mission ahead. Little Crow hoped the little miracle worker's mother was still in the land of the living; and he would not rest until he had done everything within his power to try to save her. He decided to leave within the hour and left word with his wife to keep the girl there in his tent until his return. Little Crow hoped he would return with her mother unharmed very soon; but in listening to his braves' descriptions of the half-breed that had taken her, he had a sense of foreboding that the captured woman was in grave danger. Little Crow had run across his kind before and he found most of these half breed scouts had no loyalty to anyone, and conducted themselves as savage and angry beasts, cursed by the gods because of their impurity.

Chapter 12

Eric and Peter returned back from their hunting expedition at six in the morning. They were tired and hungry and looking forward to a few hours' sleep in their beds. They had noticed the absence of both Anya and Hannah; but were not immediately alarmed, thinking they might be getting firewood or water or have personal needs to attend to, and so would be returning back to camp very soon. However, after waiting several minutes and impatient to get to his bed, Eric urged his son to go and find the women, so they could both sleep for a few hours in peace. Unfortunately though, Peter was unsuccessful in finding them, and returned in half an hour's time saying plaintively: "I can't find them anywhere, Pa." Eric began to panic at that point, remembering the bear that Hannah had encountered just a day before; and he quickly walked across the camp and woke the wagon master. Sadly, within the hour he found that no one in camp had any idea of the women's whereabouts.

After further investigation, the remaining half breed scout under the scrutiny of the wagon master, did find moccasin and horse tracks both in and outside the camp and the worst was confirmed. It was soon clear, that Indians had captured the Nelson women. Further examination of Anya's bed roll had revealed blood on her pillow and Eric's throat constricted with fear, at the realisation that both his wife and daughter were in great danger. His women had been captured by indians and Eric felt totally helpless. He blamed himself and thought miserably, "If I had been here to protect them, this wouldn't have happened. God help me, I am just a Norwegian farmer," he whispered to himself, "how can I save them?" Panic soon spread and gripped the entire wagon train and women and children alike were weeping and hugging each other, whilst men looked angry and vengeful, and the wagon master tried his best to calm them.

In the panic and confusion of the Nelson women's abductions, Black Feather was not missed by anyone in the wagon train, except Will Ryder. The half breed had often, in times past, wandered off for two days at a time, claiming he was searching out game or new routes for the wagon train. But he had come back on those occasions reeking of alcohol, and Will had a deep feeling in his gut, that somehow the half-breed scout had been involved in the Nelson women's disappearance, but he hoped he was wrong, because no one should be at the receiving end of that nasty piece of work, he thought. Will had always had a bad feeling about Black Feather, but had desperately needed another scout to help him on the trail at the time, and so had closed his eyes to the character of the half-breed and hired him anyway. The wagon master blamed himself for this turn of events and wasted no time in organising a small search party to try to find the women. But he was no fool and would make sure there were enough armed men to guard the women and children in the camp; whilst the search party was away searching for the women. Will resolved in his mind, to capture the half breed and bring the women home safely, whatever it took.

Anya woke up with her head aching and felt disorientated the next morning, and she could not immediately remember where she was. Her left eye was swollen shut and her ribs felt sore and bruised and as she looked down at her dress, she realised it was ripped to shreds. She also felt excruciating pain between her legs and numbly remembered the savage attack upon her body, carried out by the half breed, which had lasted for hours throughout the previous night. Anya closed her eyes and tried to block out the memories of the attack, while tears streamed down her face. Black Feather walked across to Anya and looked at her bedraggled state; and felt a deep satisfaction that he had at last claimed the woman for his own. He ground out through gritted teeth and said: "You are mine now woman, so get that through your head." He then dropped a dead rabbit beside her and said callously: "Now skin this rabbit and cook me some food, I'm hungry." Anya kept weeping and curled up in a foetal position, too traumatized to respond. Angered by her weakness, Black Feather grabbed her with both arms and shook her, causing her to scream and said menacingly: "If I hear any more noise from you, I will cut your tongue out woman, do you hear me?" He then roughly turned her loose and walked away, sitting down across from her, and watched her, daring her to disobey him.

Anya stiffly rose from her position on the ground, and wiped her nose with the back of her sleeve. She tried to cover herself as best she could with the rags she now wore, and pushed herself to pick up the dead rabbit and grabbed the small knife dropped beside it and trying not to heave from the bile coming up in her mouth, began skinning it. Black Feather chuckled, leering at her with a crooked smile and said: "Don't get any ideas with that knife, woman; cause I have a bigger one then you do and I will skin that pretty yellow hair off yourn head, if you give me any trouble." He threw her the water canteen and said: "Here drink some water woman, and if you do as you are told, things will not be so bad; you will see, and if you are nice to me, I might even find some blankets to cover that white skin of yours in a little bit. But we might have to have some more fun first," he sniggered and he could already feel himself growing hard at the thought of this. Anya felt revulsion and her hands and body were visibly shaking; yet somewhere within herself, she found the strength to go on, skinning and cooking the rabbit. She tried to focus by remembering the faces of her family and promised herself that somehow she would return to them.

Chapter 13 ————————————————————

Little Crow owed a debt to Hannah, "the miracle worker," this he knew. He had already vowed to himself, he would repay the debt by rescuing the young woman's mother and didn't consider the tracking of the half breed and the woman to be a particularly hard thing. His braves were expert trackers and he had given orders that the white woman must be brought back alive, at all costs, to the Indian village. He had also ordered that the half breed must be killed for dishonouring the woman in the way he had. As Little Crow and his small band of braves rode through the woods on their sturdy pinto ponies, they noticed that the white settlers from the wagon train had also dispatched a search party to look for the missing women; but strangely it was headed in the opposite direction to the tracks of the half breed and the small blonde woman. He thought to himself that probably the other half breed was trying to protect Black Feather; and in a way he thought that this was probably a good thing for now, because he didn't want any white fools interfering in his rescue operation. By his estimation he and his braves would catch up with the two before nightfall and hopefully he would have the woman back to her daughter by morning, if she still lived.

Hannah was distraught and beside herself with worry, because Little Deer had told her what her husband had gone to do; and she couldn't bear to think what her mother had suffered at the hands of Black Feather. The rough half-breed had always made her shudder with his stinking body and black teeth, and she had noticed him staring at her mama, many times before. But she had innocently believed that Anya had been relatively safe from him with her papa and the wagon master there to protect her. She now realized that her papa's lack of attention to her mother likely didn't help and she wondered with disparity if her dear mama was even still alive. Hannah squeezed her eyes shut, willing herself, not to think the worst and hoped with all her heart that Little Crow and his braves would get there in time to save her. She focused her attention on the young Indian boy she had been sent to help, and smiled at his renewed energy and healthy appetite. Hannah advised Laughing Brook to keep him in the tent for at least another day, and the child's mother nodded her head in agreement, quietly going about her daily activities in the teepee.

Hannah watched her and began to daydream about Christian, wishing he was there with her to make her feel better. His comforting words since she had come to know him, had encouraged her many times; and she sorely needed someone to encourage her just now. There was something about Christian, that made her heart feel glad and it was as if she had known him always. He had awakened feelings of excitement every time she saw him, and she had to admit to herself that she was probably in love with him. But she chided herself sharply and told herself that now was not time to think of such things, especially when her mama was in such mortal danger and resolved to put her daydreams aside for the moment.

It had been three days since Anya had begun her ordeal, and she was beginning to reach a point of desperation. During this time, she had been treated savagely by Black Feather, being forced to walk behind his horse and be pulled by a rope daily, while they travelled further and further into the depths of the forest; and she was beaten and raped mercilessly by the brutal half-breed every night. The only time she had been left alone in camp, was when he went out to hunt; but Anya soon realised that in her poor physical state there was little point in trying to escape. She was frightened of what lurked in the forest and so chose the known evil to the unknown and stayed in camp, sitting terror stricken with a blanket wrapped around her and a small knife clutched in her hand ready to protect herself from wild animals.

Eric that same day was worrying about his wife and daughter and felt the horrible weight of guilt upon his shoulders. He searched futilely through the wooded landscape with the small band of men from camp, but lost hope with each passing hour.

Would he ever see either one of them again, his heart cried out. He hung his head dejectedly and the wagon master put his arm around his shoulders and said, "Buck up man, you must be strong for your women, do you hear me?" Eric nodded his head not trusting himself to speak; because he could feel himself welling up with emotion inside and numbly walked on following the group.

Little Crow and his braves were drawing ever closer to their prey and they knew it would not be long before they found the man and woman. This was clear, because their tracks were fresher and the signs of recent campfires had been found by the chief's braves. They had also found scraps of cloth and blood believed to be from the woman, and he knew that time was running out for her, which made him even more determined to save her. He called to his braves to move more quickly, and he was deeply angered at the brutality of the savage half breed towards the woman. He gritted his teeth and made the decision then and there; he would kill the half breed himself; for what he had done; and rode on determinedly in the morning light, carefully weaving his pony through the trees.

Two hours later, his lead brave, made a whistling noise indicating that at last, they had found the half breed's camp. Little Crow knew he and his braves had to be careful, because the half breed could recognise their bird whistles. Warily, they crawled to the edge of the clearing and Little Crow squinted his eyes to see and relaxed when he noticed Black Feather sitting at the edge of the camp. The half-breed was drunk and sprawled out with a bottle of whisky in his right hand and was shouting out lewd taunts to the frail, blonde woman, who was hurriedly trying to cook a meal for her drunken captor. Little Crow noticed the haunted look on the face of the battered woman. She had swollen blackened eyes and noticeable bruises on her neck and shoulders. Her dress barely covered her body, exposing her to the elements, and a great anger consumed Little Crow, at the needless cruelty inflicted upon the poor woman. He signalled for his braves to encircle the camp and readied his tomahawk for the kill. The half breed deserved a slow tortuous death for what he had done to the woman, the Chief thought; but he decided even that would be giving the evil half breed more attention than he deserved. Instead, Little Crow decided he would do the world a favour and would kill Black Feather with one blow from his tomahawk.

Suddenly a twig snapped and Black feather staggered to his feet sensing danger. He moved quickly across to Anya and took out his big knife and grabbed her holding it to her neck. Anya shrieked and said: "Please don't hurt me again, I will move quicker to please you, if that is what you want." Black Feather laughed enjoying her terror and continued to hold her tightly looking right and left into the trees and shouted, "Who's there?" "I tell you, one step closer and I will kill her, do you hear me?" Little Crow had seen enough and quietly moved through the trees to the back of the half breed. and clutching the great axe with his hand, he threw it with a mighty sweep of his arm. The tomahawk found its' mark and the force of the weapon caused the half breed's skull to splinter and brains to spill out. Black Feather stiffened and fell in a heap on the ground. Anya screamed in terror; because the half breed's bloody corpse had fallen on top of her, pinning her down. Little Crow leapt forward to free her from the dead half breed; and ordered one of his braves to bring a blanket from one of the ponies, to cover her sore and bruised body. He gently wrapped the blanket around her like she was a small child; and then kindly told her in halting English; to sit for a moment and made her drink some water. Little Crow thought the small woman looked like she was in shock; because it was obvious her mind was in a very faraway place; but he said to her anyway: "Woman, I am going to take you back to your daughter, do you think you can ride?" Anya tried to shake herself out of the dark place she had gone to, and looked at the Chief, hardly taking in what he was saying, but the word "daughter," had somehow stuck in her mind, and she mutely nodded her agreement. He then motioned for his braves to help her mount onto one of the ponies; and decided they would ride through the night if the white woman could stand it, because the sooner he got the woman back to her daughter the better, as far as he was concerned.

The indians had travelled slower the rest of that day and through the night, out of consideration for the injured woman. When they at last reached the Indian village, Little Crow rode into the camp, leading the blonde woman's pony and stopped in front of his teepee. He then ordered for one of his braves to help her off the horse, and ushered her into his tent. Hannah had been sitting beside the Chief's son and looked up, crying out: "Mama, Mama, you are safe," and jumped up to hug her mother. But when Hannah actually looked at her mother, she was horrified at her injuries and clamped her hand over her mouth, muffling a sob. Laughing Brook noticed right away that Hannah was overwhelmed by the sight of her mother's injuries; and immediately took control and guided the beleaguered woman to a pallet she had prepared for her; and gently encouraged her to lie down. Hannah dropped to her knees beside her mama, and kissed her wounded cheek, saying "God be praised, Mama, you are still alive and you will be well again, do you hear me? I will help you and Papa, and the boys will be so happy to see you. Don't give up Mama; don't give up," she added, emotionally. Hannah wasn't even sure if her mama was hearing what she was saying; but kept talking whilst Laughing Brook removed what was left of her clothes and cleaned her wounds.

Little Crow left the teepee, allowing the mother and daughter, the privacy to reunite; and knew his wife would help; however, she could. He was relieved that some of his debt was paid to the little miracle worker; but he pondered how his path would cross with hers again in the coming days and wondered what the gods would require of him. The young woman had saved his son and now that the spirit of the "White Buffalo Woman" rested upon her; the survival of his people would be assured and Little Crow for the first time in many years, felt a hope for the future spring forth from his heart. The stories around the campfire, he had heard as a child of this Indian spirit, had not been real to him. They had just been tribal stories in his mind of long ago times. Yet now the Great Chief realised a force much greater than himself, worked within this girl; and he knew that he would gladly allow her to shoulder the burden, he himself had been required to carry for his people for so long.

Chapter 14

Eric returned to camp the next day with the other members of the search party, discouraged and empty handed. He knew that most of the other inhabitants of the wagon train had given up on his women; and believed that both Hannah and Anya were lost to them; declaring that any further rescue attempts would be futile. Eric did not believe this in his heart, however; and was confident that the gifting which Hannah possessed was too strong to be suppressed. He had to believe that this gifting his daughter carried would bring protection to her mother too; and that somehow, they would both be returned to him. Eric prayed that they would not suffer and he vowed that once his wife was at last back with him again, that he would guard her with his life, and never take her for granted again.

Anya awoke the next morning with a start and caught sight of her daughter, and lovingly gazed at her dear face. She tried to smile, but her face was so swollen and bruised, that she could only manage a slow nod of her head. Hannah squeezed her mama's hand and said: "Mama you are safe, and these people are our friends," and motioned to Laughing Brook and Little Deer. Anya looked past her daughter at the Lakota women, incredulous at their plain deerskin dresses and plaited hair; but she didn't have the strength to protest and closed her eyes to sleep again. Anya made the mental choice at that moment, that she would trust her daughter's words and not worry about the present. She slipped into a dreamless slumber, while her weakened mind sought to block out the events of the last few days.

Towards noon, Little Crow entered the teepee and motioned for Hannah to follow him, while her mother slept on. As they walked out of the tent, the Great Chief looked down at the small young woman and said: "I will be returning you and your mama tomorrow to the white man's wagon train. Will she be able to travel by then?" Relief and gratitude flooded Hannah's being. She looked at Little Crow and asked quietly: "Yes, she will be ready, but why are you releasing us, Sir?"

Little Crow looked at her with a shocked expression and responded: "You have the Spirit of the White Buffalo Woman resting upon your shoulders and the gods have used you to save my son." He went on and said: "This is just the beginning for us, and let me pledge to you now white woman, that my people are your people: and it is the will of the gods that we walk together as one for many days to come." Hannah smiled at the Chief and nodded her head humbly; not really understanding, but saying: "I will do my best Great Chief and I thank you for saving my mother."

The shocked expressions of the white settlers in the wagon train the next day; reflected the widespread amazement they felt, as both Hannah and Anya staggered into the camp. Hannah held her head high and placed her arm round her mother's shoulders protectively, as they saw the familiar faces of the camp members. Little Crow had left them as close as he had dared; in a meadow, about a quarter of a mile from the camp, and Hannah had struggled to encourage her mama to walk the short distance to the wagon train that day, but managed it, in spite of Anya's injuries..

The white settlers of the camp stared in disbelief, incredulous that both of the Nelson women had actually survived their ordeal; and had come back to the wagon train basically intact. They were appalled at the state of Anya, however; and looked at the deerskin dress she wore, given to her by Laughing Brook, and took in the horrendous bruising visible all over her face and body. Some felt great pity, while others exhibited a judgemental attitude towards her; feeling that somehow she had been contaminated by the Indians. The camp inhabitants reacted with everything from kindness to outright disdain, and Hannah was angry and frustrated at their attitudes, and defiantly met their eyes to challenge them, but no one spoke further and the crowd soon dissipated.

Eric choked back the tears, and ran to greet the women, showing immense relief and hugged them like he would never let them go. Hannah was surprised to see her normally serious Papa, showing such a display of emotion and affection; but Anya seemed oblivious to her surroundings and her husband. She stared with glassy eyes at the crowd surrounding them,and remained isolated in a sober world all her own, when they lost interest in her.

Several days passed, and Anya's bruises started to fade; yet her internal scars continued to shadow her everyday activities, and made her somewhat of an oddity in the camp. Some women even considered her defiled and not fit to be in their company. Nevertheless, Hannah and Eric kept her shielded from their cruelty and treated her like a small child, much of the time. Never mentally strong, Anya's unstable mind seemed to be replaying her ordeal and nightmares plagued her, night after night. Eric blamed himself for his wife's diminished state, and worked hard to comfort and care for her each day.

By the end of the week, Will, the wagon master, made the decision that the wagon train must resume its' journey to Fort Webster. The wagon master had announced they would break camp and move on in two days' time. The Nelson family were glad of his decision, due to the bad memories the place held for them. Only Hannah felt differently, and although she, like her family, was anxious to get to her destination, she knew that she had experienced a life changing event in the heart of the Lakota Woods; and that this would forever link her with the Lakota Sioux Indians and shape her destiny.

That same day, Hannah sat with Christian at the riverbank in the early hours of the evening and said: "My mama is still acting quite strange, Christian; I can't seem to get through to her." Hannah knew she was relying more and more on Christian's comforting words lately. For his part, Christian seemed only too glad to be there for her. He had been taken with Hannah, from the first moment he had laid eyes on her; and he felt a fierce protectiveness towards her. While he listened to her pouring her heart out about her mother, it all seemed very right to him.

Christian was a muscular, fair haired young man and would have turned the head of any girl. Yet, the unconquerable spirit of

Hannah Nelson; had captured his heart; and although there was a six year age gap between them, he knew he would wait for her and marry her one day. Inexperienced in matters of the heart, Hannah was naturally a passionate person, and knew the attraction between them was very strong; but felt too overwhelmed to think of their future, after the events of recent days. So he waited patiently, giving her comfort and friendship for the time being, of which she was grateful.

Since her return to camp, Hannah had taken walks by herself daily, seeking guidance through her gifting. In contrast to her mama's demoralised state and lack of popularity amongst the white settlers, Hannah's fame, amongst the white settlers, had reached even greater heights recently, which was a surprising turn of events, to her. The story of her time with the indians, she had told only to a few people in camp, yet the details had somehow spread quickly throughout the wagon train, and as a result, at least five to ten people would be waiting for her after her walks every day; begging her for prayers of guidance and healing. Hannah tried not to mind this invasion of her privacy; because she felt it was her duty to attend to these people, even though her mama was usually the one who mostly needed her help the most and she didn't have much time to spare.

Peter felt ashamed of himself, because he could not show the same kindness that his papa and Hannah did towards his mother. Yet every time he thought of her being manhandled by the indians, he felt sick. Hannah had explained it was not the indians that had dishonoured her; but the vile half breed, Black Feather. And even though he understood her words, he couldn't shake the revulsion he felt over the situation; and so he used the excuse of chores or hunting outside the camp; to stay away from Anya; as much as possible. Otto and Lars, his small brothers, knew Anya was ill; but being very young, had little understanding of the ordeal she had suffered; and so their attention seeking behaviour and confusion was often quite overwhelming for their mother. Consequently, when she couldn't respond, the boys turned to Hannah to meet their needs.

Chapter 15

The white settlers collected their belongings and packed their wagons and chattered excitedly about the next leg of their journey. Much had happened in the last six weeks, particularly whilst they had camped along the Lakota River. There was still a lot of unrest in the camp and many blamed the indians for their delays; but the settlers that thought badly of the indians were perplexed by Hannah's praise of Little Crow and his braves, and their respect for her, kept them quiet most of the time.

On the morning of their departure, it was a sunny and bright day, and Eric rounded up his family, putting his younger sons and their mama in the back of the wagon. Anya was still withdrawn and quiet, although the bruises on her body had mostly healed, with only traces of the previous violence she had experienced, marking her body. Hannah climbed in behind her mama and desperately wished she could somehow bring her back from the dark place she had gone to. She had to feed and dress her mother most days, because she would not do these things for herself; which drew attention and even ridicule, from many others in the camp. She settled her mama and the boys in the back of the wagon; and then crawled into the front to sit on the buckboard beside her papa. Her father had been feeling the strain since the return of her mother; and the burden of guilt Hannah knew; weighed heavily on his shoulders. She looked at her papa and saw the shadows under his eyes; and vowed to try even harder to support him; so he would be able to get through these tough times. She would not let her parents down and her gift told her, they would all overcome this terrible ordeal, even though hard times were still without a doubt, ahead of them.

The wagon master signalled for the wagons to line up single file and Peter rode his horse directly behind his family's wagon. Will waved the wagons forward, shouting to them "Wagons Ho" and the wagons at last, started their journey northwards to Fort Webster. Will knew he would have to report the indian troubles they had experienced, when they arrived at the fort, in a few weeks' time. He dreaded having to do this though; because he knew the relations between the indians and white settlers were already extremely poor. In truth, Will had "no axe to grind" with the indians; and he believed they had been treated very badly by the white man, for the most part. He kept his opinions to himself, but in his mind, the white man had not only stolen their lands; but had brought disease and violence to the tribes in equal measure. Will was careful though, because in his line of work, he could ill afford to be branded an "Indian lover."

Little Crow sat with the elders in the smoky tent; while talks continued for several hours about the white army patrols that had been spotted recently in the Lakota woods. Little Crow knew his people were in extreme danger; because his tribe was one of the last ones to refuse to be forced onto the white man's reservations. His people were children of the forest and were used to the lush, green forestlands and rivers of the eastern Lakota Territory. The Great Chief and his people had managed to effectively evade the white soldiers in the last few months; but he feared for his tribe's future, because there were many who were vulnerable amongst them. He also knew of the viciousness of the white soldiers; and that they would stop at nothing to wipe out his entire tribe, killing every man, woman and child. In fact, many of these soldiers viewed the extermination of the indians, a divine right.

After several more hours, it was evident the leaders of his tribe wanted to make war with the white soldiers and settlers; making them pay for their atrocities. Yet Little Crow did not agree with these actions, and although he understood his brother's love for the Lakota lands; he knew his people would suffer greatly at the hands of the white man, if war was the path they chose to take. He did not want pride to be the downfall of his people and suggested they escape to Canada to make a new life; rather than risk their lives against such a formidable enemy. Nevertheless, anger burned hot in the hearts of his people, and the elders turned a deaf ear to his entreaties for peace.

In recent weeks, several young braves had returned from hunting expeditions with a variety of gunshot wounds caused by the white soldiers; which caused an outcry for revenge to spread venomously throughout the tribe. During this time, bitterness and a desire for the white man's blood ran deep in the hearts of the Lakota Sioux. Little Crow knew it was only a matter of time; before war was the inevitable result. But for now, until they were ready for such an action, he told the elders he would create a diversion to lead the soldiers away from the Indian village. There were too many women, children and old ones in the village to make a successful escape; and Little Crow was convinced, he must act quickly to save them. Reports had come, in the past week that the white soldiers were getting closer to the Indian village each day, and were now only seven miles away. After receiving approval from the elders, Little Crow nodded and walked out of the teepee, giving orders to his braves to assemble themselves, right away. His plan was to depart at dawn and head straight for the white soldiers, to act as a decoy, to lead them far away from the Indian village. Little Crow knew it was imperative he succeed; because the lives of his family and people depended on it. Whilst he was leading the soldiers away from the Indian camp, the elders would then move the inhabitants of the village into caves further northwards, where Little Crow was confident, they would be safe.

Little Crow hugged his wife and child the next morning; and rode hard with his braves throughout the day; at last reaching the white soldiers' camp that afternoon. He decided he would wait until the dawn of the next day, and then position his braves for escape, so the chase could ensue without hindrance. His plan was to fire a single gunshot to initiate the diversion, and to lure the white soldiers as best he could away from the area. The plan went like clockwork and as the gunshot fired the next morning; the soldiers assembled themselves quickly and gave chase to Little Crow and his braves, which continued for most of that day. The white soldiers were surprisingly adept at following the Lakota braves throughout the forest lands. Nevertheless, the Indians galloped their ponies expertly through the woodlands, boldly shouting mighty war whoops; as they drew the soldiers further and further away from their tribe. Little Crow's braves led them through dense forest paths and shallow rivers, in an attempt to slow them down; but essentially they wanted the soldiers to keep following them, so the braves continued to lead them in the planned chase, even though shots were fired and some of Little Crow's braves had fallen and bravely died of gunshot wounds along the way.

Suddenly, a gunshot sounded and the Great Chief gasped, when the buckshot from the white soldier's gun, entered his back. Running Bear, one of Little Crow's braves, leaped across from his pony to the back of Little Crow's pony, holding him upright, and rode the Chief's mount as fast as he could to safety. The Great Chief was bleeding profusely and his blood ran down the chest of Running Bear. He frantically stuffed his breech cloth between them to help staunch the Chief's bleeding and hoped that Little Crow would not die. He desperately looked for a shelter to hide the Chief in; and he bird whistled, signalling for his brothers to keep leading the white soldiers northwards. Running Bear then spent the next few minutes searching through the woods for cover, and at last spotted a cave in the crevices of a rock face, beyond the next clearing; and quickly rode the pony inside the cave. He hoped no rogue soldiers had followed them to the place and dismounted his pony and lifted the wounded Chief gently to the ground.

Running Bear did his best to bandage Little Crow, cleaning the wound with water from his animal skin, then placing ginger root on the wound and covering it with a tightly bound cloth torn from his own shirt. He had been taught from a young age that ginger root had the power to reduce swelling and was good medicine for wounds; and so Running Bear had always brought some with him when he rode with his brothers. The Great Chief looked deathly white and Running Bear feared he had lost too much blood and would not survive. He was frightened that Little Crow might be headed for the Land of the Dead; and wondered desperately how he could help him. He prayed to the gods to help him and to give him guidance; and hoped for a miracle, because in his mind, Little Crow must not die, for he was the hope for the future and the Lakotas needed him.

Chapter 16

The causes of the Dakota Conflict, as the ongoing battles between the Sioux Indians and white soldiers and settlers, came to be known, were many and complex. Sadly, peace treaties were signed by both the indian and white man, in 1851 and 1858; but served to escalate tensions rather than relieve them. This is true, because the treaties served the interests of the white man and undermined the Lakota Sioux Indians and their way of life. The corrupt practice of using indian traders and agents was born during this time; reducing the proud status of the Lakota Sioux Indians to dependants.

In actual fact, payments from the government for the feeding and welfare of these indians on reservations; was made to individual agents and traders, who were by and large motivated by greed. These individuals sold goods to the indians on the reservations with an inflated 100% to 400% profit. Tragically, no effective resolution for these practices was ever available to the Lakota Sioux, which led them to choose other options such as robbery and violence, against the white man to hold onto a way of life that was fast disappearing.

The injured Chief lay quietly in the deep recesses of the cave, fading in and out of consciousness. He couldn't remember how he had gotten there and wondered why he was alone. He was lying on his side and his back had a searing hot pain running down it, which was like none he had ever experienced before. He prayed to the gods for a miracle and hoped his wife and child were safe, and fell back into a dreamless sleep to escape from the endless pain.

Running Bear had decided he must find the white miracle worker for his Chief. She had saved his son, Wowinapa; and Little Crow said: "She wore the mantle of the White Buffalo Woman, so why would she not come to the Great Chief in his hour of need?" He had been gone for several hours, tracking the wagon train and at last, caught sight of the white people setting up camp for the night. Running Bear looked impatiently for Hannah, walking around the camp, hiding in the trees just outside it; and finally spotted her at a nearby stream, getting water for her family.

Hannah was weary from the day, because both her mama and younger brothers had needed her constant help and supervision, whilst the slow and tedious wagon made its' way north. She leaned over the stream and took her handkerchief, dipping it in the cool water and cleansed her face. She then dunked the bucket in the water filling it to the brim; and turned to go back to camp. But when she turned, a movement caught her eye and she paused, calling out: "Who is there. Little Crow, is that you?" Running Bear looked to his right and left and saw no one coming; and so stepped out of the trees to reveal himself. Hannah caught her breath, taken aback by the dishevelled brave; but putting her fears firmly aside, she waited for him to speak.

He finally responded in broken English and said: "It is not the Great Chief; it is I, Running Bear." Hannah looked at the Indian brave, her eyes large with anxiety, but she told herself to stay calm and asked: "What is it you want Running Bear?" He did not waste any time and said: "My Chief has suffered at the hands of the white soldiers and has been shot in the back; and I fear he may die unless you help him." Hannah's throat constricted and tears welled up in her eyes, when she heard what had happened to Little Crow. She then replied hastily: "I must tell my Papa that I am going, and then I will go with you. Please wait here." Hannah hurried back to the camp and found her papa tending to his livestock. She dreaded telling him that she needed to leave the camp again; but she didn't want him to worry and so boldly blurted out her news. Rallying her courage, she said: "Papa, Chief Little Crow has been shot and I must go to him. His brave, Running Bear, is waiting for me just by the stream," and she pointed through the trees, but quickly put her hand down, not wishing to draw attention to herself. Eric looked at his daughter, shocked by her news; and waited a few minutes, mulling over what she said. Finally, with a resigned expression on his face, he said: "Go my daughter and may your gifting keep you safe; but don't be too long or people in the camp will wonder about your whereabouts."

Hannah kissed his cheek and whispered "Thanks Papa," and turned to go, rushing back to the stream. She mounted Little Crow's pony which had been brought for her to ride by Running Bear; and both rode as fast as they could, frantically hoping to reach the sick Indian Chief's side, before the worst happened. Hannah sensed that another event was about to take place, which involved her gifting; and she tried to keep herself peaceful, not letting anxiety or fear intrude upon her thoughts. During the evening hours, prior to their arrival, Little Crow had stopped breathing; and when Hannah and Running Bear finally reached the cave, quite late at night, fear and anxiety gripped Hannah's heart, when she saw the cold and lifeless body of the wounded Chief. His tan and muscular body was unmarked from the front, except for the blue and red war paint he wore upon his cheeks and forehead. In fact, he looked to be in a deep sleep and wore his war bonnet upon his head looking every inch the Sioux Indian Chief that he was. Hannah sensed the Chief's spirit was still in the cave and no matter what the obstacles; with purpose in her heart, she was going to do all she could with the gift she had.

Running Bear saddened at the sight of the dead Chief, watched in awe, and waited, whilst Hannah rolled up her sleeves and said to him: "Please go away from this cave and leave us, as I must seek direction so that the Chief may still live." Amazed at her words, Running Bear quickly nodded, knowing after looking with his own eyes; that the Chief was indeed dead, yet he hoped against hope; that Hannah's powers could somehow resurrect his leader. Hannah had never faced such a challenge in her young life; but regardless of the dead Chief's body laid out before her; she sat quietly in faith, open to her gifting's direction and closed her eyes tightly, bowing her head. She waited a full hour and when guidance finally came, she was surprised at the simplicity of the instructions.

Hannah knew from experience though, not to question the voice within; and moved to carry out the actions without question. She moved to the back of Little Crow and removed the crude dressing Running Bear had placed over the wound. She then picked up sand from the mouth of the cave and spit six times into her hand making it damp, and plastered the damp earth on to the Chief's back wound and waited. Hannah further leaned over the Chief, as directed by her gift, and breathed into his mouth, several times and called to him saying, "Awake Great Chief, your night has now turned into day and God has made you well."

After the third time calling out these words, warmth starting returning to Little Crow's body, and Hannah always astounded herself at the power of her giftings; saw the puckered gunshot wound totally close, showing no signs that the Chief had ever even been shot. A few moments later, Little Crow shuddered, took a deep breath and sat up. Looking across at Hannah he spoke solemnly, saying: "The spirit of the White Buffalo Woman has used you to save not only my son, but now me as well, little one, and I am very grateful."

Hannah rejoiced, raising her hands to the heavens; and let the tears stream down her face, showing her thankfulness that this miracle that had just taken place and especially that Little Crow had truly been raised from the dead. Running Bear rushed in, hearing his Chief's voice and dropped to his knees in reverence of what had just taken place. He gazed at the radiant face of Little Crow and the young woman, and he was a true believer that the Spirit of White Buffalo Woman truly rested upon her, and vowed to protect and serve this young white woman and his Chief for the rest of his days.

Chapter 17

The white settlers' wagon train had received a visit from a regiment of army soldiers and they had been warned about the "Indian hostiles" in the region; but Will thought it best not to mention they had already encountered some. The wagon master saw the murderous look in the hardened soldier's eyes, and didn't want to make matters worse. He also did not want to expose the Nelsons to any unnecessary scrutiny from the military; because in his opinion, the family had been through enough. Will didn't really believe the stories young Hannah had been telling about the healing of the Indian Chief's son; but still felt protective towards the girl and her mother and the guilt of their capture still played heavily upon his mind.

The morning after Hannah's disappearance for the second time, Eric anxiously waited for his daughter to return. He knew the wagon master would be urging the wagon train inhabitants to break camp and press on towards Fort Webster; but he was determined to delay the wagon train until she returned. He quickly whispered in the ear of his eldest son and then Peter picked up Otto and placed him in the wagon, saying to him, "If you will lie down beside Mama and pretend you are sick, I will give you a ride on my horse later." Otto quickly agreed and laid down beside Anya, pulling the blanket up to his chin; and moaning in pitiful manner. Anya watched her sons, staring blankly at them, but did not interfere in their antics, thinking it was some new game they were playing. Eric then swiftly went across to the wagon master and said: "My son is too ill to travel, can we delay for a few hours?" Will, being a reasonable man, agreed; but said, "The wagon train must make a move by noon," and Eric agreed, desperately hoping Hannah would make it back to the camp by then.

Laughing Brook tried to comfort her son, Wowinapa, because he had experienced another nightmare in which his father had died at the hands of the white soldiers. His conviction that his dreams were real, distressed her greatly; but she tried not to let her anxiety show, and stroked his brow to settle him back to sleep. She had not heard from her husband or his braves for several days and feared for their safety. Yet, being a Chief's squaw and an elder's daughter, she knew of the great burdens they had to bear, and accepted her fate; surrendering her life to the will of the gods. Laughing Brook had to admit the young miracle worker had given her hope for the future, when she had healed Wowinapa; especially when her husband told her the White Buffalo Woman's Spirit rested upon her. She stood up and stretched, smoothing out her buckskin dress and raked her fingers through her long black hair. "No," she told herself, "I will be strong for the sake of my son and believe my husband will be returned back to us very soon, it is the will of the gods." It was still early morning, but Laughing Brook decided she would go to the medicine man and get something to help her sleep. She was with child and three months gone, and she knew she would need Little Crow's love and support in the hard days ahead. Her pregnancies had never been easy and she had experienced several miscarriages in the past; and her heart's desire was to bear her husband another son.

After the resurrection of the Great Chief had taken place, Hannah was taken back to the white settlers' wagon train by Running Bear; by mid-morning of the next day. She walked tiredly into the camp, amazed that it was still there, because she had fully expected them to have broken camp and moved on in the early morning hours of that day. She walked over to her family's wagon and heard the loud moaning of her younger brother, Otto, and worriedly crawled into the wagon to examine him closer. Otto looked at her guiltily and stopped his noise abruptly when he saw her; and Hannah removed the blanket and asked: "What is the matter, are you ill??" Otto sat up and grinned, shaking his head and said: "No. I just want a ride on Peter's horse, and he told me if I pretended to be sick, he would let me ride 'em." Hannah stared at Anya and said: "Mama is what he says, true?" Anya jumped at her daughter's question and replied shakily, "Yes,

I think they are playing some game." Hannah swiftly left the wagon to let her papa know what was going on; and to inform him she was back, and found he was leading the oxen to the wagon, in order to harness them for the next leg of their journey. The great black and white beasts snorted and stomped their feet in impatience, when they saw their master stop and hug Hannah in relief, saying: "Thank God you are safe; I was beside myself with worry, are you alright?" Hannah nodded and said, "Yes." "I am fine, just tired; but none the worse for wear, but what is happening with the boys?" "Well, it's a long story" Eric chuckled, "I think it's best though that your brother stop pretending he is sick, because the whole camp is tired of hearing him moan like a cat in a heat cycle. He was pretending he was sick, so the wagon train would be held up until you got back," he explained. Hannah laughed with him at his joke. "Does the Chief still live, Hannah?" he asked. Hannah looked at her father jubilantly and said: "Yes, the Great Chief lives and my gifting enabled me to raise him from the dead, Papa. His fate is to live for many days yet, on this earth," she added.

Eric held fast to the oxen, trying to take in her words, his eyes wide with wonder. At last, he spoke saying: "That must have been a wondrous thing to behold my daughter. "Truly, you are destined for a higher purpose on this earth."_ The oxen continued to snort and stomp their hooves and Hannah said gently: "Papa, let us go back to normal now; alright, it is me, your only daughter, Hannah and we must get the oxen harnessed and prepare to break camp." Matter of factly, she turned to go and retrieved water from the stream; and took control of her small brothers, like nothing at all had happened out of the ordinary. Christian greeted her with affection, kissing her on the cheek, when he saw her at the stream and commented: "I haven't seen you since yesterday, have you been tending to Otto?" Hannah looked around and saw several of the wagon train's inhabitants close by and whispered: "No, something extraordinary has happened; but I will have to tell you later in private, I hope you understand?" Christian gave her a surprised look and searching her face, he asked: "Is all well with you, Hannah?" Hannah stood on her tip toes and kissed his cheek and replied, smiling: "Yes, all is very well."

Little Crow and Running Bear knew that by now, his band of braves would have led the soldiers very far north and well away from both the cave they were in; and the Indian village further south; so they decided to return to their tribe to check on the women and children. The Great Chief had missed his wife and child and was concerned about Laughing Brook, because he knew she carried his child and was in a weakened state. After riding all day south, they finally entered the quiet Indian encampment and his wife's younger sister, Little Deer, was the first to spot the men as they rode their ponies into the village. Elated at seeing the men, she ran to tell her sister the good news. Laughing Brook wasted no time in coming out of her tepee to greet her husband and smiled up at him, looking lovingly at his dear face. He caught her eye and smiled back, while he dismounted his pony. And although their custom was not to embrace in public, the love between the couple was undeniable. Wowinapa ran out of the tee-pee at that moment and shouted joyfully: "Papa, you are home and safe from the white soldiers, this is good." Little Crow smiled and ruffled his hair and responded: "Yes, my son, this is good."

Later that evening, whilst the family huddled together and ate their meal of venison and dried pemmican; Little Crow told his wife of the great miracle that had taken place in the Lakota cave that brought him back to life. Laughing Brook exhibited shock and great joy when she heard the story, and they both expressed delight at their good fortune and embraced. Little Crow watched his wife and saw how tired she was. He knew she would have to endure many months of hardship through the winter months before the child was delivered; and feared for her health, especially with the village under threat of attack from the white soldiers. But for tonight, he would put these worries out of his head, because the gods had made it possible for him to live to fight another day, and his wife would bear him another son before the year was out. He was indeed a lucky man.

Hannah felt it was only right to report to Will Ryder, the events that had transpired in the last few days, and also what was happening between the white soldiers and the Lakota tribe. He in turn, thought it was best to hold a public meeting around the campfire, the next evening after supper; to let the people of the camp know what had happened. That evening, the wagon master stood up and detailed the happenings, which occurred between Hannah and the Lakota Indians, and also reported the actions of the white soldiers, and when he finished, a great hush descended upon the crowd. Soon after, a large woman named Elsa, stood up and said loudly: "Hannah, why would you want to save a filthy savage, who would be happy to murder us in our beds?" Hannah stood up and squared her shoulders, looking directly at the woman, and said firmly: "These savages as you call them, are people just like you and I. They have wives and children, and hurt and bleed just like we do," she declared, "and I am called to help them just like I am called to help you." She then sat down quickly, choked up with emotion and Christian protectively placed his arm around her shoulders

After this turn of events, Eric and Will both stood up and tried to disperse the crowd. Eric shouted: "All of you go on back to your wagons now; my daughter has nothing more to say." As Hannah and Christian walked back to the Nelson wagon, Eric closely followed and thought to himself: "Hannah's gifting is both a blessing and a curse." He also realised that Christian was just beginning to find this out. He fervently hoped with all his heart that Christian could safeguard his daughter properly if they married; because it would take a special man indeed, to bear up under this kind of pressure for the rest of his life.

Chapter 18

In the next few weeks, Hannah settled back into a normal routine by acting as a mother figure, in attending to the needs of her family. She performed the tasks of washing, cooking, and child-minding admirably; never complaining about her burdens, and cared for her fragile mother continually in the bargain. Anya's mental deterioration had taken a downward spiral and she continued to exhibit childlike behaviour and oftentimes she could be heard, even talking to herself. Equally alarming, was the fact that Hannah had noticed her mama's monthly cycles had stopped entirely. Both mother and daughter had always seemed to have their monthly cycles at much the same time; and would wash their linens out together at the streams or rivers nearby. Yet, since Anya's ordeal at the hands of Black Feather, she had no further need for this task; and Hannah knew this could only mean one thing, that she was carrying the half breed's child. Hannah wondered how she would ever break the news to her Papa; because she knew this harsh reality would truly devastate him. She had to admit, that this would make her mama's life even more unbearable; because of the physical symptoms and humiliation she would undoubtedly suffer, as a result of the treatment of others in the camp.

Hannah knew there was only one person that she could confide her fears to in the entire camp; and that was Christian. She sought him out that evening, so that he could help her decide what to do; and as the couple sat in a secluded part of the camp, Hannah shared with him her shocking conclusion. To his credit, Christian was sincerely sorry to hear of Anya's predicament, especially since she was still so damaged from her ordeal. He also advised in order to save her from being made an outcast of society; that Hannah's father must claim the child as his own, and said that no one would dare question such a thing, not out loud anyway. He urged Hannah to tell her father and to do so quickly, before the baby started to show. Hannah knew he was right, but wondered if her papa would agree to this action. She decided though it was early days yet; that she would keep him in the dark for now, until she knew for sure at least, that Anya was indeed expecting a child.

A few days passed, and the entire camp decided to conduct a celebration to honour Hannah for her contributions to the camp. Will decided the wagon train could break camp a bit earlier that day, so that preparations could be made for the celebration; and the inhabitants of the camp were relieved to have something pleasurable to look forward to. Hannah, in their eyes, was a celebrity and the men and women of the camp were intent on making the celebration one to remember. Fortunately, there were several musicians in the wagon train and the cooking smells of good home-style Norwegian and Swedish dishes were wafting across the camp, continually throughout the afternoon. The women of the camp pulled out their colourful frocks and the men took baths and spruced up for the occasion, because dancing was planned after the meal; with violins and harpsichords at the ready, for the much anticipated event.

Later that evening, the dancing was in full swing, while couples waltzed and two stepped to both slow and catchy tunes in time. Hannah happily looked out at the lively occasion and felt out of breath, because she had danced so much with Christian. She had even danced once with her papa and Peter. Since she was the guest of honour, Hannah had borrowed one of her mama's dresses, which she felt made her look more grown up. It was a gingham blue dress with puffed sleeves that nipped in, showing off her tiny waist. She also had a blue ribbon tying back her auburn hair. The people of the camp did not approach her for blessings, prayers, or advice that night, for once; leaving her entirely alone to celebrate her day and Hannah was very relieved about this. It felt good just to be fifteen for a change, and not have a care in the world; and it felt like the burdens of the last few months, just melted away that night.

Midway through the night, a cake was presented to Hannah; and the well-wishers sang her a hearty rendition of 'For She's a Jolly Good Fellow'. Her papa gave a touching speech and tears rolled down her cheeks, after hearing his words of appreciation. After the cake was served to everyone, Hannah went to check on her mama, who was seated quietly with some of the ladies of the camp. Hannah noticed that Anya had dribbled both food and spittle on her dress. She tenderly dabbed her mama's chin and clothing to wipe the stains clean. Anya seemed oblivious to her daughter's efforts and in her customary childlike manner, thanked Hannah and swayed in time to the music. Several of the women shook their heads in disgust and mumbled amongst themselves. Angry at their reaction, Hannah's eyes flashed as she looked at them and she sharply rebuked them saying, "Shame on all of you, for your unkindness, and not one of you will lift a finger to help her." "She needs your support right now, do you hear me?"

Christian watched Hannah whilst she chastised the ladies of the camp, and admired her feistiness, but also pitied her for the burdens she bore with her mother. He walked across and took her hand to lead her back to the middle of the camp to dance, and was determined that her night would not be spoiled by the small minded women of the camp. Hannah danced with Christian like there was no tomorrow, and the starry night and sweet music did indeed restore her spirits. She didn't want to think about anything but being alive and fifteen, right then; and she knew deep down to her toes; that somehow it was all going to be alright.

Chapter 19 ─────────────────────────

While the white settlers' wagon train began its trek to Fort Webster; the weather had been mild, although cool winds began to blow, making them shiver in the early mornings, which marked the changing of the seasons from summer to autumn. The families felt great urgency to get their homesteads built, before winter came and most were unhappy at the time they had lost; due to the indian trouble they had encountered on their journey.

Will had made it known, that they should arrive at the Fort in the next few days; and instructions had been given that the white settlers needed to go to the Land Office and stake their claims, directly after they arrived at their destination. The apprehension and excitement was apparent on the faces of the Scandinavian families, when they heard the news; and most were very relieved that at least, the journey part of their adventure would soon draw to a close.

It was early evening and Hannah had removed her stockings and shoes and was soaking her feet in the cool trickling stream, located just a short walk from camp. She enjoyed the solitude this short rest afforded her; because lately Hannah had experienced very little time to herself. Especially, since after her two disappearances from camp, it seemed like her papa and Christian were afraid to let her out of their sight, most of the time. Also, the constant stream of people begging her to help them, through use of her gifting; was tiresome and stifling to her, even though she tried very hard to meet their needs during these times.

In addition, Anya had been experiencing morning sickness on most days; and Hannah knew now without a doubt, that she was with child. She had however, improved somewhat mentally; and seemed to take more interest in the outside world; and for this Hannah was thankful, for surely any progress would mean her eventual recovery. Also, fortunately, Anya was not showing her pregnancy as of yet, and Hannah decided rather than expose her parents to possible ridicule or shame, whilst in the wagon train; that she would wait to break the news to her papa, until they arrived at their own homestead in the next week. As she sat by the peaceful waters, Hannah wondered why she had been called twice to save the lives of Little Crow and his son. Was there a higher purpose to be discovered, because of her involvement with the Indians? she asked herself. And would her intervention somehow fuse a greater understanding between the indian and the white man? Well, only time would tell, she thought, and she hoped with all her heart, that she would be up to the challenges facing her ahead. Hannah was unsure about a great many things concerning the indians; but one thing she did know for sure is, that she had been given a rare glimpse of their way of life. She had seen with her own eyes that they were not savages like many said; but rather real people with families; who had hopes and dreams, just like anybody else. Her mind then turned to Christian, and at the young age of fifteen; she knew that she had womanly feelings towards him. He had certainly made his feelings clear concerning her and Hannah wondered if he would be able to wait until she was sixteen; before they married. Her papa had made it plain to both of them; that he would not give his permission for the pair to marry, until that time, and so like it or not, they would just have to wait.

Hannah knew that Eric needed her at home with the precarious health of her mama hanging in the balance; yet the urgency of Christian's kisses every time they were together and the physical longing they both felt for each other, made it difficult to quench the fire building up between them. Being new to the physical side of love, it was both shocking and exciting to feel Christian's male member grow hard against her, when they embraced; and her own swollen breasts told the same story and confirmed the physical longing she felt for Christian. Hannah had grown up on a working farm and knew about the mating practices between males and females in the animal world; and felt exhilarated knowing she was the object of Christian's desire.

Her body had developed in the last six months, and Hannah was now quite big breasted with a narrow waist and was looked upon with appreciation by most men of the camp, which embarrassed her greatly. And even though she was not a classic beauty, she had an earthy sensuality that most men found very appealing. That combined with her sharp wit, only served to increase her revered status amongst the white settlers.

Another deterrent to escalating the physical longing that both she and Christian felt, was the responsibility that was hers and hers alone. This responsibility singled Hannah out, as a sort of spiritual leader and miracle worker amongst both the indians and white settlers. With this in mind, she knew she could never do anything to bring reproach upon herself or her family; and it was unthinkable for her to dishonour the gifting that she had carried with her, since she was a small child.

Hannah's responsibility to her family and her mama's health, along with the deep calling of her gifting, would have to take centre stage for now. She felt certain that Christian would wait for her; after all, it was only ten months until she was sixteen, at least she hoped he would. Hannah had asked her friend Helga to watch Anya while she was at the stream, and dutifully turned to walk back to camp. She was determined to meet life head on, and with the help and direction of her gifting, she would embrace whatever challenges came her way.

Two days later, the wagon train at last, entered the gates of Fort Webster. Excitement erupted amongst the families of the wagon train, and cheering and clapping could be heard across the travelling settler's wagons, whilst they drove their vehicles into the Fort's encampment. Eric knew that he and his family had sacrificed probably more than most, on the long journey; and was determined to get to the Land Office and stake his claim for a prime piece of farmland, as quickly as possible. He jumped down from his wagon buckboard and threw the reins to Peter to take control of the livestock; and made his way to Will Ryder to find out where the Land Office was located; and then made sure he was one of the first in line to speak to a land agent about his claim.

The Homestead Act of 1862 had been drafted to entice settlers to transform the wild Dakota lands into a place filled with communities, towns and farms. There were stringent requirements enforced by the Land Agents; which were spelled out to the settlers; as they staked their claims and signed the paper work. Most took these requirements in their stride with unbridled enthusiasm, because the prospect of owning their own lands was their ultimate goal. These requirements stated that the claimant needed to be at least twenty one years of age and be the head of the family; and also that they must agree to live on the lands for five years; and additionally, that they must show evidence of improvements of these lands during this time.

The difficulty of settling such lands with families in tow; was that the lands were literally nothing more than flat grassy prairies with very few trees or plant life. Consequently, the settlers could not erect the normal wood cabins they were used to; because unlike the Lakota Woods, these lands offered very little by way of resources; except for future farm crops or possible grazing fodder for livestock. However, unwilling to let the circumstances beat them, the settlers would resort to building mud hovels erected with mud and buffalo dung; better known as buffalo chips; and most of these were nothing more than one room dingy homesteads at the best of times.

After hours of waiting, Hannah was relieved to hear her father's voice, which indicated he was at last returning from the Land Office. She had been trying to keep the peace between Otto and Lars who had argued continually for the past two hours. Feeling as if she wanted to knock their heads together, Hannah knew they were tired of being restricted to the wagon, yet was determined to keep them there and follow her papa's instructions, in spite of their unruly behaviour. Her mama was very little help, and sat quietly folding and refolding her families clothing in the upper corner of the wagon bed. Hannah couldn't help but be jealous of Peter, who she knew had been exploring the fort; yet she chose not to complain, because it would do very little good and she wanted to keep the peace for the good of her family. She often wished she had been born a man; because of the freedom they enjoyed, but being a realist, she soon dismissed the thought and waited for her papa to approach the wagon.

Eric returned, smiling broadly with Peter at his side, and stuck his head inside the wagon and said: "Daughter, our new life now begins and we are presently the proud owners of 160 acres." Peter let out a loud whoop, and Hannah returned his smile and said: "Papa, I am so pleased, so when do we leave to see our new home? Also, can we set up camp soon?" she continued, "because the boys are restless and Mama needs to stretch her legs?" Eric smiled at his young sons indulgently, feeling on top of the world; and looked fleetingly at his wife. He then replied and said: "Hannah, we will camp on the north side of the fort for tonight, so I can replenish our provisions; then we will make a start in the morning." She nodded her agreement and Eric leaped up to the buckboard and drove the family's wagon to the campsite, feeling happier than he had in a very long time.

Hannah was worried Christian would not be able to find them, because she had not seen him, since entering the fort. She knew he had been busy helping to stake his own family's claim and her papa had told her that Christian's family's lands bordered the Nelson's lands to the south. She felt very happy that he would still be living reasonably close, even though they would be at least three to five miles away from each other. Once the family set up camp, Hannah made sure that they were fed, and further settled her mama in bed; and at last, was able to search out Christian, feeling strongly she needed to see him before they left for their land parcels.

She started to walk to the other wagons camped within the fort walls, and smiled when she saw Christian walking towards her and felt love rush to her heart. He took her hand and led her a small distance from the camp, and walking behind the fort's general store, he kissed and embraced her, showing he was very glad to see her. Hannah started weeping and said with feeling, "I don't want to be parted from you, Christian, when will I see you next?" Christian took her face in his hands and replied: "My dear sweet girl, don't you know by now, how much I love you? I promise, we will be married when you turn sixteen Hannah, and this is my pledge." He then hugged her tightly and let her continue to cry until her emotions were well spent, and the two parted, vowing their undying love.

Chapter 20

The next day the Nelson and Peterson wagons headed west on the two day journey to the land claims they had been allocated. When Hannah had returned back to camp the evening before, feeling calm and secure in the man she loved, her papa had been there waiting for her and questioned her about his wife's sickness. He had noticed Anya's morning sickness and had his suspicions. But Hannah hesitated to break the news of her mama's pregnancy to her papa, just yet; sticking to her plan to tell him once they reached the privacy of their own lands. So, she placated him and said: "Ah Papa, you know she is still getting over her ordeal, you must be patient and give her time to get well." Eric nodded, but still in his heart, felt something was wrong; yet with no answers from his daughter, he let the matter drop.

On the afternoon of the second day, the Nelson wagon finally came to a halt; and Eric called out to his family in a cheerful voice and said, "We are here family, these are our lands and at last we have arrived!" Hannah climbed out of the wagon with her young brothers quickly following and uncharacteristically Eric went to the back of the wagon and beckoned for his wife to come out of the wagon, as well. She meekly obeyed; taking her husband's hand as he gently lifted her down to the ground. He looked at her face, pitying her and said; "My wife, we are finally here." "There will be no more travel for us and we are now home."

Anya looked uncertainly at her husband and studied his face; then looked around at the grassy plains surrounding them, with large eyes. She felt overwhelmed by his words, and suddenly anxious; but kept silent, bowing her head. Hannah walked across, to help her mother and said: "Papa, let me get her settled and then we can set up camp." Disappointed and somewhat deflated by his wife's response, Eric allowed Hannah to take control of the situation and beckoned to Peter to help him set up camp. Further saying: "Son, you and I can ride out and look at our lands a bit later; so work quickly whilst I see to the livestock." Hannah looked at the grassy prairie around them, thinking it was so very different to the rocky, hilly terrain of Norway and the Lakota woodlands; and she wondered how people actually lived here. Nevertheless, Eric remained upbeat and whistled while he worked and seemed oblivious to the challenges ahead. He gathered his family and said: "Peter and I will have a scout around today and tomorrow and find a suitable place to build our cabin." "I have taken advice from the Land Agent and know what we can use to build it. We will have a proper home very soon," he added.

The Peterson wagon had stopped not far away from the Nelson wagon, and Christian strode across to the Nelson camp and said: "Hannah, I must go on to our lands now with my auntie and uncle; but I will come to see you very soon." He squeezed her hand and whispered in her ear, "Be strong now my love," and kissed her on the cheek. He then turned without speaking further, and returned to his family. Tears welled up in Hannah's eyes, as she watched him go; but she squared her shoulders and lifted her chin, determined not to cry. Christian could not bear to look back at her, and walked with his back straight to his family's wagon, and vowed to return to his love as soon as he could.

That evening and the following day, Eric rode with his son throughout his lands and was shocked to see that there were flattened grassy plains and very little else. Although, there were a few shrubs here and there, there were virtually no trees to be found. He refused to be discouraged though; and decided to build his family's cabin, where they were presently camped. The site was only one hundred yards from a nearby stream and in truth; there was not a better option to be had. In the next week, the hot sun beat down on the family, whilst Eric and Peter laboured hour after hour to build the family's mud cabin. Both Eric and his son struggled to erect the structure, but through dogged determination, they persevered while waiting for the hot sun to dry the mud-blocks solidified by buffalo chips. The stench from the buffalo chips assaulted the family's nostrils, carried along by the hot dry prairie winds; but with the family having very little choice, the builders continued their task. At last, the one room structure was built by the struggling men; and after four days, the family moved into the mud cabin.

Hannah did her best to make the humble dwelling habitable; and laid out the bedding and their belongings inside. But she was not happy because she would have to continue to cook outside over an open fire, for there was no chimney indoors. She also wondered how the structure would hold up during the winter months; but kept her thoughts to herself, not wishing to discourage any members of her family. One evening, when the family had all gone to bed and Hannah and her papa were sitting around the outdoor fire; she at last felt it was the right time to break the news to her papa, about her mama's pregnancy. Eric had been questioning her about Anya's health that night; and with a trembling voice she blurted out the news. Hannah quickly said: "Papa, I believe Mama is expecting a baby, because she has not had her monthlies since her ordeal." Eric's eyes widened when he heard her words and he stared at Hannah, shocked at the news. After some time passed, he lowered his head in his hands and spoke in anguish saying: "How can this have happened; my poor wife has been dirtied by a filthy savage, and now she bears his child, what am I to do?" "My God, what am I to do?" Feeling overwhelmed at her father's words and tears; Hannah searched for the right words to give him comfort, but before she had the chance to speak again, Eric left the campfire and walked away into the dark, trying to come to grips with the heart breaking news.

Chapter 21

Little Crow and his people remained on the run from the Federal army soldiers for two months, and the Great Chief came to the conclusion that the soldiers would not stop chasing them until he and his tribe were hunted down and murdered. Little Crow forced himself to face up to the reality, that if he and the elders did not agree to a plan soon, that they would all die. The diversion he and his braves had initially created, to lead the soldiers away from his village in the Lakota woods; had worked well for a time; but Little Crow knew that his people could not survive such an existence in the long term, and he felt the burden for his people weigh heavily upon his shoulders. Yet, the option of being starved on Crow Creek Indian Reservation was an equal and terrible fate in the eyes of the Lakota tribe; and the Great Chief vowed he would do anything to stop this from becoming a reality.

Little Crow's hope was that he could persuade the elders to agree to his plan to move his tribe further north to the Canadian woods, where the army soldiers held no power over them. However, in the meantime, until he convinced them, his people had to remain in caves and hiding places for safety, staying well away from the soldiers and the white settlers, to ensure their survival.

The numbers of Little Crow's local tribe, totalling men, women, and children, was nearly four hundred; and the wider adjoining Lakota tribes tallied up to more than two thousand people. Relocating that many of his tribe to Canada, Little Crow knew; would be no small feat. Perhaps, he thought to himself, this is why the gods had sent the White Buffalo Women to guide them. He took solace in this knowledge, and hoped that her protection would keep them safe from the hands of the white soldiers. Sadly, both the white soldiers and settlers had proven they would shoot the indians on sight, if they were caught; and the dangers that faced his tribe were very real and life threatening. Little Crow had ultimately hoped the Indians and white man could somehow learn to live in harmony, but he was resigned to the fact the white man would not stop, until all indians in the Dakota Territory were either trapped on reservations or dead.

The Great Chief had sent two of his braves to track the progress of Hannah and her family; because he had come to the realisation; that he would need to count on her and her powers in the dark days ahead. Somehow, this young woman inspired courage and hope in not only his own heart; but also in the hearts of his people. Little Crow decided to wait for one of his braves to return with news of her, before further decisions concerning his tribe could be made; and he said as much to the elders, which they seemed to accept at least for the time being. The other brave would remain upon the Nelson lands to watch over her; as she was now sacred and a good omen to his people, and she must be kept safe at all times.

As the weeks passed and the Nelsons tried to acclimatise to their new home, it was not easy for any of them. The mud hovel they now lived in was worlds apart from the spacious wooden cabin they had resided in, whilst in Norway. Hannah had tried her best to see to the comforts of the family and had taken the role of mother for the Nelson clan. In addition, Anya's pregnancy was now noticeable with her belly swollen and cumbersome. It had not been an easy pregnancy for her, and Hannah tried hard to alleviate her mama's discomfort, by taking on all of the heavy lifting and household tasks; and urging her to rest for much of the time.

Peter and the boys didn't ask any questions regarding their mother's delicate condition, and Hannah didn't feel it was her place to enlighten them either. Eric seemed to accept the situation and had not spoken again to Hannah about his wife's pregnancy. He had insisted that Anya still slept with him, in spite of her advancing pregnancy and sickness caused by another man; for in his mind, she was still his wife and even though he had failed her in the past, he had purposed in his heart to protect her from now on, with his very life. Eric also made the difficult decision that he would claim this innocent child as his own, trying somehow, to atone for the guilt he felt for not protecting her.

Eric had been to Fort Webster and bought a much needed plough and tools that he required to initiate his farm work. He had also purchased a milk cow and some chickens at a good price, and turned to go home; happy to focus his mind on the development of his farm. He preferred to come home in the evenings; completely worn out from ploughing and clearing the fields; so that he could eat his meal and fall into bed, without thinking about what was happening to his wife. Eric had already made the decision, that he would do the right thing by her; but that didn't mean that this decision was easy for him, especially when he saw her belly growing larger and larger every day. It was too late in the year to plant seed in his fields for crops, but at least he could clear his fields and prepare the way for spring planting. Eric had been told by the Land Agent that it would be a tough winter; and he hoped the family's resources would stretch until the first crop came in. The burden was his to bear alone, and only sleep could help him escape these pressures for a time, for the worries of his family's survival, in this harsh place and his wife's pregnancy plagued him day after day.

Since there was a decided lack of trees on their land, Peter seemed to spend half the day, collecting buffalo chips for the fire. The animals roamed free in herds throughout the plains, and their massive heads rose from grazing to watch him, from time to time. He didn't really mind the great beasts watching him, and revelled in the freedom he now had; but sometimes he did worry that they might start a stampede and trample him. One day, his father even shot one of the massive beasts for food for the family; and the buffalo hide had been used as a rug for the hovel floor to keep them warm in the winter. Peter had felt bad for the buffalo when his papa had shot it; but understood the need his family had for food, and tried to toughen up for his family's sake. But the memories of the bleating, dying beast would be with him for some time to come. Peter had to admit though, the buffalo meat when cooked, although tougher than the goat and lamb meat he was used to; had a delicious taste and aroma. Also the sheer size of the slain buffalo would ensure that his family ate well for many days ahead.

Hannah looked across the flat grasslands of the outstretched prairie, and was struck by the wild beauty of the land. She pondered the events of the last few months, and sat by a nearby stream about a quarter of a mile from the Nelson homestead. Her papa didn't like her going off by herself, but Hannah felt the need to get away from the small dingy mud homestead, at least once a day. Usually it was when her mama was napping and Hannah had dispatched her younger brothers to do one task or another to keep them busy. Anya was six months pregnant now and still trapped within her childlike mind; which worried Hannah greatly and gave her misgivings about the future. She had to admit however, that her papa seemed to accept the plight of his wife, and was making the best of the situation. She missed Christian desperately, because she had been used to seeing him every day, whilst they were on the trail. He had only been across twice in the last three months to see her, which made her yearn for his company. Hannah knew he was working night and day to help his family establish their farm; but her head could not quite convince her heart, that all was still well between them and she worried about their future.

One day as Hannah sat beside her normal spot by the stream, she felt a presence behind her, and turned quickly to find out who or what was there. Her eyes widened and she caught her breath in her throat; when she saw Little Crow standing not five feet away from her. The Great Chief stood proudly and waited for her to collect herself, then he took a few cautious steps forward to get closer to her and spoke quietly, saying: "Do not worry little one, I have come to seek your guidance about my people and where they should live." Hannah was used to people approaching her for advice in much the same way; but her gifting told her that Little Crow would not humble himself to seek out her help, unless there was something desperately wrong with his tribe. She spoke haltingly in response and said: "How may I help you Great Chief."

Little Crow didn't waste any time in answering her and said: "My people still run from the white soldiers and we need your protection until we move to Canada. The white man has stolen our lands and seeks to murder us; and we can no longer stay on our lands," he added. Hannah looked bewildered at Little Crow's words, and said, "But how can I protect you, I am just one girl and these are my father's lands?" Undaunted by her logic, Little Crow responded and said: "You are bound to our people and have been chosen by the gods to wear the mantle of White Buffalo Woman. Let us stay on these lands for a time. There are small caves we can stay in, that will hide us from the white soldiers; and they will not think to look for us there," he explained.

Hannah felt the gift strong within her, and knew that she must agree to the Chief's request. Somehow, she would have to convince her papa of this fact; but Hannah wasn't sure how she was going to do that. She looked into the eyes of the Great Chief, keeping her composure and said: "Yes, do what is necessary to hide your people on our lands, I will tell my father this evening." Little Crow bowed his head giving her respect, and said quietly: "We will move the old ones, women and children here in two days' time," and then turned without another word, walking away as silently as he had come.

Hannah felt fear grip her heart; because she knew her life and the lives of the ones she loved, was about to drastically change. Yet along with her fear, conviction burned strong in her heart and she was convinced that she was walking in the right direction. Hannah tried to prepare herself to meet the challenge of telling her papa about the Indians moving onto his lands; and she knew very well that her father's overprotective nature towards the ones he loved would be a giant obstacle. Nevertheless, Hannah also knew that he respected her gifting; and would see it her way in the end, even if it would be an uphill struggle in the beginning.

Chapter 22

Two days later, Hannah searched the horizon, hoping to catch sight of the Lakota tribe. Feeling a sense of foreboding, she had not had the courage to tell her papa about what she had agreed to, and realised she couldn't put off the dreaded task any longer. It was early morning, and her papa had not yet left for the fields, and so she took her opportunity and forced herself to head towards the makeshift shed he had built to shelter the animals. Hannah tried to go over in her mind, what she would say to her father, to explain what she had done; but nothing came immediately to her mind and Hannah's stomach churned with the thought of his reaction to her news.

When Hannah entered the shed, Eric was bent over examining one of the oxen's hooves. When he heard her coming, he stood up and gazed at her with a quizzical look on his face. "Daughter, what are you doing out here this time of day, is everything well with your mama?" he asked. Hannah assured him "All is fine," and replied with a sheepish look on her face: "But I do have something to tell you, Papa." Eric waited patiently for his daughter to tell him what was on her mind, and at last she blurted out: "Papa, Little Crow came to see me two days ago, and he is moving his people on to our lands." She hurried on to explain and added: "The tribe are being hunted like animals by the army soldiers; and they asked if they could stay in some of our caves for safety, just for the time being." Hannah then stopped speaking, completely out of breath; and intently watched the face of her papa, waiting anxiously for his response. Eric stared at her in shock and then resignation crossed his face, as he asked her: "When do they arrive, daughter, and how long are they staying? You know this can only be a temporary arrangement, don't you?" Hannah nodded, feeling relieved, and said accommodatingly: "Yes Papa, it is only for a short while, I am sure of that, and they should be arriving sometime today, I think." Eric looked beaten at that point; and said in a wooden voice, "I know your gifting has told you to take care of these indians; but you know as well as I do; if the soldiers catch them on our lands, we all could be paying a very high price." Hannah looked at him helplessly and replied, "Papa we have very little choice, but I will do all I can to ensure we are all safe." Eric shook his head, not knowing how to respond to her words; and finally urged her to go back to the house. Upon returning to his tasks, feeling disgruntled, he muttered to himself: "How can a fifteen year old girl keep anyone safe?"

Later that day, Hannah heard hoof beats galloping towards the homestead, and she wondered if it could possibly be the Lakota Chief and his braves, telling her that his people were safely settled in to the Nelson caves. She had been scrubbing clothes in a wash basin and stood up, rubbing her aching back and removed her apron. She rushed out to the front of the homestead; and her expectant expression turned to joy, when she saw that it was Christian riding towards her. Christian smiled broadly at the sight of Hannah and dismounted his horse, hugging her tightly when she ran into his arms. However, his delighted face shifted to concern, after a time, and he said: "Hannah, there are masses of Indians camping on your Papa's lands; where is Eric?" I must let him know right away." Hannah took him by both shoulders and looked up at him, saying: "Christian, Papa already knows, and it must be this way for now, according to my gifting." Amazed at her calm words, Christian replied cynically and said: "Surely not, after all your family has been through. Don't you realise that allowing this to happen could put you and your family in grave danger?" he demanded. Ignoring his remonstrations, Hannah stayed quiet and after a few moments asked: "Have they camped in our caves, Christian then, as I must go and see that they have settled in well?" Christian stared at her in disbelief, and replied: "You can't be serious; you can't just ride up there and check on them like they are houseguests. These are fully fledged Sioux Indians with arrows and tomahawks; and they might just decide to put you in their cooking pot," he added dramatically and Hannah laughed. He took in the determined expression on her face though; and said seriously: "Well then, if you are set on going, then you are not going without me."

Hannah looked at him lovingly and replied: "Chris, I would not deny you this, you can go with me of course; and remember the indians see me as a sort of spiritual guide, we will not be harmed by them. They are hiding from the soldiers and Papa knows and understands," she explained. "I will ask Peter to look after Mama and then we can leave right away and hopefully be back by supper time," she added. Christian shook his head, knowing he was beaten and said, "What am I going to do with you?" and dutifully tied his horse to the hitching post Eric had built the previous week; and followed her inside the homestead.

After settling her mama and informing her brother of her plans, Peter grudgingly agreed to watch Anya and his young brothers for the afternoon. Christian knew the Nelsons only owned one horse, and so he helped Hannah onto his own horse and climbed up behind her. Holding her securely, Christian navigated his horse to the north side of the Nelson property to see Little Crow and his people. On their journey to the Indian camp, Hannah and Christian detoured to the field Eric was working in, to let him know the news of the indian's arrival. Upon hearing the news, Eric tipped his hat to the back of his head and whistled in a low voice, saying: "May God help us, if the soldiers find out; but I guess I owe my dear Anya's life to this Little Crow; so I must do what I can to help him and his people." Hannah felt a glowing sense of pride at her papa's words, and kissed him on the cheek. She felt greatly relieved that he and Christian were supporting her in this decision, and said to both of them: "Thanks, you are both being perfect angels about this."

A half hour later, Hannah and Christian rode into the caves the indians had chosen. Hannah was impressed with the industrious activities of the women in the camp, whilst they worked at cooking, weaving, and the tanning of buffalo hides. Christian's eyes widened in amazement, as this was the first time he had seen the Lakota Indians, up close; and he took in the many families within the cave; and felt glad that Hannah had taken the decision to help them, in spite of the many dangers it might inflict upon her own family. Both he and Hannah had talked whilst travelling to the indian camp, and expected the Lakotas to be half starved and desperate; yet the sense of pride that emanated from these people was truly admirable. The Lakotas got on with the business of life, despite the terrible conditions they had been forced to live under. Hannah had nothing but respect for the spirit and courage these rare people exhibited; and knew deep down within her heart she would do anything she could to protect them.

The Lakota women laughed and joked amongst themselves, paying little attention when Christian and Hannah rode into the camp. They had been alerted ahead of time by the men of the tribe; that they would be visited by Hannah and her family whilst staying in the cave. The Lakota children chased each other back and forth in the cave, shouting with careless abandon, and Hannah and Christian searched the sea of faces for anyone they knew. At last, Hannah caught sight of Laughing Brook and her younger sister, Little Deer; and the women pointed to them, and beckoned for the young couple to join them. Laughing Brook smiled delightedly at Hannah, and Little Deer ran to meet them, pulling Hannah's hand to come back to their campfire, whilst she gazed shyly at Christian.

Hannah had learned after her time spent with the Lakotas that Christian would not be allowed to remain with the women, unless Little Crow was nearby, so she asked: "Is the Great Chief home?" Little Deer nodded and Laughing Brook continuing to smile, said: "My husband is home. Come and sit Hannah; and bring your young man with you, we are most glad to see you," she added.

Hannah and Christian joined the women respectfully; and Hannah's throat tightened and eyes glistened with tears, when she saw Little Crow and Wowinapa, also join them by the fire. The Great Chief looked at them and nodded solemnly; and motioned for the two young people to take food. Neither she nor Christian was hungry, but Hannah knew; that if you were offered food in the Indian camp, that this was a sign of respect given to guests; and no matter what; you must eat it. Christian tried to follow Hannah's lead and sat cross legged at the fire and took the crude bowl filled with steaming pumpkin mash and buffalo jerky.

Hannah whispered to him to eat with his hands, and they ate the food; trying not to show any expression on their faces, while they kept their heads bowed. It was evident Little Crow was not going to speak to them, until they had finished eating; and so she and Christian did their best to get the food down as quickly as they could. At last, they finished the meal, and the Great Chief finally looked their way and said quietly, "It is an honour to have you and your young man at our fire. We are pleased that we are safe on your father's lands and the Lakotas will remain hidden in these caves, until the gods tell us, it is time to move again to our future home." Hannah responded humbly and said; "It is my very great honour to have your people on our lands, and may God protect us all." After the meal and the exchange of words, Hannah and Christian said their goodbyes, and left the Lakotas, feeling comforted that all was well with their friends, at least for now.

The days and weeks passed, with very little change, and it was as if an invisible barrier protected the Indian encampment during this time. Soldiers would ride to the perimeters of the Nelson property from time to time, but would then travel on during these occasions, paying little attention to the inhabitants of the land, and not knowing that they harboured the indian fugitives. Each day, one of the Nelson clan would ride out to the Indian camp to check all was well; and some days, Hannah would bring one of her younger brothers along to play with the Indian children in the camp, whilst she visited the Great Chief's wife, Laughing Brook. During these times, Little Crow would either be with the elders, or patrolling the Nelson lands.

As the seasons changed, the winds blew cold and the leaves dropped from the trees whilst the Lakota land prepared itself for a long hard winter. Anya's pregnancy had reached its final stages and Hannah stayed close to her mama, during this time; to ensure her safety. Anya's stomach had grown enormous and in spite of the physical changes her body underwent; her mind had now cleared and all remnants of her childlike behaviour seemed to have disappeared. Hannah was greatly relieved at this turn of events; and hoped it would last, for not only her mama, but for the unborn child's sake. Nevertheless, she was still very careful in what she said to her mother; for fear she might suffer a setback at any time. On Friday afternoon of that week, Hannah had been outside collecting eggs in the chicken coop, not far from the family's homestead; and she heard a high pitched scream come from the house, which made her jump. Hannah shivered and dropped the bucket of eggs, which now lay cracked and dripping at her feet. Not caring about the eggs, Hannah ran to the homestead and burst through the door. Upon entering the homestead, she saw her mama standing at the kitchen table and clutching a chair with both hands. A clear fluid could be seen gathering in a pool at her Mama's feet; and the whites of Anya's knuckles were showing, while she gripped the chair and a labour pain wracked her body with fierce intensity.

Hannah had witnessed many labours in the past, back in Norway, but was very frightened because she had never been the one entirely responsible for helping someone to give birth to a baby before. She was especially worried, because this was her mother; but there was not a doctor within a hundred miles, in this wild land, and so she squared her shoulders and washed her hands and hoped that what she knew would be enough. Hannah shooed her younger brothers out of the small house, and helped Anya change into a white cotton gown and then get into bed. After this, she called outside the front door to her brothers and said: "Go and tell Peter to find Papa; because mama is having her baby, do you understand?" The little boys looked frightened; but ran to the front field to tell Peter the news. He had been gathering buffalo chips and wasted no time in saddling the horse to fetch his father. Hannah returned to the task at hand; and determinedly vowed to herself, that she would make sure that her mama birthed her baby safely.

The delivery of Hannah's new sister thankfully progressed very quickly and by the time Eric arrived back to the Nelson homestead, and rushed through the door; his wife's raven haired child lay sleeping in her arms. Anya was glowing and smiled tiredly at Eric. He walked uncertainly to the side of her bed, taking in the idyllic scene. The infant although small; had a cherubic face, with a small upturned nose and a tiny rosebud mouth. Eric looked at this small girl child and thought she was the prettiest thing he had ever seen in his life and a great love for her swelled in his chest. Eric squeezed his wife's hand and kissed her cheek, saying: "She is a pretty little thing; just like her Mama. Wife, you have done very well," he said in a gentle voice. Tears streamed down Hannah's face, as she looked at her parents and the perfect child, she had helped to deliver. She was emotionally and physically drained from the day; but was hugely relieved at both the beautiful baby and her father's reaction to the child. "At last," she thought, "my family can get back to normal."

Eric continued to beam at his wife, and said: "Well Mama, what shall we call her?" Anya looked down at her sleeping child, lovingly and said: "I think we should name her, Marguerite, for my mama; but we can call her Maggie, if you like." Eric feeling emotional at his wife's words, kissed her on the cheek, and said, "That is a fine name, Anya, and she will make a fine addition to our happy home."

Chapter 23 ─────────────────────

Hannah had been out to see the Lakotas a few days before, and was stirring the family's laundry in a big pot of boiling water over the fire in the front of the homestead. Suddenly, when she glanced at the horizon, she spotted a large regiment of army soldiers headed towards the Nelson property. Panicking, Hannah wiped her hands on her apron, and went in to tell her mama to watch the fire. For once, the horse was close by, grazing in a field by the house, because Peter had gone to help his father in the fields. Hannah saddled the horse and rode it, as fast as she could, to the caves where the Indians were camped; and hoped she hadn't been seen by the soldiers, during her rushed journey. The soldiers were still miles away, but Hannah knew she must act quickly to protect her friends. She was aware it would take at least a half an hour to reach the camp; but pressed on, determined to reach the caves.

Hannah finally arrived and was shocked to realise that all the women, children and old ones were missing. She was puzzled as to where they could have gone in such a short time; and quickly found Little Crow to tell him about the soldiers and ask about their whereabouts. He realised when he looked at the panicked expression on her face, that he needed to calm Hannah's fears, and quickly said: "Little one, do not be troubled, I have known of the white soldiers coming and moved the women and children and old ones, on to a safe place. We found more caves not far from here; that have deeper recesses to hide my people and this is a place, the white soldiers will not think to look."

Hannah replied in a small voice: "But what about you, Little Crow?" "You must not die, you are a great leader among your people?" Little Crow looked intently at Hannah, surprised at her question, and answered, saying: "The mantle of White Buffalo Woman, rests upon you; and you have been used two times to save me and my son. We will live and we will survive, for this is the will of the gods, little one," he added. He then turned to give orders for his braves to continue packing the camp items, in order to move them on to the new site, and not wishing to disturb him further; Hannah said goodbye and rode her horse back to the homestead, worrying the entire journey about the Lakota's welfare. She was convinced their lives were in grave danger and there was very little she could do to help them; unless she received guidance from her gifting. And for now, the gifting was not telling her anything at all.

Anya had much improved since the arrival of her baby. She understood Hannah's instructions and took more and more responsibility for the household tasks each day. A day had passed since the sighting of the soldiers, and Hannah was jumpy and nervous and was thankful for her mama's help. She had time to go off by herself and sought guidance from her gifting. and she paced back and forth, wondering what to do. Around mid-afternoon, she heard a thundering of hooves coming towards the homestead: and expecting the soldiers, she patted her hair and straightened her dress, because Hannah knew she would have to put on the best performance of her life. At last, when she heard the riders come to a halt in front of the homestead, a man's voice shouted, "Ho, soldier's halt." Hannah stepped outside the front door, and smiled sweetly, greeting the hard-faced army sergeant and asked: "Morning Sir, what can I do for you?" The brawny sergeant stepped forward and looked her over from head to toe, and it was obvious he liked what he saw. Yet Hannah remained unmoved at his blatant scrutiny, and he gruffly queried: "Who lives here, Miss?" Hannah looked at him innocently and replied: "Just me, my brothers and sister and both my parents, why do you ask, Sir?" The sergeant was amused at her curiosity and obliged her question and replied: "We have reason to believe, there are Indian savages in these parts, Miss; may I enquire have you seen anything?" Hannah looked wide eyed and tried to look convincing, as she said: "No, not anything unusual, Sir; but to be honest, I don't stray too far from home. Can I offer you any water before you ride on?" she asked.

The grey bearded sergeant seemed satisfied with Hannah's answer, and grudgingly tipped his hat and said: "Well, thank you Miss, but we have enough water, I think we will be on our way now; but remember we don't take kindly to anyone covering up for the indians, cos' those savages are animals and would kill you in your sleep if they were given half the chance." Hannah clapped her hand over her mouth, feigning horror at his words, and the sergeant cackled with laughter along with several of his soldiers, whilst he mounted his horse and the regiment of soldiers galloped away.

Hannah was relieved to see the soldiers riding in the opposite direction to the Indians; yet she had to admit, that the interchange with the soldiers was a little too close for comfort. The next day, Hannah rode out on the Nelson's only horse, sitting in front of her papa to warn Little Crow of the soldiers' visit. Both she and her papa were surprised to find, however; the cave the indians had been in, was completely empty when they rode into it, without an indian in sight. The disappearance of the indians remained a mystery for the next week and Hannah was frustrated that she had no idea where the Lakotas were hiding. The only information she had, was the clue that Little Crow had mentioned, that the tribe were hidden in caves not far away. Eric had no idea where these caves might be, and tried not to interfere; and kept quiet for most of the week; until he decided he couldn't bear to see the worried expression on Hannah's face any longer.

Deciding to bring the matter up one evening after supper, Eric was determined to speak to his daughter about her worries. He asked her to take a walk with him, and Hannah agreed absently and wrapped her heavy shawl around her shoulders, even though she was not really feeling like a walk. Eric was not fooled though and Hannah's hunched shoulders and downcast eyes told him everything he needed to know. He finally broke the silence as they walked and said; "Hannah you must realise these indians are not your sole responsibility. I am sure your time with them is not finished yet." He saw the tears in Hannah's eyes, as she gazed at him; but he also felt a sense of pride when he saw her compose herself and respond: "Yes, you are right Papa. I must not lose hope; because I don't know how or when, but somehow I am meant to protect them." Eric squeezed her hand encouragingly, saying: "You will find a way, both you and your gifting; but it may not be today or maybe not even tomorrow, but soon, and you must be patient." Hannah looked at him comically and said; "You know I am not very good at being patient, Papa; but I will work on that." Eric neither agreed nor disagreed with her statement and replied: "Now, let's get back to the house, because the wind is making it powerful cold out here." Hannah smiled indulgently at her papa and they walked back to the homestead, arm in arm.

Eric had also promised that evening, under the stars, that he would take Hannah out on the Nelson lands from time to time, to look for the indians. On these outings, she was usually seated in front of her father, as they rode the Nelson's single horse over the flat plains. Eric had forbidden her to ride alone across the fields, with both the rogue soldiers and indians, a constant threat. He did not so much mistrust Little Crow and his braves; but he had heard of warlike bands of Indians that answered to no one, who would like nothing better than to capture a young white girl and dishonour her.

One day, Hannah and Eric were riding on the north side of the Nelson property, and they suddenly caught sight of an emaciated wolf running towards them menacingly with white froth streaming from its' mouth. Eric's horse was terrified at the sight of the approaching wolf and it jumped and pranced whilst he tried to control it. The frightened horse whinnied nervously and was desperate to escape; and Eric tried to think fast and noticed that the wolf seemed to be more focused on his horse, rather than himself or Hannah. He quickly placed Hannah on a nearby boulder and told her to hide behind it; and rode the horse the opposite direction to lead the wolf away from his daughter. The rabid wolf continued to chase the man on the horse; and paid little attention to Hannah; and started snarling the closer it came to the horse's legs. Standing up behind the boulder, Hannah watched and started screaming, when she saw the wolf bite the rear leg of the horse and saw the terrified beast rear up on its' hind legs and fall backwards onto her papa.

At first, all was quiet, after the terrible incident, and Hannah completely horrified by what she had just seen, was too stunned to move. She desperately prayed, "Oh God, please help us," and sprang into action, running to her papa, with tears streaming down her face, and hoped against hope, he was still alive. Upon reaching him, unbelievably she saw that, although her father had one of his legs trapped underneath the injured and groaning horse, the wolf was still alive and stood over him snarling and was ready to pounce at his throat. Suddenly, in a matter of seconds, six arrows ploughed into the neck and body of the rabid wolf and it fell to the ground, its' wounded body breathing its' last breath, as it died. Emotions overcoming her, Hannah ran across to her papa and cradled his head in her lap.

Eric's body was limp and he lay unconscious in his daughter's arms. Hannah heard footsteps behind her and she was relieved to see Little Crow and his braves standing all around her. Little Crow called to Hannah to: "Look Away," and then quickly chopped the throat of the injured horse with his tomahawk to stop its' suffering. When the suffering beast finally went quiet, Little Crow then knelt beside Eric to check his breathing. The Chief was relieved to find the white farmer was still breathing; but noticed the large lump on the back of his head and ordered his braves to lift the horse off the man's leg, so that he could pull the injured man out from under the dead animal. When Little Crow was finally able to examine the white man's twisted and injured leg, it was obviously broken in several places. Although Little Crow did not have any wood to set the unconscious man's leg right away, he did his best to reposition it and decided once he was able to get the man back to his homestead; he would retrieve tent poles from his tribe later on, to set it properly.

Hannah was still quite traumatised by the wolf attack; but nevertheless managed to thank Little Crow in a small voice, for his help. He and his braves had fashioned a make shift pallet with buffalo hides for her father to lie on, and Little Crow eyed Hannah and responded to her saying simply: "You have done much more than this for me and my son, White Buffalo Woman, and I have vowed that I will protect you and your family for the rest of my days."

The journey of five miles back to the homestead was tedious and to Hannah, it felt like it would last forever. When they finally did arrive at the homestead, the indians carried the injured man inside the Nelson home and placed him carefully on his bed. Anya and the children were extremely frightened at the sight of the indians; but were too concerned by the injuries of Eric to let it show. Anya cried out when she saw her unconscious, bruised and bleeding husband; but Hannah quickly reassured her and said: "He is alive, Mama, but he has a big lump on his head and his leg is broken. He will be fine, but needs us to stay calm and we need to help him right now," she added. Anya quickly shook herself and assured Hannah, contritely, "I will do all I can to help," and the two women set about making Eric comfortable.

Having witnessed the arrival of his papa and the indians from the front field; Peter rushed through the front door, soon after their arrival, and ran across the homestead to grab his father's gun and aimed it pointedly at the indians. "What have you done to my papa, you savages?" he demanded. Hannah gasped at her brother's actions, especially when she saw him aim the gun at the indians. "Peter," she shouted, "what are you doing?" "These Indians saved Papa from a rabid wolf, and we owe his life to them." Peter looked at his sister slowly comprehending her words, and lowered the gun; but remained belligerent and eyed the indians and his sister darkly.

Little Crow had raised his arm to his braves to stop them from raising their weapons against Hannah's brother, and he was relieved when the young man finally lowered his gun. Hannah then said quickly: "I will explain it all later Peter, but right now, I must get Papa comfortable in his bed, so go and get some water so I can wash his wounds." Peter obediently walked out of the cabin without saying a further word; and Little Crow said to

Hannah: "I will go back to my people and get some tent poles to set your father's leg and be back as soon as I can." Hannah nodded her thanks and the indians left the homestead, and the Nelsons to care for the injured man.

The Lakota Chief and his braves never returned to the homestead as promised though, and Hannah was both worried and surprised by this in the following days; because Little Crow had never broken his word to her, so she knew something must be desperately wrong. Fortunately, Christian had ridden across to visit Hannah, two days after the incident, and when he found out what had happened, he rode all day and all night to Fort Webster and found a military doctor, who had just arrived from the east coast. The doctor had agreed to come to the Nelson homestead to treat the injured man, and when he arrived at the farm, Eric was running a high fever, and seemed semi-comatosed from his head injury. Also, his wounds to his leg had become infected, and the doctor was not hopeful about his patient's chances. The doctor set Eric's leg as best he could, and advised the women to do all they could to break his fever; and he left the farm, worried that the poor man would not live to see the winter.

————————————————

Chapter 24

Although Hannah listened to the doctor's advice, she did not agree with the man's abysmal conclusions concerning her papa's chances for survival; and sought her gifting for a way to bring about his full recovery, despite the odds. Two nights passed and it was touch and go for her papa; but at last morning broke, and Hannah had direction from her gifting, and she knew how she could help him. Again and again, the stream she went to on a daily basis, came before her eyes, and then it was clear what she must do. That morning, after breakfast, Hannah instructed Christian and Peter to carry Eric to the stream; persuading them by saying: "It is the only way to help him."

Both young men looked at her with disbelieving eyes, but they knew better than to question her, and went to their father's bed and picked him up to take him to the stream, being careful not to put any undue stress on his injured leg. Hannah had prepared her papa for the strange outing and had explained why it was necessary. The sick man had very little strength to argue or question his daughter; and weakly agreed to her plan, putting his trust in her gifting.

It was not easy to transport Eric to the stream and a twenty minute walk turned into an hour long ordeal. Anya could not bear to see her husband in pain, and elected to stay back at the homestead with the children. This suited Hannah just fine, because she could not risk being distracted from the force of her gifting in any way, in order for the miracle to take place successfully.

When they finally arrived at the water bank, Hannah told Christian and Peter to keep walking into the muddy stream and to go to the deep part of the water. She explained they would need to fully emerge her father's leg in to the water, to take full advantage of the healing power of the stream. Peter started to protest about the ludicrous instruction, but one look at Christian's face convinced him to keep quiet and he did as he was told. As they lowered the older man into the water, Eric passed out, and was unaware of the cold muddy waters seeping over his leg. Hannah further instructed the young men to dip her father's leg into the river six more times and then to take him back to the homestead and to remove his wet clothes and put him back into his bed.

Christian and Peter noticed the peace on Hannah's face, and shrugged their shoulders, doing as they were told; and slowly carried Eric back to the homestead and put him back to bed. Afterwards, Eric remained in a deep sleep and Hannah and her family expectantly waited for the results of the young girl's healing powers, throughout the night. The next morning there was excitement in the Nelson household. Eric awoke from his deep sleep, looking peaceful and refreshed. He smiled brightly at Anya and Hannah, saying: "I feel better than I have felt in ages, can you make some breakfast for a starving man?" Hannah looked uncertainly at her papa and said: "Yes Papa of course; but can we get you to sit up and test out your leg first?" As if forgetting he even had an injured leg; Eric looked surprised at her request and looked down at his splinted leg. He then stretched it and sat up with ease at the side of the bed and removed the splint trappings. Anya, Hannah, and Peter gasped simultaneously and then whooped and clapped their hands with joy, when Eric stood up and danced a jig. Christian, who had just come in from tending the livestock, witnessed the older man's dance of victory and tears pricked his eyes. He went across the homestead to hug Hannah and shake Eric's hand, and declared. "This is truly a miracle, sweet Hannah, surely the power of your gifting rests heavily upon you, and you should be very pleased." Hannah, humble as always, reciprocated his hug and smiled from ear to ear, enjoying her family's joy and celebration; and looked with joy at the sight of her papa, renewed and well.

Life at home, was at last getting back to normal, and Christian stayed on to help Eric with the clearing of the fields for a few days, to make up for the time that had been lost during his ordeal. When Christian did finally return to his family's lands;

he decided to leave his horse for the time being, at the Nelson's farm to help out, choosing to walk the distance back to his uncle's homestead.

One day, Hannah felt the need to get away; and although her papa and Christian had warned her time and time again, that she should not ride out alone; she saddled Christian's horse and galloped across the plains; feeling all the tension melt away. The wind whipped across her face and when Hannah reached the perimeters of the Nelson property, she decided to explore the area of the canyons. She let the horse meander through the narrow paths between the canyons for a time, and after travelling a short distance was amazed to see that there was a narrow path barely large enough for a man's body to slip through, in one of the rock faces. Intrigued, she decided to explore it and dismounted her horse and tied it to a nearby bush. Hannah made her way through the narrow passage, wondering where it led to. She had to admit that she was taking a chance by going on foot, because wolves, bears and mountain lions were an ever increasing threat in the wild terrain; but she could not resist following her instincts and exploring the trail.

As if emerging into another world, Hannah was fascinated to see that the path led into a deep recess of caves, but became frightened when pitch blackness descended over her, as she walked into the underground chambers. She tried to adjust her eyes to the darkness of the caves, and continued to move forward, and was delighted when she smelled the unmistakable aroma of pumpkin mash and buffalo jerky wafting through the cave towards her. Hannah continued walking and was comforted to hear the rumbling of voices within the cavernous caves and the unmistakable language of the Lakota Sioux, echoing across the cave walls. After walking another half an hour, she also saw a multitude of fiery torches lighting up the temporary home of the Lakota people. Hannah made her way into the well-lit portion of the cave. As she looked above her head,, she saw there was daylight showing at the top of the chamber, and that fresh air was still coming into the cave through the rocky crevices, giving much needed fresh air to the people who lived deep within. She also saw there were buffalo hides stretched horizontally from the ceiling of the cave to the ground, which subdivided each family and gave them privacy. Hannah never ceased to admire the Lakotas for their adaptability and resourcefulness. She thought to herself, these people have the will to survive like no one I have ever seen.

Excited, chatter erupted when the Lakota women caught sight of Hannah, but she kept walking, not acknowledging their faces, and sincerely hoped to find Laughing Brook or Little Deer soon, to ensure they were both safe and well. As if reading her thoughts, the graceful form of Laughing Brook walked towards her. She smiled and embraced Hannah, greeting her warmly and said: "I knew you would find us; welcome White Buffalo Woman to our new home." She led her back to their partition and seated Hannah on animal furs and offered her something to eat. Hannah dutifully ate what was offered to her, and then asked Laughing Brook, if she might see Little Crow. Laughing Brook's face looked strained and she said, "No, he is not here, White Buffalo Woman, he has gone to Fort Webster, because the soldiers have captured Wowinapa and some other young boys from our tribe."

Hannah noticed Laughing Brook's trembling voice and immediately concerned, asked: "Why have the soldiers done this, Laughing Brook, surely they have not found your hiding place?" Not waiting for Laughing Brook to respond, Little Deer who had slipped in during the conversation, answered and said: "Wowinapa went with a group of our young braves to get some chicken eggs and a white settler's wife has been shot and killed." Shocked, Hannah jumped when she heard a baby's cry and she noticed a small baby swaddled in blankets sitting to the right of Laughing Brook. Hannah remembered when she saw the child; that she had seen him in a dream only a week before. She had been shown in the dream, that this was the child that would succeed Little Crow, as Chief of the Lakota people; not Wowinapa, and Laughing Brook said: "His name is Walking Bear." Hannah leaned over the child and touched his small head, feeling the softness and warmth of his sturdy body. She then turned to Laughing Brook and said to her: "Fear not, Laughing Brook, all will be well, with your husband and sons, and this one will be a blessing to his people." Hannah then kissed the baby and rose to her feet and said: "Now I must go home, as there is much to do, and not much time to do it" and squeezed the older woman's hand to encourage her and turned to make her way out of the caves.

Wowinapa was now thirteen and a tall, arrogant child, who was headstrong and did not listen to the council of others, choosing to go his own way. Because of the burdens which continually weighed upon his father's shoulders; Little Crow spent very little time with Wowinapa; and as a result, he had not restrained his son from foolish behaviour nearly enough. Tired of being treated like a child and angry that the white soldiers caused his people, in his words: "To hide like scared rabbits, rather than stand and fight;" Wowinapa bragged to his friends, that he would steal a horse from the white man to prove his manhood. But the young teenager knew he could not take the horse from anyone linked to Hannah. Wowinapa had also never stolen anything before, and so he and his friends decided that they would practice on a white farmer's chickens first, just to make sure they were doing everything right.

The Indian boys had out the next morning for a white settler's neighbouring farm, and crept out of the Lakota caves, travelling on foot the eight miles to carry out their plan. The youths arrived at the white settler's farm around four in the afternoon and agreed they must wait until dark, before the chicken eggs could be stolen. Wowinapa bragged to his friends and said: "Stealing these eggs will be easy, because the white man is weak; and this will prove that I am a fierce warrior to the white man." He further bragged that he would kill the white man, if he tried to stop him and raised his tomahawk and knife to show his courage. His friends laughed and slapped him on the back, cheering him on, as they were still a quarter of a mile from the farm and could not be heard.

When darkness fell, Wowinapa crawled on his belly with his knife, clenched in his mouth; and the young brave made his way to the chicken enclosure. The chickens were clucking when they caught sight of the boy, but the birds had been nesting since it was night time and the eggs were easily taken by him, and he leapt over the enclosure and made his way back to the top of the field, with very little effort. After Wowinapa returned to the rest of the group, however; he was ridiculed by the other Indian boys and told that the egg stealing had been too easy and was not real proof of a brave warriors' manhood. Upon hearing these words, Wowinapa became frustrated and angry, and threw the eggs to the ground, shouting: "Ok, my brothers, if these eggs are not good enough for you, I will go to the farm house and kill the farmer and his family," and he walked angrily back towards the house, turning his back on the young braves.

Chapter 25 ─────────────────────

The Nelsons in the last year, had developed a close friendship with a kindly Episcopal priest named, Henry Wipple, who had established a small church in the area and was a jolly and well loved soul and a pillar of the community. Hannah especially had a soft spot for the older man, because he told many stories about his interactions with the indians, as an Indian emissary dispatched by the government; and was a self-professed ardent admirer of the Lakota Sioux tribe.

One such story he told, was of when he first journeyed to the Dakota Territory in his youth, and had contracted small pox and had been left to die in the wilderness by his terrified travelling companions. After two days of lying at the brink of death, in the abandoned campsite, the priest was found by some Lakota Sioux women, who had been foraging for berries, and they took pity on him and moved him to the edge of their Indian camp and took care of him. And although it took several weeks, slowly these women nursed him back to full recovery. At the time, Henry had come to admire and appreciate the Lakota tribe and vowed he would repay them for their actions one day, if ever given the chance in the future.

Since that time, he had been sickened to hear of the endless stream of prejudice and tyranny lodged against the Lakota people by the white man; and in his private moments; did not really blame the indians for striking back with violence, even though he hoped, one day, that peace would be agreed between the two sides. Henry was comical in his descriptions of his day to day activities in the community and always brought laughter to the Nelson household when he came to visit; and even though food was sparse in the Nelson household, there was always plenty of buffalo meat and lively conversation to be had, which made for a pleasant visit.

Before leaving for Fort Webster, Little Crow searched the various passages of the caves, where his people now lived; and had come to the conclusion that Wowinapa and his friends were not in them, and even worse, that they had been gone the entire day and that night was fast approaching. He was not initially concerned, as many times the young boys lost track of time, when they were out hunting; but as the evening progressed, Little Crow became more and more worried. The white military patrols had become more frequent recently and he knew the boys could easily be apprehended by the white soldiers, if they strayed too far from the caves.

The Great Chief approached one of his braves, Bright Eagle, whose son was also missing and asked; "Do you know where our sons have gone, my friend?" Bright Eagle's shoulders slumped and his face grew serious; because he did not wish to give his leader bad news, but he answered him truthfully and said: "My Chief, my younger son tells me that your son wanted to prove his manhood by stealing eggs from the white man; and that he has taken many of our boys with him to accomplish this task, this day." Little Crow's eyes widened in disbelief when he heard the man's explanation and he went quiet, not knowing how to respond to such a statement. Finally he said: "My friend, bring your youngest son to my fire, as I wish to hear his words, so I can best decide what to do." Bright Eagle bowed his head and agreed, and went to find his son, as Little Crow requested; and brought him to his leader's fire to tell all that he knew about the boys' whereabouts.

During the conversation around the Chief's fire, a series of shouts could be heard at the mouth of the cave, because two young braves had just run into the cave breathless and panic stricken, and they asked to see Little Crow right away. The two youths were brought to Little Crow's fire and were both close to tears, when they told their disjointed tale of what had happened to the Chief's son. They explained: "Wowinapa went to steal the white farmer's chicken eggs and when he returned from the farm, he was goaded by the other boys that this was not enough." They continued and said: "Wowinapa became angry at their words and said he would go and kill the white farmer and his family himself to prove to them that he was a man and left by himself to do so."

Little Crow's throat constricted at their words, and he steeled himself to hear what happened next. The youngest boy continued and said: "He left then to go back to the farmer's homestead and we saw Wowinapa sneak inside the farmhouse, and we heard a rifle blast sound very soon after. We ran then, because we were scared we would be killed by the white farmer like Wowinapa had been; and we ran for our lives," he declared. Shocked, Little Crow bowed his head after the boys finished their stories, and tried to regain his composure, trying with all his might not to show the deep grief he felt at their words.

Christian anxiously waited for Hannah in the Nelson homestead, pacing the floors and wondered where she had gone. He knew with her inquisitive nature that her first inclination would be to search for the Indians; and he had made up his mind that he would check on her every few days to make sure she was still safe. Finally, after several hours, he heard the sound of hoof beats coming close to the farm house. Relieved, he hurried out the front door. When he saw Hannah's small frame riding in on his horse, Christian noticed the troubled expression on her face and called to her: "Where have you been Hannah, my love, I was worried for your safety?" She looked up surprised, and feeling happy to see him there, she replied: "I am fine Chris; I was just going for a little ride and lost track of time." Christian knew her too well, to believe she was telling him everything, and waited until she dismounted the horse before questioning her further. Once Hannah had stepped down from the horse and they had unsaddled the animal and given him food and water; she asked: "How is your family Chris, is everyone well?" Christian looked at her impatiently and said: "Yes, they are all fine, but now tell me where you really were, and no holding back." Hannah met Christian's eyes and smiled at him, but kept silent. "Well?" he said. She sheepishly stared at her feet and finally said: "Well I found the Lakota's hiding place and I am desperately worried, because Wowinapa has been taken by the white soldiers and Little Crow has gone to look for him." "Slow down," Christian said, "and tell me everything and we will see what we can do to help." Tears filled Hannah's eyes, as she entered his open arms. He then kissed the top of her head, while she cried out her fears.

The next week came and went, and the routine of the Nelson household settled in. "But the trouble with routine," Hannah thought, "is that people start to relax and tend to be less cautious, which is a mistake in this part of the world, with all this trouble brewing between the Indians and the white man." She had not told anyone but Christian, about the shooting; but one day Eric came home, and informed his eldest children and wife, about the shooting on the neighbouring farm. He recounted how he had heard that the farmer's wife had been killed by indians, whilst the farmer was out hunting. Eric described how the farmer had tragically come home and found his wife dead from a gunshot wound in the head. Eric had waited until the smaller children had gone to bed before he broke the news; and then he looked at Hannah and asked pointedly: "Are the Lakotas responsible for this woman's death?" Hannah stared at her papa and wished that Christian was there to support her; but then straightened her shoulders and decided to tell Eric what she knew of the tragedy. When she finished her story, Eric gave a low whistle and said: "All hell will break loose now Hannah, you must not get involved and let the soldiers sort this out." "Yes Papa, I see your point, but we don't know if this was an accident or Wowinapa meant for this to happen," she pointed out. "You can't condemn a young boy, without knowing the truth," she declared. Peter raised his voice, frustrated at her words and responded: "When will you get it through your head, that the soldiers view the Indians as less than animals in this territory, and that young boy does not have a chance in hell of going free now." Hannah burst into tears, and Eric immediately regretted his words, because he knew what the Lakotas meant to her. Yet unless another miracle took place, Eric could not see how the fate of this young indian boy could be altered, because as surely as he was Norwegian, Little Crow's son was headed for the gallows and very soon.

Chapter 26

The days ran into weeks, and the white army soldier patrols increased around the Nelson homestead. Hannah did not dare make the frequent trips to the Lakota Indian caves to check on her friends; for fear she would be spotted and endanger the Lakotas further. She had heard through Henry Wipple, that Little Crow had gone to Fort Webster to give himself up in exchange for his son, which terrified her; because she knew the Great Chief had been a wanted man for some time, and that the army soldiers would not hesitate to execute him in order to make an example of him to put the indians in their place. Little Crow had successfully eluded the soldiers for almost two years, many times wearing white men's clothing, to achieve this purpose; and was fast becoming something of a legend amongst the white people. In fact, it seemed like every atrocity carried out by rogue indian braves against the white settlers; such as: rape, murder, and burned out farms, was often blamed on him and his tribe, because of the notoriety he bore across the land.

When Wowinapa had been ridiculed by his friends, after stealing the white settler's chicken eggs; and then he had bragged he would go and kill the farmer and his family, he immediately wanted to retract his words, once he'd spoken them; but his pride did not allow him to do so. And not feeling he had a choice, the young brave crept back to the farmer's homestead and quietly slipped through the back door, intent on proving his manhood, but not really wanting to hurt anyone. He decided he would slip in and out of the farmhouse, and tell his friends that no one had been at home; but what he found when he entered the farmhouse, was a rather slim young white woman asleep in a chair and a baby asleep in a nearby crib and no man in sight.

Wowinapa had no intention of killing the woman or child; and turned to go out of the homestead, as quickly as he had come; but when he turned his back to retrace his steps and leave the farmers' home, he heard the young woman wake and scream and the undeniable cocking of a rifle behind him. She then shouted in a high pitched voice: "Don't move or I'll shoot." Wowinapa froze, and hoping the white woman would be too frightened to shoot; he turned and ran towards her, grabbing the rifle she held with both hands, and tried to wrestle it from her grasp. The young woman struggled with the young Indian boy for several minutes, both intent on taking control of the rifle; and suddenly the rifle discharged itself, and the young woman fell heavily to the floor, after the gunpowder entered her head, instantly killing her.

Shocked beyond words, Wowinapa sobbed when he saw the young mother fall to the floor, and he ran out the door, too frightened to even think about what had just happened. To make matters worse, an army soldier patrol had been riding only a quarter of a mile from the farmer's property; and had heard the gunshot. Ten minutes after the shooting had occurred, the regiment came thundering on their horses to the white settler's homestead; and the soldiers immediately dismounted their horses and ran into the farmhouse finding the dead woman and her crying baby. Not long after the grisly discovery, the army sergeant in charge of the patrol, shouted for his men: "Spread out and search the area to find the woman's killers."

When a nearly hysterical Wowinapa ran to where he thought his friends were waiting for him, all of the young indian boys had run for their lives, but in spite of their panic, several of the young braves were captured by the white soldiers and Wowinapa was singled out as the murderer once apprehended; due to the murdered woman's blood being found on his chest and hands.

Although heartbroken, when Little Crow had heard of his son's capture, he set his mind to formulating a plan to save his son. He knew deep down that Wowinapa was not a murderer, but he was realistic enough to know, that if his son was accused of killing any white settlers, that sadly his fate would be sealed. Owning up to this truth, the Lakota Chief realised he must move fast, in order to save his son.

Hannah had been riding out on the Nelson lands with Christian, soon after the incident had occurred and her eyes widened, one day, when suddenly an army regiment rode past them in the distance and they saw Wowinapa walking behind one of the soldier's horses with several other young braves in leg irons, with their heads bowed. Both she and Christian rode closer to the soldiers, and noticed that Wowinapa and the other young braves were bruised and bleeding, like they had been beaten, and that one of Wowinapa's eyes was swollen entirely shut. Hannah's hand covered her mouth and she gasped when she saw the state of Little Crow's son; and Christian squeezed her hand, warning her to stay quiet until the soldiers had safely passed by.

Once the soldiers were at a safe distance, Hannah, clearly distressed, said: "It is true, they are taking Wowinapa and these other young Indian boys to Fort Webster and God help them, Chris, did you see what they had done to those boys?" Christian nodded and said: "There is serious trouble afoot that is for sure, what do you want to do Hannah, it won't be easy to help them, you know?" Hannah responded: "We must go to Fort Webster to see what the white soldiers are going to do to Wowinapa and Little Crow, and then hopefully my gifting will give us direction after that, Chris." Helpless to disagree with her words, Christian said in a resigned voice, "Ok, but we must make sure that your papa and Henry are aware of what we are doing, and then we will leave tomorrow morning; because there is not much time to lose." Lost in her thoughts, Hannah looked up lovingly at Christian and said: "Thank you, Chris, for supporting me in this; I would be lost without you."

Hannah dreamed that night a dream that was more of a nightmare, as the very real and terrible details of the night tale unfolded. In the dream, she rode up to the Lakota caves on her horse and dismounted and entered the caves. Once in the caves, Hannah heard the unmistakable sounds of weeping; and suddenly she started running through the caves, frantically looking everywhere for Little Crow. In the dream, at last she found him sitting woodenly with some of the elders, with his face devoid of expression and downcast, and he didn't meet her eyes at first. Hannah did not want to embarrass the Chief; but she could feel his terrible sadness as he sat motionless before her. Finally, the Great Chief signalled for her to sit beside him, and she did as she was told and noticed that the elders and the Chief were looking into the fire, with their eyes riveted on the flames. She herself, then focused her own eyes on the fire, and terror and fear gripped her, when she saw herself the same scene that they did, in the unforgiving flames.

A vision more terrible than any she had ever seen before, assaulted her, when she saw a mass number of young Lakota braves appear before her. These braves stood on a great wooden gallows, with nooses around their necks, awaiting their executions. Amongst the doomed braves, was Little Crow's son Wowinapa. In the dream, the keening of the Lakota women could be heard continually, echoing throughout the caves and the unmistakable outcome of the gallows was made clear.

After dreaming the terrible dream, Hannah sat up in her bed with a start, and she put her head in her hands, wondering what she could do to stop this terrible thing from happening. She already knew that Little Crow was headed to Fort Webster to save his son, and she was convinced he would try to bargain with the white man for his son's safe release. Yet, with the price on his head, Little Crow, in her mind; had little chance of succeeding, and she desperately sought her gifting, because it was clear that only supernatural intervention could save the Lakota Sioux Chief and his son now.

At last, dawn came, and Hannah knew the direction she must take. Fortunately, Christian had agreed to come that day and she would ask him to stand with her, when she explained her plan to her papa and Henry Wipple; because she knew, without a doubt, there would be objections coming from both men. But it didn't matter, she thought to herself; because she would carry out her plan to save the Lakota Sioux, and would be successful, whatever it took.

Later that evening, Hannah with Christian by her side, courageously laid out her plan to both of the older men and waited for their reactions. And although Eric looked uncertain, Henry Whipple smiled when he heard Hannah describe her plan, impressed by her plucky ideas. Amazed at his reaction, Hannah asked him: "Do you not find my plan to go to Washington D.C., to tell President Lincoln of the plight of the Lakota Sioux, crazy, Henry, because I would like you to go with Christian and me, if you would agree?" Henry's laughter could be heard reverberating around the farmhouse, at the courageous audacity of the young woman; and finally regaining his composure, he responded and said: "Yes, although your ideas to most might be crazy, my dear, I would be happy to accompany you, because President Abe and I are old friends and he will listen and reflect upon our words and act accordingly." Hannah squealed in delight and ran across the room and kissed him on the cheek, saying: "Thank you Henry, your faith in my gifting and your knowledge of the indians, will be invaluable on this trip; and I am sure we could not do it without you." Embarrassed, the frontier priest patted her on the shoulder, repeating: "I am happy to help dear, happy to help."

Eric then followed up the other man's words and said; "Well, I guess there is no stopping you three now; but make sure you two take care of my Hannah on the journey, mind; because I want her back here safe and sound very soon, do you hear me?" Christian stepped forward and shook Eric's hand, saying quietly: "You have my word, Sir; we will return your daughter back to you safely, very soon."

Chapter 27

On the journey to Fort Webster, Little Crow prepared himself for the bargain that must be struck between himself and the white man. He did not want to involve Hannah at this stage; because he believed the Spirit of the White Buffalo Woman would guide her and that he must surrender all the events that were currently happening to him and his people, to the will of the gods. Nevertheless, although he didn't let it show, a great fear and sadness gripped his heart, and these feelings almost overwhelmed him, at times.

Henry felt the success of the planned trip to Washington, rested heavily upon his ability to influence President Lincoln to reach out and provide assistance to the Lakota Indians. He realised that with the Civil War on, the conflict between the Indian and the white man was not something the President could afford to spend much time on; especially since many of his supporters were avid opponents of the "indian savages in the west." Yet, he also was aware that the President was an intrinsically fair man, and that he would not be able to hear about the injustices levied against the Indians, without doing something about it. There was also something about the courage and commitment of the young Norwegian girl, Hannah, that compelled Henry to help her; and although he had a feeling their journey would not be an easy one; he would do all he could to make it a success.

It was planned by Hannah and the men that they would travel to Fort Webster for supplies and discover what was happening with their Indian friends, before they set out on their journey back east. Christian brought an extra horse from his Aunt and Uncle's farm for Hannah and the three set out for the fort, just after breakfast. Henry warned Christian and Hannah that once they reached the fort, they must not show too much interest in the indians, because the soldiers would not hesitate to throw them into irons and accuse them as co-conspirators to the indians, if they noticed they had any sympathy for the Lakotas. This was especially true, since the white woman had been killed very close to the Nelson lands.

The trio rode for most of the day, finally reaching Fort Webster in the late afternoon. They rode into the fort gates and Hannah tried to stifle a gasp, when she immediately spotted Little Crow being led out from the military stockade in shackles. Little Crow kept his face unreadable and had been stripped to his waist with his head dress removed by the soldiers, in an effort to humiliate him. Christian reached over and squeezed Hannah's hand and tried to quietly support her; because he knew the sight of the humbled Chief must have been a tremendous blow to her. But to his amazement, he saw a steely glint enter her eyes as she straightened her shoulders and lifted her chin. She angrily declared in a low voice: "We cannot let this happen, Chris; we must leave as soon as possible to stop this from going any further." He agreed with her and said: "Yes, but try to calm yourself for now. We will leave at first light and do our best for them, Hannah." Henry looked across at the distressed girl and realised that he and Christian would have their hands full, in keeping Hannah away from Little Crow, while at the fort. He warned her firmly, trying not to let his heart soften when he saw her eyes glistening with tears, and said "We cannot risk you showing any closeness to the Lakota leader in plain view of the white army soldiers, Hannah, do you understand?" Hannah nodded her head glumly and wiped her eyes trying to collect herself. The older man decided at that moment, he would not tell her that Little Crow's likely fate would be torture and death in the coming weeks.

Later that day, even worse news came to their ears, when Henry overheard, whilst buying supplies at the fort general store, that not only Little Crow and his son were being held; but that there were plans to arrest three hundred indian braves on and off the surrounding reservations. These indians would be tried for murderous crimes against the white settlers in the Dakota Territory, in the coming weeks.

Hannah took the news of the impending arrests very badly and wept copiously, whilst Christian held her against his chest, trying to console her. Curious stares from passers-by were the inevitable result, and Christian quickly fabricated a story, saying: "My fiancé has just heard about a family tragedy back east, and we are travelling there very soon to attend the funeral." The soldiers seemed to accept this explanation from the tall fair haired man and went about their business without further comment, not wishing to intrude on the young woman's grief. Henry breathed a sigh of relief and was thankful for the younger man's quick thinking.

Henry was well aware of the political intrigues of Washington D.C.; and had decided prior to his leaving; to wire the President to get an invitation for he, Hannah, and Christian, before they set out for the long journey back east. In due course, an invitation came inviting Henry and the young people to a tea party at the White House with the President. Of course, the excitement of such an invitation, gave Hannah even more hope that they were going on the right course; however, Henry worried that the influence of the Attorney General, Edward Bates, would be a deterrent to their cause, because his influence over the President was well known. In addition, his son, John Bates, was 'according to his sources,' about to be appointed the US Army Chief of Staff. Edward Bates, had in fact, grown up as a young boy on a plantation full of slaves, and both father and son had a tendency to label anyone who was not white, as "lower life forms." But, Henry thought it best not to mention these details to Hannah or Christian; because he didn't wish to dampen the young people's enthusiasm. "Anyway," he thought to himself, "there is something special about little Hannah Nelson, and if anyone can change the course of history, she certainly can." So, the three friends rode out of Fort Webster on a sunny September day with high hopes and sturdy hearts.

Henry advised Hannah to dress as a man for most of the journey for her own protection, and Christian lent her some clothes for her to change into once they had ridden out of the fort. It was truly a comical sight to see her swallowed up by a heavy overcoat and a man's shirt and trousers; and even worse, Hannah had to keep the trousers bound with a rope, to keep them from falling down around her ankles. Her attire made her appear like a small boy in men's clothing, which Henry thought was indeed the perfect disguise.

It was faster to travel by horseback rather than wagon train to Washington D.C.; and the plan was, that the usual journey time of five to six weeks would be reduced to 21 days. During the journey, Henry emphasised to Hannah and Christian, that when they finally did meet with the President, that the human rights of the indians must be the central theme. They listened to the wise advice of their friend, agreeing to let him take the lead in the future discussions. However, Henry was adamant that Hannah should tell the President about the chain of events that she and her family had experienced during their time in this country, so President Abe could see the passion and conviction they all felt, in pleading the cause of their indian friends.

The immensity of Little Crow's plight was made even more real to Hannah, one night on the trail, when she dreamed again of the Great Chief and several of his braves standing on wooden gallows with ropes around their necks, waiting to be hanged. Suddenly, awakening from the nightmare, she sat up and screamed, crying uncontrollably. Christian, awakened by her distress, reached out to her and said, over and over: "It was only a dream." But Hannah's gifting told her that this was more than just a dream; but rather a sign that they hadn't much time and that the fate of the Great Chief and his people was totally dependent on the success of their meeting with the President. She settled herself though and allowed Christian to comfort her, and was happy she was not alone in her burden.

Even though the burden of the Lakota people's plight was ever present in their thoughts; the beauty of the landscape all around them, gave Hannah some semblance of peace, as they travelled the long trek back east. She seemed to notice things that she had not seen on her first trip to the Dakota Territory, and the lush plant and animal life all around them made her appreciate the land she had immigrated to immensely. But when the night fell, it was an entirely different story, and Hannah couldn't help but be fearful when the darkness and sounds of the eerie woodlands, brought to life how truly vulnerable they all were. The men took turns, keeping watch over the little camp and their horses; because the threat of large predators, whether it be bears or wolves, was a stark reality in the wild and fierce woodlands and hills of North America.

One night, Hannah had settled down to sleep and Henry was already snoring as he laid on his bed roll, across from her, having left Christian to keep watch. Suddenly, their horses began snorting and stamping their hooves anxiously in the meadow beyond the camp; and in the next few minutes the horse's nervousness seemed to worsen and their whinnying echoed throughout the night in high pitched and panicked tones. Concerned by the horse's fearful state, Christian decided to go and see what had frightened them, clutching his rifle close to his body. The noise of the panic stricken horses had awakened both Henry and Hannah; and they quickly jumped up from their bed rolls to join Christian, to find out what could be causing such a ruckus. The three feared the worst, as they moved together in the direction of the horses. The weary beasts had been staked in a meadow close to camp after a long day's travel, so they could graze during the night. The trio stood determinedly trying to look up and down the meadow to spot the threat to their horses. Then all at once, Hannah caught her breath when she looked across the meadow, and stared directly into the green eyes of a white wolf, just coming out of the trees and looking hungrily at the horses. She pointed to the fierce looking creature and shouted "Look there, just across the meadow, there is a white wolf."

Not wasting any time, Henry and Christian caught sight of the fierce animal, and made ready their weapons to shoot the creature. Hannah placed her hand on both their shoulders and shouted, "No, please…don't shoot it." Amazed at her words, the men watched Hannah stand very still, making eye contact with the white wolf, and saw the massive beast turn his head to look at her for several minutes. Hannah knew after spending time with the Lakota Sioux, that the sighting of this white wolf meant more than just a hungry predator looking for a meal. The Lakotas believed a white wolf to be a symbol and a confirmation of good fortune and success. She had also learned that, to the Sioux Indians, a white wolf was sacred and represented a Great Chief watching over his tribe. Hannah felt her gifting stir within her, and felt greatly comforted by the sighting of the white wolf, and was sure, that Little Crow's spirit was there with them, watching over them. After several minutes, the silent communion, between the wolf and Hannah, ended, and the creature turned and ran back into the woods. Christian and Henry lowered their guns, and Henry scratched his head in amazement. Finding his voice, he asked: "What was that all about Hannah, did you use your powers to frighten the beast away?" Hannah still wide eyed and very affected by the experience, turned to the men and said breathlessly: "No, he never meant to hurt us, or our horses, he was sent by the Great Chief Little Crow to let us know that we are on the right path and that the Indian guardians will be watching over us."

Not quite knowing how to respond to her forthright explanation, Christian put his arm around her shoulders and said: "Well, that is good news then for us. Now you and Henry go back to your beds; because dawn is fast approaching and Washington D.C. is still many days ride, so we will need to be well rested." Hannah nodded, still somewhat fazed by the experience and Henry stuck his arm out and said: "Here young Hannah take my arm and I will escort you back to camp," and back to their bed rolls they went, to settle down for a good sleep.

The following days came and went uneventfully and all three of the riders were tired and hungry by the time they finally reached the nation's capital. The travellers rode into the bustling city with its' miles and miles of shops, saloons and boarding houses; and were impressed by the men walking the wooden pavements in business suits and top hats; and by the women, who were wearing stylish dresses with hooped skirts and elaborate hats, of all shapes and sizes. Embarrassed by her men's clothing, Hannah declared to Christian, "Look at those stylish ladies, Chris; I must change out of these clothes because I must be a terrible sight in comparison." Christian smiled and looked at her tenderly, "You look good, no matter what you are wearing my love, but we will find a resting place soon enough." After exploring the city for some time, the weary travellers finally found a clean and respectable looking boarding house and were determined to be fed, cleaned up, and fully rested before meeting the President in two days' time. Hannah though, was so eager and excited at the prospect of meeting the President, that it was very hard for her to focus on eating or sleeping, at all. But Christian and Henry remained firm with her and Henry said grumpily: "You will be no good to anybody, least of all the Lakota Sioux, if you don't settle yourself down and do what you need to do, to keep your strength up." Hannah, feeling contrite, apologised and agreed, saying "You are both right." and asked "Can both of you take a walk around the town whilst I take a bath?" Without waiting for an answer, Hannah promptly turned to the landlady and asked: "Can you arrange to bring a tub with some water up to my room, so I can have a wash?" The landlady readily agreed, and although the men did not want to leave Hannah unprotected, in the unfamiliar boarding house; they respected her need for privacy and agreed to leave her in the hands of the landlady, Mrs. White.

Mrs. White, at first acquaintance, had a gruff exterior with her hair tied back into a severe grey bun; but the men decided she had a good heart underneath her severe looks, and left, as Hannah requested. They intended to find a bathhouse themselves to clean off the trail dust, promising to return in a couple of hours. Mrs. White was a nosy soul and immediately after the men left, asked, "Why have you three travelled from so far to get to Washington D.C.?" But Hannah had been warned by Henry not to reveal the true reason for their being in the bustling city, and Hannah remained tight lipped, only saying vaguely, "We came to visit a sick family member." The older woman seemed satisfied with her answer and went to collect the necessary items for Hannah's bath.

Later, when Hannah removed her clothes, she was relieved to be able to bathe again properly, and sank relaxed into the soapy water. Even though the tin tub was a bit small for bathing, she revelled in the feeling of being clean again and felt glad to have finally arrived to the city safely. Hannah was both eager and frightened at the same time, to meet with the President. She was petrified, that she might not be up to the task, but as she collected her thoughts, a bold determination filled her heart, and she spoke firmly to herself, saying: "I must be strong and save the Lakotas, and it will work, I just know it will."

Chapter 29

Unbeknownst to the weary travellers, army officials had long ago branded the trio as 'Indian sympathisers' and had assigned army operatives to monitor their actions for many months now. John Bates, the newly appointed US Army Chief of Staff, and the son of Edward Bates, who was President Lincoln's right hand man, had a lot to lose; if these so called 'Indian sympathisers' influenced President Lincoln. Bates was well known for his views on the Indians, because he had called them 'brutal bloodthirsty savages', throughout his career, and had vowed he would ensure the safety of white settlers, even if he had to exterminate every last indian on planet earth, which had won him much praise in the newspapers and ardent support far and wide from both polite society and the immigrant hordes, who arrived daily from distant lands.

He sat at his desk, examining the numerous confidential reports, which had arrived in recent months describing the activities of the young woman and the two men who accompanied her, Christian Peterson and Henry Wipple. He had heard talk of Hannah's gift of healing and her ability to see into the future; but had put it down to fanciful Norwegian folklore. John Bates was a no-nonsense sort of man and was determined that he would not jeopardise his political career by allowing indians to run rampant, killing and pillaging the lives of law abiding white citizens; and he reckoned if these 'Indian sympathisers' wanted a meeting with the President, then this meant trouble. Bates was determined not to let them undermine what he had worked so hard to achieve, all these years, which was a solid base of supporters. The Army Chief of Staff had his eye on the office of the US Presidency next; and he would not let an uneducated Norwegian peasant block him from his destiny. She will have to be stopped whatever the cost, he thought to himself. The 30 year old officer had early on, developed an intense hatred for all indians; because he had lost, a very dear sister who had been five years his senior, over a decade ago. The young woman had been travelling west with her husband on a wagon train; and they were viciously attacked by indian renegades; who left every man, woman and child killed by the brutal assault, including Bates' sister and her husband.

The respected Chief of Staff had learned, that from time to time, unsavoury characters, which could be trusted to carry out unpleasant tasks; in his line of work; could be very useful. Thinking about the problem, a plan soon formulated in his mind; as to how to get rid of the Norwegian peasant girl, once and for all. He treated himself to a glass of whisky and chuckled, when he realized the simplicity and brilliance of his plan, and he decided to put it into action, as soon as possible.

Hannah had not properly explored the bustling city, since arriving in Washington D.C; because the men had insisted she rest after her bath and wait until they had returned from their own wanderings around the nation's capital. But the next morning, she was determined that she would have a proper look around, of her own, and glanced across at the sleeping men who were both snoring without any signs of waking any time soon. To save expense, the three had told the landlady that they were a family; and so were all placed in the same room. This had been fine with the landlady; due to the fact that there had been only one room left in the boarding house anyway.

Hannah quietly put on her clothes and boots and plaited her hair, pinning it in place. She then slipped out of the quiet room and headed down the hall, determined to make good her escape. Hannah could never resist a sunrise and a chance to spend some time by herself; and couldn't wait to breathe in the fresh air just past the boarding house doors. When at last she escaped from the stuffy boarding-house and hurried through the back gate, she relaxed her pace and looked to her right and left taking in the lively city's sights and sounds. Hannah watched with interest, as a milk wagon drove by, pulled by two magnificent

Clydesdale horses. She marvelled at their rippling muscles and the sheer size of the equine beasts and walked on for another fifteen minutes; taking in the many shops and large townhomes on the tree lined street. Hannah tried to remember landmarks, so that she would be able to find her way back to the boarding-house and knew she should be returning there soon; but she couldn't bear to turn back just yet.

Nevertheless, she knew that both Christian and Henry would be worried about her, so after several more minutes, she finally made herself turn around and started retracing her steps back the way she had come. Lost in her own thoughts, Hannah hardly noticed when a black hansom carriage started slowly moving along the street beside her, until it came to an abrupt halt and two large men jumped out of the conveyance and promptly grabbed her, with one of the men clamping his hand over her mouth to stop her from screaming. Hannah frantically struggled with the two men, whilst they dragged her inside the carriage; but they were too strong for her; and before she knew it, a gag had been tied around her mouth and her hands bound together with a coarse rope. She couldn't believe what was happening and tried to clear her mind and wondered who in this great city would even know her, much less want to kidnap her.

Hannah looked curiously into the hardened faces of her kidnappers and one looked at her mockingly and said: "There will be a taste for what you've got to offer, little-un. I can't wait to show ya to Miss Lil." Both men cackled and one left the carriage to climb on top of the carriage to drive it on to their next destination. Hannah tried to calm herself and wondered what the crude men meant by their remarks; and deep within her, she knew she was in desperate trouble. She wondered how Christian and Henry would ever find her; because they seemed to be moving farther and farther away from the boarding house. Hannah hoped with all her heart that it would not be long before the men awakened and noticed she was gone.

The carriage journey seemed to last a very long time and Hannah was very surprised that after a certain amount of travelling that the carriage stopped and a sour faced woman with a mop cap and high waisted dress, boarded the carriage. She seemed discontented with her lot in life and looked upon Hannah with a loathing that she knew was unmistakable. Hannah shuddered to think what the next leg of the journey might bring; if this woman was anything to go by.

After several hours, the carriage finally ground to a halt and Hannah hoped that at least, she might get a drink, because her throat felt like shoe leather, it was so dry. She also wanted to relieve herself. Also, her wrists were bleeding from the tightness of the rope bound around them, and she hoped they would loosen the bindings soon. Hannah refused to let herself cry and did not want to show fear; but the truth was, she was terrified. The sour-faced woman elbowed the man snoring beside her and said: "Wake up you big lout, we have reached Miss Lil's place and I need you to remove this here girl's ropes; because her hands are bleeding and the customers won't take kindly to damaged goods and neither will Miss Lil, come to think of it." The man jumped when she elbowed him and irritably barked back. "Calm yourself Maude; can't a man get some peace and quiet after a long journey? I will loosen her bindings now. I reckon between the three of us we can keep this little 'un under control," he added.

The woman who Hannah had just learned was called Maude, further said: "And get that gag out of her mouth and give the girl a drink and let her have a pee in the outhouse; cos' we don't want her keeling over anytime soon." Obediently, the man did as he was told and upon her return from the privy, Hannah rubbed her sore wrists and gratefully took the canteen of water that was offered. At last, Maude addressed Hannah in an authoritative voice and said: "Now Miss, you will do as you are told; because from this moment on, your life hain't no longer your own. You are now Miss Lil's property, do you understand?" Hannah gasped at her words, but kept her composure, even though her eyes were glassy with emotion. Maude continued undaunted by Hannah's distress and said: "As I said, you are now the property of Miss Lil, the grandest madam in all of New York City, and untouched virgins like yourself, fetch a pretty penny from the gents that frequent our establishment."

Hannah thought about the older woman's words and although innocent in many respects, she understood her meaning and shook her head vehemently, saying: "No, I am meant to meet with the President this week; and I already have a man I intend to marry. I think this has all been some terrible mistake. I have just arrived from the Dakota Territory," Hannah added. Maude listened impatiently and said to the man beside her, "They always say the same thing, that there has been some terrible mistake, but the truth is, she has been bought and paid for by one of our most distinguished clients from Washington D.C; and she has little choice in the matter." She added: "Let's get her inside, so Miss Lil can have a look at her. I can't imagine why she is so special anyway," she commented, "she has nice eyes and a few assets; but this little 'un is not as pretty as some I've seen." Hannah angrily flashed her eyes at Maude and declared: "I have a name and it is Hannah." Both the man and woman cackled at her show of spirit and the man crudely replied: "That's right girlie, show a bit of spirit; the punters will love that too." He roughly pushed her through the doorway of the old brick building and Maude said gruffly to him, "You wait here with her, while I go and get Miss Lil."

It seemed like a very long time before the woman returned accompanied by a large woman wearing a garish purple sequinned gown and with blonde hair piled on top of her head. The woman, who Hannah supposed was Miss Lil, had a painted face and the low cut gown she wore, was designed to show off her massive breasts, which Hannah could see attracted the attention of the man's eyes, who stood beside her; so much so, it took him several minutes to realise he had been dismissed from the building. He finally left sheepishly when Maude shouted good-naturedly at him and said: "Leo, if you can tear your eyes away from Madam Lil's baps, you can leave now cos' we can take it from here." Madam Lil paid no attention to her employees' banter and looked at the young girl that stood before her, moving her eyes up and down. Looking appraisingly at Hannah, she finally spoke and said: "There is a man who has paid me a princely sum to have you brought here for him to plough your innocent loins, so I don't want any trouble from you girl, do you hear me?" Hannah nodded, seeing the hardness in the woman's expression and the madam responded to her approvingly, saying: "Good then, Maude will oversee your bath, and get you all prettied up and we already have some dresses for you to try on. Oh and don't try anything funny, because Chu-Ling, my bodyguard, will be in front of your door at all times."

Hannah's eyes widened when the frame of the large Chinese bodyguard seemed to appear out of nowhere. "Chu Ling take this one up to her room and lock the door," Madam Lil instructed. Hannah shrieked in surprise when the giant bodyguard picked her up, like a sack of potatoes, and she was carried unceremoniously up the stairs to the second room on the first floor and deposited on the large wood framed bed. He then looked at her on the bed and said to her in broken English: "You be good and me no hurt you, yes Miss?" Hannah nodded numbly, as the large Chinese man exited the room and locked the door. She then crept to the door and stood on her tiptoes to look through the peephole of the door, to see if he had gone; and shrank back suddenly when she saw him standing in front of her door with his arms folded. She would just have to wait for the right time to make her escape, Hannah thought, and escape she would.

Chapter 30

Back at the boarding house in Washington D.C; Christian and Henry had awakened to find Hannah gone. Neither man was immediately concerned, because they knew she had an insatiable curiosity and liked to have time to herself; but as the hours passed; and midday was fast approaching, they finally came to the realisation that something was desperately wrong and they couldn't wait for her any longer. Christian immediately wanted to go to the police to report Hannah's disappearance; but Henry thought it best to search the area first, just in case Hannah was lost. "Surely," he commented to Christian, "she cannot just vanish into thin air." Christian agreed and both men left the boarding house to search the nearby streets to seek out any sign of Hannah. They felt frustrated and helpless; and after two hours of searching the area without success, it was decided between them to save time; to split up and that Christian would go to the police to file a missing person's report and Henry would make contact with friends and colleagues in the area, to try to piece together what may have befallen Hannah, which may have led to her disappearance. Christian's frantic face showed his anxiety before the two men parted and Henry patted his back trying to console him and said: "All will be well, my lad, our Hannah is strong and smart; and with her special gifts, she is a force to be reckoned with, don't worry we will find her." Christian nodded his head mechanically, trying to make himself believe the older man's words; and the two agreed to meet by late afternoon back at the boarding house; to discuss what they had found out. Henry made a mental note that he would have to get in touch with the White House to delay their meeting with the President and he was resolved to get that done before the day's end.

As the afternoon progressed, Hannah was tired from her ordeal and tried to rest on the bed, whilst looking around the room she was now imprisoned in. She noticed there were several paintings of nude women placed on the walls around the room and that the bed linens were silk and of the finest quality. The upmarket bordello had spared no expense in ensuring the rooms would be an enticement to their customers; and Hannah shuddered to think what these people might have in store for her. She tried to get some direction from her gifting, but nothing came; and so she began to daydream, remembering a story she had heard in Norway as a small child. Her country of birth, was well known for its' superstitions and folklore and this particular tale had always made an impression on Hannah above all others; and so she tried to put the details of the story in motion, in her mind to distract herself, and then she dozed off to sleep.

The story is told as follows: "One priest who had dealings with the evil one by delving into the black arts had been tried for his crime and condemned to die. He begged continuously for his life and was only reprieved by the judges of the land on the condition that he would exhibit his supernatural powers by preaching at a cathedral over four hundred miles away. He agreed to do this task and summoned an evil winged spirit and said to him, 'How fast can you carry me to this cathedral, which is four hundred miles away?'" and he replied: 'As fast as a horse can go.' "But that would not do, so he summoned a second evil winged spirit and asked him to fly him to the cathedral as fast as he could go. However, the spirit declined to do his bidding. At last, a third evil winged spirit offered to take the priest to the cathedral on the condition that he might have all the souls of those that fell asleep during the priest's sermon. The priest now desperate to save his life agreed and the unearthly travel began.

The winged creature flew with the priest on his back and went around the coast and when out above the seas, he asked the priest to repeat his vows to God and country, knowing that if he did so, he would be compelled to drop him into the ocean. But the priest was too wise to be fooled by the trick and urged the winged spirit to travel faster. When the priest finally arrived to the cathedral, the sermon was delivered and was so earnest and powerful, that the priest didn't cause anyone to fall asleep and the evil winged spirit was not delivered any souls that day. And all was right and good in the land and the priest was hence, set free."

Hannah awoke from her dream filled sleep with a start and tried to remember where she was; and upon remembering, wondered if once she performed some good task, if she too would be set free, like the priest. Several hours had passed, and it was dark in the room and she felt groggy and not herself at all. Hannah wondered if she might have been given something to drug her, when she drank a cup of tea earlier; because she had never felt so tired in her entire life. It seemed like the house had come alive outside her door, because she could hear a lot of male and female voices both laughing and shouting, as the sounds of these mysterious people reverberated around the bordello.

Hannah turned on a kerosene lamp in the room and walked across to the windows which she had previously noticed were nailed shut with wooden shutters over them; and she felt her gifting flow strong within her. Suddenly, the window shutters flew open and the glass window flew upwards supernaturally and a blast of cool air blew into the room. The window looked out upon Newbury Street and Hannah could see there were many unsavoury people, milling about on the streets below. She was not foolish enough to call out indiscriminately to the people below and it was too high a place to jump out of, without injuring herself; so Hannah waited and watched, hoping that no one would enter her room from the hallway, before she made contact with someone to help her.

At last, Hannah caught sight of a young policeman and her gifting leaped from inside of her and she knew, this was the man that was meant to help her. Before she could utter a single word, she saw him gazing upwards at her and he said quite loudly; "Missy, do you need some help, you don't look like you belong in Miss Lil's place?" Relieved, Hannah nodded gratefully and replied as quietly as she could: "Mister, I have been kidnapped, since yesterday and brought here, can you help me please?" The young policeman, whose name was James Mitchell, in truth was a regular customer at Miss Lil's establishment, and had enjoyed her services many times, which were free of charge to him; because he had always made sure that the bordello was not targeted by the police, in anyway. James liked Lil, and her girls were clean for the most part; but he had heard rumours that the middle-aged madam was starting to get too greedy with her takings; and was offering virgins and even children as sexual fodder to her customers, which in his book 'crossed the line'.

James gazed up at the young copper haired girl with the Scandinavian accent and said reassuringly: "Yes Miss, I will try, just close the windows and sit tight for now; because I need to think of the best way to get you out of there, okay?" Hannah excited at his self-assured words, called out: "Thank you," and desperately hoped he would come back for her; and decided for now, to do as he asked and closed the windows, settling herself on the bed to wait. Hannah knew her gifting was never wrong and that this was the man destined to help her. She prayed he would have the courage to carry out her rescue very soon.

Around an hour after her interactions with the young policeman, Maude entered Hannah's room carrying several shiny dresses and looked appraisingly at her young shape and hair saying: "Okay girlie, we need to get you into the bath and then fixed up for the customers, because you are on show tonight; and we want you looking your best. I have sent Chu-Ling to get the washing tub, so we can do your hair as well; then we will paint you up like a china doll and get you dressed for tonight's showing," she explained. Hannah stayed mute, not sure how to respond to the older woman's plans; but was horrified at the look of the dresses, as they looked skimpy and the front of the dresses were cut extremely low and were sure to show her bosoms. Also, Hannah wondered what Maude meant by tonight's showing and hoped that she would have the strength to get through whatever it was these people had in store for her.

Chapter 31

Henry and Christian met back at the boarding house as planned, just before the evening meal; and both men were frustrated at the lack of progress they had made in finding Hannah. Henry had contacted the White House to delay the meeting with the President and had heard ominous reports from his contacts, about young ladies being kidnapped and taken to the seedy bordellos, in the streets of New York for sexual trafficking. He desperately hoped this had not been Hannah's fate; and reluctantly shared this information with Christian and saw the young man's face grow sick with worry. Henry said: "Christian, my friends say there are only two reasons a young lady would be abducted in these parts; ransom money if you are rich and a prostitution house, if you are poor." Christian clearly distressed, asked: "Well if this has happened to Hannah, where would the blackguards have taken her?"

Having genuine compassion for the younger man, Henry answered him and said: "New York City, my boy, we must go to every bordello in that wretched city; if need be, to find her, and we must leave right away." The men decided between themselves to leave immediately and went to tell their landlady and gather their belongings, so they could ride through the night. They then went to the nearby stableyard to retrieve their horses and pushed the beasts as hard as they dared to get to unknown city. They had been told it was an eight hour journey from Washington D.C. to New York City; and they hoped to cut down their journey time to six hours, if possible. Henry and Christian had discussed that the sheer size of New York City and the number of bordellos in it; was bound to make finding Hannah a daunting task. However, Henry's Washington contacts had come in useful, and had shared with him that there was only around five bordellos in the city that were delving into the kidnapping and sexual trafficking of innocent women and children. These same contacts had given Henry the names of these places and they were scrawled on a piece of paper in his vest pocket. Henry intended for them to start searching for Hannah in these places, immediately upon reaching New York City, and Christian had readily agreed.

After Hannah was scrubbed within an inch of her life, Maude made her dress in a white frilly chemise and gave her a silk robe to wrap around herself; and then began to dress her hair. Her hair was curled into ringlets to create an even younger effect and Hannah's eyelids were painted blue and also her cheeks and lips were painted a rose pink. Maude stepped back to admire her creation and smacked her lips, seeming well satisfied with her work, and then directed Hannah to dress in the pink satin dress lying on the bed behind her. Although ashamed to put the garment on; Hannah did as she was told and glanced down at her body. She was ashamed to see how much of her pale white skin was exposed by the dress. Yet she was determined not to let her distress show, and straightened her shoulders, raising her chin and looked defiantly at the older woman and asked: "Where are you taking me in this vile costume?"

Surprised and amused at Hannah's show of spirit, Maude gave her a calculating look and responded: "Chu-Ling will be escorting you to the gentleman's parlour, so the punters can have a look at you, girlie, so you better get used to the idea. You are only reserved for one client, who will be arriving next week; but you will attract business, so we may as well show you off a little in the meanwhile," she added, laughing crudely. Hannah shuddered at the smell of the older woman's unwashed body, mixed with cheap perfume; but she didn't challenge her further, because she could see the ruthlessness in the woman's character and decided it would just make matters worse. Maude then said: "Right if you are done with your jabbering, Chu-Ling will take you to the gentleman's parlour and don't even think about trying to escape; because he could snap your neck like a twig if he had a mind to."

Maude then opened the door to let the giant bodyguard into the room and Chu-Ling grabbed Hannah's arm and ushered her into the hallway and steered her down the stairs and across several ornate rooms, until they reached the gentleman's parlour. The lush red oriental rugs and thick oak and leather furniture reflected the prosperity of the bordello; and Hannah could hear the noise of at least thirty men talking, laughing and drinking in the next room. Chu-Ling opened the double doors and pushed Hannah into the centre of the room and a great hush fell over the men, as they openly stared at her exposed young body while she stood trembling before them.

Madam Lil spoke out loudly when Hannah entered the parlour and said: "Ahh here she is, our newest acquisition, a young nubile woman, who is a virgin in every way and has come fresh from the Dakota Territory. I am sure there are many of you, who would enjoy spending a night with her. She is a right tasty little piece, isn't she gents?" the Madam added. The men leered at Hannah, openly commenting on her large breasts and narrow waist and she grew red with embarrassment; and steeled herself, praying the ordeal would be over soon. Then after several minutes, Madam Lil signalled for her bodyguard to remove Hannah from the room, and she said tantalizingly to the group, "But not tonight gents, we will leave you salivating over her tempting body for now; and we have plenty of other beautiful girls, to take care of your every need this evening." The men laughed raucously at the Madam's words and before Hannah knew it; as swiftly as she had entered the gentleman's parlour, she was being removed by the large bodyguard and for that she was grateful.

He returned Hannah back to her room and locked the door behind her; without a word, and at last letting the floodgates open, Hannah let the tears flow, and cried quietly, whilst sitting on her bed. The humiliation she had suffered at the hands of these people was like none she had ever known, and the realisation that others were probably subjected to the same fate on a regular basis, was a sobering thought indeed.

Finally, the tears stopped and Hannah hastily removed the hated pink dress and wrapped the silk robe around herself. She then walked to the bedside table to pour a glass of water from the china pitcher, which sat on the night stand; and suddenly heard what sounded like mewing noises from the next room. Hannah listened intently, and moved towards the wall where she had heard the sounds, and noticed a tiny hole where she could see into the next room perfectly. She peered with one eye through the hole and noticed two small children who looked to be brother and sister sitting on the bed dejected and crying. The boy and girl were blonde and blue eyed and looked to be no more than two to four years old. The young girl seemed to be the oldest, and Hannah called to them saying: "Hello, are you alright you two? My name is Hannah."

The children seemed shocked when they heard her voice, and it was clear they did not understand her, so Hannah tried again in Norwegian and immediately the little girl ran to the wall. The child whose name Hannah learned was Helga, asked: "Lady, do you know where our mama is, her name is Nelia, and we were playing in the street when some bad men grabbed us and brought us to this place and we need to find her?" Stopping to catch her breath, the little girl then pointed to the young boy in the corner of the room and added: "My brother's name is Olaf, and he cries every night for our mama. Can you help us please?" Delighted that the little girl understood her, Hannah, replied: "Yes, of course I will, but we must first get free from this place, and then we can go and find her together, if you like?" Helga clapped her hands excitedly and said: "Would you really help us, Lady?" "My brother and I have been here for such a long time and we are so sad." Hannah tried to appear comforting to the small girl and said: "Yes, but you must call me Hannah and please don't worry, it will be fine; but it must be our secret, do you understand, no one can know that we plan to leave here together?" Helga nodded solemnly and responded: "Ok Lady, I mean Hannah; but please, we must leave very soon, 'cos our mama will be very worried about us."

James was disgusted that Madam Lil had decided to expand her bordello's services to the sexual exploitation of innocent young women and children; but he was not surprised she had decided to branch out in that direction, because although it was a risky business, the financial rewards for providing such services, more than compensated for the risk. He had thought through the best way to rescue Hannah and decided to confront Madam Lil and threaten her with a police raid. She seemed tough and unbreakable, but he knew that like everyone, Madam Lil had her weak points; and would not want a scandal.

She seemed to be in high spirits when he entered the bordello, and he watched her for a time, as she talked and gave banter to her customers. He was amused to see that her great breasts nearly broke free from the tight satin dress she wore, and James decided to approach the soused madam directly after the disgusting display of Hannah in the gentleman's parlour. He had felt compassion for the frightened girl when he saw the depraved customers leering at her young body; and with a firm resolve he crossed the room and waited until Madam Lil was alone and said: "Lil, the Mayor of New York City is planning a police raid on your place and you will have to clean up your act. There must be no more abductions of young women and children or he will shut you down, do you understand?" he added, looking directly into her eyes. She laughed openly at his statements and said: "His honour himself, has his own mistress and she is not more than a girl, barely 15, I'll wager."

James shook his head, not willing to be swayed by the strong willed madam and declared: "No, this is different and you know it, you can't just pluck people off the street against their will and use them to slake your customer's sexual lusts, like it is common practice." He added: "Times are changing Lil, the mayor has committed to the people of New York City; that he is going to clean up the opium dens and prostitution houses; and he will ask the police to raid this place soon, so things have to change?" The madam, looked uncomfortable and asked the young policeman, "Well what do you expect me to do, just release them all?" "I have spent a lot of money getting these people in and I am so close to reaping a fabulous profit, I can smell it," she said drunkenly, slurring her words. "Let me take care of it," said James, "I am a copper and I can protect you; but you must first of all let me be in charge of making the Norwegian girl disappear without a trail leading back to you." The madam eyed James suspiciously, trying to determine if he had an angle and asked: "What is in it for you, James, why would you want to take on the young girl and make her disappear, do you fancy her for yourself?" James tried to stay calm and said convincingly: "I have a little racket of my own Lil, and I reckon I could get a fair amount for her as an indentured servant out West: so if I can sell her for a good price, this can mutually work out well for the both of us. Just give me the keys to her room and this will all go away," he added. "That better be the case or that young girl will not be the only one disappearing, do you understand me, young copper?" she snarled and then she reached in her pocket and passed James the keys.

James nodded curtly to her and left the parlour and felt better about himself then he had in years. He knew he had to move quickly or Lil would change her mind, once she sobered up from the alcohol; but she had given him the keys to the room that Hannah was being held in, and the Chinese bodyguard was now down having his evening meal, so there was no time like the present to get this rescue operation underway, James thought to himself, with a big smile on his face.

As Hannah stood talking to the frightened children through the wall, she felt a great sense of purpose and her gifting told her: 'the reason she had come to the bordello was to save these children.' Now everything suddenly made sense to her and she jumped when she heard keys rattling in the door behind her. She rushed back to sit on her bed and was terrified that the giant bodyguard, had heard her talking to the children. Hannah let out a great sigh of relief when she saw the young policeman walk through the door, and said gratefully. "You came for me, Thank God." James grinned and said: "Yes, I am officially your knight in shining armour, but we need to leave quickly before that big ugly bodyguard comes back. Come on, let's get out of here," he urged. "That's fine we can go, but we are not leaving without the children," Hannah replied in a determined voice. "Okay, I heard there were children here, but where are they being held; because we haven't much time and by the way I am James Mitchell and what is your name Miss?" he asked in a rushed tone. "I am Hannah Nelson and the two children I am talking about are next door. I saw them through that hole in the wall." Hannah then pointed to the small hole of which she had peered through, just moments before. "Come on then, get some clothes on and let's get them and go; but remember you must keep the little 'uns quiet; because we can't risk being heard by anyone," the young policeman warned. James, at that point ran quickly out of the room leaving Hannah to hastily pull her dress over her head and without delay she followed him out of the room.

James opened the door to the children's room and Hannah rushed in and hugged them both and advised them to remain quiet in Norwegian. The children's eyes widened and they looked frightened at her words; but they both nodded solemnly and took her extended hands, when Hannah told them gently, "Helga. Olaf, it is time to leave, so we can find your mama. Are you ready?" she asked. They both eagerly nodded and the hastily assembled group banded together to begin their escape from the tawdry bordello, once and for all.

A hurricane was headed for the city of New York and the floods of rain which engulfed the beleaguered city, were only the first stages of dangerous weather which would come blasting into the perilous night. James knew the only place that would be a safe haven for the three escapees in the storm, was the Savoy Theatre, a popular West-End theatre, not far from the bordello. He was a friend of the night watchman at the theatre and after hearing weather reports at the police station he reported to; James had arranged before even speaking to Madam Lil, to bring Hannah there after rescuing her. But now he had two small children in tow and he hoped his old friend Sam wouldn't mind them coming to stay, as well.

The Savoy had a well built balcony and James was convinced that if the worst happened and the waters rose high in the city during the storm; that they would be high enough to remain safe.

To hurry things up he offered to carry the smallest child, Olaf; and Hannah gladly handed the sleepy child over to the young policeman and adjusted the shawl around his older sister, firmly taking her hand. Helga was also tired but kept her trusting eyes on Hannah and followed her gladly without complaint. The rain was pummelling down torrentially and the trio ran carrying the small boy, as fast as they could, through the streets, taking refuge under store fronts, when passing carriages would come their way.

Finally, they arrived at the stalwart theatre, and James ushered the small party to the back door of the large building and pounded on the door. A thin, black and elderly night watchman opened the door and looked at the bedraggled young woman and children. Then he looked at James and said with a grin: "Well, I guess you wet ducks better 'git yerselves in here before you drown." James smiled back and shook his hand and said: "Thanks Sam I won't forget this, you are a real friend."

Chapter 32

As the drenched arrivals walked through the back door of the grand theatre, the kindly watchman beckoned them to follow him into the actor's dressing room to get dry and to change their clothes. The realisation that James had brought with him, not only a young woman, but also two small children that had no dry clothing with them, prompted him to think of an idea. James made the introductions on the way; and the fair haired boy and girl, were amused to be replacing their saturated clothing with a fairy costume and monkey suit, and enthusiastically donned the costumes. As for Hannah, she was only too glad to exchange the hated pink costume supplied by the bordello, for a nun's habit. James and Sam smiled at the newly glad trio; and not to be outdone, James, himself, found a knight's tunic that would do for the night. The elderly watchman leaned down to the children and asked: "Are you young'uns hungry, I believe that some of the actors have left some bread and cheese in the larder, after the last show?" The children looked quizzically at the old man and then to Hannah for interpretation, and she grinned, translating in Norwegian, what the night watchman had said. The children clapped their hands and called out "Ja, Ja" in unison; and Hannah smiled gratefully saying: "I think you have a firm answer there Sam; that would be wonderful."

After the bread and cheese were brought to the dressing room and was quickly consumed, along with apple cider poured from a large jug, in to tin cups; the exhausted children were all but asleep on the floor. There was no bedding at the busy theatre; but James, Hannah and Sam improvised and heaped large swathes of set curtains, one upon another, to make large comfortable beds for the group; and then Sam bade them all a good sleep, saying, "I must go make my 'rounds now; but I will be in the front pavilion warming my 'ole feet in front of the pot belly stove with a nice cup of java, should you need me," and off he went leaving them to get comfortable for the night.

The surreal circumstances struck Hannah as quite comical when she looked at the four of them getting ready to bed down for the night, and she couldn't help but giggle and quipped: "Am I dreaming James, or am I really looking at a knight, a fairy and a monkey, sleeping in the same room with me tonight?" The young policeman, joined in on the joke, and bowed in front of Hannah and the children and said "Sir James at your service," putting on a posh British accent. Finding this even funnier, Hannah started laughing in fits of giggles after his comedic gesture, and poured out a much needed release after the fear and stress of the last few days. Both James and the children giggled with her, enjoying the sight of her laughing and all of them felt greatly relieved that at least for this night, they were fed, safe and warm.

The next morning, the four overnight guests at the theatre, awoke to the sound of raging winds and pouring rain blasting the theatre. The frightened children scampered over to Hannah after hearing the noise and she hugged them close trying to comfort them. James took in the three and said: "Those little ones have really taken a shine to you, Hannah, keep them close; because it sounds like this hurricane has hit the city with full force, and we may need to move to the balcony to get above the water." Hannah nodded solemnly, and replied: "Yes, it sounds bad out there, I hope my fiancé Christian and our friend, Henry, are not stuck out in it; because they are bound to have come looking for me."

Hannah turned to the children and said in Norwegian: "Come on you two, let's go and get a little wash and then we will find something to eat." Helga and Olaf got to their feet obediently and started following Hannah out of the room; however; before leaving, she touched the young policeman's arm and said: "James, thank you for helping us; because if it weren't for you, we wouldn't have escaped that terrible bordello." Turning red, James bowed his head and cleared his throat a few times and finally answered, saying: "I couldn't do anything else; it is just wrong what Madam Lil is up to these days." Hannah responded and said: "Well the next thing we need to do after the storm passes, is to find these children's mama, she must be frantic with worry for them." James looked at Hannah, admiring her courage and said good naturedly: "I will help all I can little lady," and then he bowed saying, "your knight in shining armour is at your service."

Upon returning to the actor's dressing room, Hannah saw that James had changed back into his police uniform. She commented to him: "The storm is still very bad out there, and maybe we should all move up to the balcony, because the streets look really flooded." James agreed and said: "Yes, let's relocate up there; it is probably best to take our bedding too." After all four were properly settled, James and Hannah resumed talking and the young policeman decided it was time to divulge some information, he had been keeping to himself. He cleared his throat and said: "Hannah, there is something I have been meaning to tell you; but what with the storm and our escape, it slipped my mind." Hannah looked at him expectantly and waited and James said: "Your fiancé' and your friend apparently did come to the police station on the east side, looking for you." He hurried on and said: "The police sergeant told me they were really anxious to find you; and I would say there is no way they are leaving this city without you." Hannah sucked in a breath and exclaimed: "But with this terrible storm, anything could have happened to them." James tried to calm her fears and said: "They told the police sergeant, they were staying at the Carlton Arms Hotel. Hannah, don't worry, the sergeant seemed to believe they were quite sensible men," he added. "Anyway once the storm dies down, we will find them and also the children's mother too," James soothed.

"What do you know about the children's mother then, Hannah?" James asked, trying to get her mind off her loved ones. "Well I can only assume she is their stepmother; because she doesn't have a Norwegian name, and I think they said her name is Cornelia Wright," Hannah said. "They also said she works in a laundry, and that they went against her wishes to play several streets over from the laundry she works in, after school; and that they were snatched by bad men and taken to the bordello," "Cornelia Wright sounds more Irish then anything," James exclaimed. "In fact, I have several Cornelias in my family," James chuckled. "We will see if we can start trying to find her tomorrow or the next day, if the streets are passable," he commented.

The massive hurricane had hit the city of New York hard and the fallout from the giant storm had caused mayhem amongst the inhabitants of the bustling metropolis. Water damage had caused endless damage to shops and homes and looters ran amuck in the city, breaking windows and stealing goods; after the worst of the storm has passed. Hannah had spent a restless night worrying about Christian and Henry and hearing the noise outside; yet her gifting spoke to her that they would be together again very soon.

The great windows in the front of the Savoy Theatre afforded the night watchman and the four stranded guests, a clear view of the watery world outside; and they were appalled to witness the masses of looters milling in noisy crowds outside. By the afternoon of the next day, the rain had stopped and remnants of the sun peaked through the stormy clouds, and Hannah breathed a sigh of relief.

She didn't waste any time in tracking down the young policeman, for she knew he had gone to check all the doors of the theatre to ensure their safety. It seemed that the raucous crowds had no interest in the large theatre, but he wasn't taking any chances. When Hannah found James, she said: "The rain has stopped and the crowds have moved towards the shops on the west side; so we must take this opportunity to find Christian and Henry, and the children's mother." James looked at Hannah's determined face, and replied: "Yes we should, but we will do it my way, Hannah; you must stay here in safety with the children; and I will go and check at the police station to see if they have visited there again." Hannah was not happy to stay behind, but could see the sense in James's plan and reluctantly agreed, saying. "Yes, alright I will stay here, if I must; but you must not take any unnecessary risks and come back as soon as possible. Also, we are running low on food, so do you think you could buy some cheese and bread and maybe some milk for the children?" She asked. James grinned at her bossy tone and said compliantly, "Yes, I will do what I can, Hannah; and try not to worry in the meanwhile." James patted her on the shoulder, because he could see she was fighting hard to hold back tears. He added, sensitively: "I will go ahead and leave then, but remember to keep the doors locked and do not open them to anyone. I will try not to be long and if you have any concerns just let Sam know," he added.

Hannah watched him go, and realised how much she depended on the young policeman. For a moment, she panicked with fear when she saw him go; but tried to get control of herself, because she realised she must be strong for the children.

James was shocked to see the desolation in the city, when he ventured out of the theatre; but he kept his focus whilst he made his way to the East End police station. The looters were everywhere, but seemed to pay little attention to him and he made good time; as he walked through the flooded streets. James had to make several detours because of the flooding and massive crowds; but he knew the city well and after two hours, he finally caught sight of the familiar police station. Breathing a sigh of relief, he walked the remaining distance and entered the crowded police station and said to the police clerk; "Where is the Sarge?" The frustrated clerk had a long queue of people waiting for his help, and looking up from writing a report, he said in an annoyed tone: "Look James, can't you see I have my hands full here? Just go look yerself, he is back there somewhere," waving the young policeman on. James chuckled and walked through the double doors towards the police sergeant's desk, and was relieved to see two men fitting Hannah's descriptions, seated, and speaking to the sergeant. He walked over to the men and said: "You wouldn't happen to be the famous Christian and Henry that Hannah has talked about nonstop?"

Both men stood up smiling, and Christian shook his hand, and asked urgently: "Do you know where she is? Please can you take us to her?" James answered calmly and said: "It is a long story; but yes she is safe and sound and I will take you to her, I can tell you the details on the way."

The men quickly left the police station together and made their way to the Savoy Theatre. The relief on Christian's and Henry's faces was evident, and James filled them in on the details of the last week. At last, they reached the theatre, and Christian all but burst through the doors, shouting out Hannah's name. Hannah had taken the children up to the balcony to feed them, because it was reaching late afternoon. She jumped at the sound of Christian's voice, and sobbed in relief, and with tears running down her cheeks, she said in a quiet voice to the children: "Stay here, I have friends who have just arrived and I will bring them to meet you." The children's eyes widened in confusion at Hannah's show of emotion; but they nodded in agreement and continued eating. Hannah trying not to alarm them, walked out of the balcony, and then when they could no longer see her, she ran down the stairs as fast as she could.

When she reached the foot of the stairs, Hannah saw Christian and their eyes met, and the grateful young people ran into each other's arms. They embraced each other, and both were crying and held each other, like they would never let each other go. Henry and James looked at the reunited young couple and smiled indulgently. A hint of tears misted the older man's eyes and Henry walked up to both Hannah and Christian, and put his arms around them both and said: "God be praised, we are together again and all of us safe, it is a miracle." Hannah literally beaming, responded and said: "Yes, isn't it wonderful and we also have James to thank; because not only did he rescue me from that awful bordello, he rescued two innocent children, as well."

Christian held Hannah at arm's length and said: "Wait, let me take a look at you, Hannah; did the people from the bordello, hurt you in anyway? I am so sorry it took us so long to find you." Hannah shushed him, putting a finger to his lips tenderly, and said: "I am fine and anyway we are together now." Henry then asked: "You said there are children here, as well, Hannah, where are they?" Hannah answered: "They are waiting in the balcony, a little boy and girl, who were also held prisoner at the bordello." The men digested her words and Hannah continued, saying: "I have promised them we will find their mother, and her name is Cornelia Wright. She is Irish and works in a laundry, they have told me," she added, "will you all help me?" Recognising the heartfelt determination in her voice, the men laughed and James said comically: "Well, I guess we know what we will be doing in the next few days."

Two small faces peeped around the doorway of the theatre foyer, and the older child, Helga called: "'Hannah, you were very long, so we came to find you, are these your friends?" Hannah led Christian by the hand across to the children, and said in Norwegian: "Helga, Olaf, I would like you to meet Christian and Henry," pointing to Christian and the older man, "they are my dearest friends and you can trust them." The children smiled shyly up at the men and then moved to Hannah and clutched her skirts for safety.

Chapter 33

The men and Hannah had talked long into the night, and decided that because they were expected in Washington D.C. very soon; that they must quickly initiate a plan to find the children's mother. Christian, James and Henry laid plans together and were determined to be successful; because the trio knew that Hannah would refuse to leave New York City, unless they had actually found the young mother. The children, although young; were able to describe where their mother worked; and knowing the city very well, James had a fair idea where to go and look for the woman.

Through many conversations with the children, Hannah had pieced together why they called this woman their mother and recounted to the men, what they had told her, saying: "While the children were travelling on the great ship across to America; their real parents died of some sort of fever." She continued and said: "And this woman, Cornelia, whose husband and child had also died of the same fever on the ship, kindly, took over as their mother. The young woman's parents, of whom the children call Nanny Sarah and Papa Ben, apparently had also been travelling on the ship, and survived the journey, but Helga does not know where they live," she added. "The children also told me that Cornelia was able to learn their language, and that she has a funny way of talking; and that she has bright red hair and is very beautiful," Hannah concluded.

"Well," Henry said, "we have a lot of good details about the woman, so it shouldn't be too hard to find her." "Yes," said James, "I know this city well, so there is hope in finding her; but with the looters and the flooded streets, it will still be dangerous out there." Christian joined in and said: "We will find her; but we just need to keep our eyes open for danger and it probably would be a good idea to map out our route." Taking his point, the men did just that, and then readied themselves for bed.

The next morning, the men set out to look for the children's mother, and were surprised to see that in spite of the devastation caused by the hurricane and the many looters everywhere; that shops and businesses were trying to get back to normal and were open for business. The men made their way westwards in the city; to the Italian quarter, to a place called "Little Italy" on Mulberry Street. The older child, Helga, had remembered pizza shops and said her mama worked on 'Mooberry Street, so the men thought it a good place to start looking. Almost 10,000 Italians; lived there; and James knew that a red haired, Irish woman would stand out in that community; so he took the men to Mulberry Street and asked for the nearest laundry.

The three men went from shop to shop, asking if anyone knew the whereabouts of a woman fitting the children's description of their mother, and after an hour of questioning people on the busy street, they subsequently visited two laundries without success. The men entered a third laundry, and found no one at the counter; but did hear shouting at the back of the premises. "Get your fat hands off of me, you filthy lecher," a woman's voice shrieked shrilly; and then a sharp slap resounded throughout the laundry. The men heard a man's voice angrily shout back in a heavily accented Italian voice, saying; "You hussy, I will kill you for that." The men thought it best at that point to intervene, and stepped across to the back of the counter to get a better view of what was going on. What appeared before their eyes was a beautiful red haired women struggling to get free; whilst a dark-haired and furious looking man held her fast around the waist and had his other hand balled up in a fist, ready to strike her. Christian and James jumped on either side of the man to restrain his arms, while Henry stepped forwards and spoke quickly to the woman, saying: "Madam, come with me, these two will hold this man, until we get away from here." Without saying a word, the woman nodded and took Henry's hand and they both ran out of the laundry, and headed east back to the Savoy Theatre.

Henry decided, he had never seen a more beautiful creature in his life, and he found it hard to keep his eyes off of her. After travelling through several streets, whilst narrowly avoiding both looters and flood waters; the pair decided to stop for a moment to catch their breath and introduced themselves to each other. Henry went first and said: "My name is Henry, Henry Whipple; and you are Cornelia Wright, I presume?" The woman ran her fingers through her hair and skirts to smooth them down and smiled appealingly, looking up at him with twinkling eyes and said: "Well top of the morning to you, Sir, and how is it, that you would be, knowin' my name?" Henry quite bewitched by the small, pretty woman with the fiery red hair, said; "Well Miss Wright, my friends and I have found your children, and I know you must be aching to be reunited with them. They have told us all about you," he added.

Cornelia looked at him with a shocked expression, and tears of relief filled her eyes, "You have found my little Helga and Olaf? I had thought that they were lost to me forever and that I would never see them again," she said emotionally. Cornelia smiled broadly and asked: "Well, where are they, Sir? I must see them right away and let them know their mama has not forgotten them." Henry answered gently and said: "The other men will no doubt be joining us soon; after they have tied up that lecherous boss of yours, so we can go a little slower going back to where they are. But they are safe and happy, do not worry," he assured her. "Let's just catch our breath for a few minutes first," he added. "Your children are waiting for you at the Savoy Theatre," he added. "Oh Saints be praised, take me to them, Henry, I can't wait to see them." she said excitedly. He smiled back and took her arm in his and replied: "I would be happy to, Cornelia" and the pair set off walking the long journey back to the theatre.

Christian and James wasted no time in forcing the man into a chair and tied him up securely, to give Henry and Cornelia enough time to get away from the laundry. James said to Christian, "I will make sure that this fellow gets locked up for his sins; you go on and get back to the theatre." Christian replied: "Do you suppose that woman really is Cornelia Wright?" James answered and said: "Well she fits the children's description of her to a tee, so if I was a betting man, I would put money down that she is." Christian responded as he was leaving, and said: "Well I hope you are right, because it would certainly make those children and Hannah very happy. Anyway, I will see you, when you get back to the Savoy, James," Christian said and he began retracing his steps back to the theatre.

Christian made good time and soon caught up with his friend, Henry and the red haired woman, and he caught sight of them from a distance on the next street ahead. But as he drew closer, he noticed crowds of people between him and the pair ahead; and was alarmed to see his friend fall down suddenly on the wooden boardwalk. The woman looked distressed when a group of looters gathered around them; and Christian ran to help Henry, and the loud crowd moved off at his approach. He was shocked to see a pool of blood gathering towards the bottom of Henry's left thigh; and Christian turned anxiously to the red haired woman and asked: "What happened to him?"

Clearly upset, Cornelia choked out: "One of those fools stabbed him in the leg, when he told them to stop crowding me." She tore off a strip of her petticoat beneath her skirt, and then sensibly tied it around Henry's leg to make a tourniquet to stop the bleeding. Christian said: "He looks really pale and we need to get him back to the Savoy, as soon as possible. Is your name Cornelia?" he inquired.

After applying the tourniquet, she looked up and answered, saying: "Yes it is, and I hear my children await me there; saints be praised; but we will both need to walk on either side of Henry's arms, to help him walk; if he is to make it that far. He has lost a lot of blood, you know," she added. Christian nodded and said: "Yes, that sounds a good idea, Cornelia, my name is Christian. Let us begin, because I fear he will lose consciousness entirely before we reach the Savoy," he said, growing seriously concerned for his friend. Henry groaned, when he was lifted to his feet, the pain of the wound evident on his face; yet, he struggled to walk with his friends, even though a permanent grimace remained on his face.

Chapter 34

On the long walk back to the theatre, Christian asked Cornelia: "Have you had to endure that treatment at the laundry for very long? That man you were struggling with; seemed to have it in for you?" he added. Cornelia looked across at Christian while her small body tried to support Henry, and she finally spoke, saying: "It was the only job I could find, after my parents died. It seems like no one wants to hire a middle-aged Irish woman in this city, and I needed to feed and clothe Helga and Olaf, so I just put up with him." Christian looked with sympathy at the woman and responded: "I can understand your reasons; but it is better you are away from that brute. How are you holding up, can you manage until we get back to the theatre?" he asked in a concerned voice. Cornelia set her jaw and looked at Henry's face and her eyes softened, when she replied: "Henry seems a good man, and I will do my best to help him." Henry groaned with every step he was made to take, and appeared semi-conscious for most of the journey. His bleeding from his thigh had slowed, since Cornelia had tied the petticoat tourniquet around it; but blood still seeped from the wound and he looked deathly pale.

After walking for some time in silence, Cornelia said bluntly; "I don't think he can take much more, is the theatre close now?" "Yes, Thank God," Christian declared, "It is just on the next street, it won't be long now." "Bless the Virgin Mother Mary, I didn't think we would ever get here, lead the way," Cornelia exclaimed. As the three walked onwards, the large theatre loomed before them, and finally they reached the large back door. Christian pounded hard on it, to draw either the night watchman's or Hannah's attention. Hannah had been anxiously waiting hour after hour for the men and jumped when she heard the pounding on the back door, and was afraid that maybe a looter was trying to get into the theatre. She cautioned the children to stay in the dressing room, and ran to the back door with her heart thumping in her chest. When Hannah reached the door, she looked through the peephole, and she was relieved to see it was Christian; and unlocked the door eagerly with the jangling keys she kept in her pocket. She opened her arms, ready to embrace Christian, and then she saw the pale and bleeding body of Henry, and noticed the small red-haired woman standing on the opposite side of him, and said in a shocked voice: "What has happened Chris, Henry looks terrible?" Before Christian could answer, Cornelia cut in and said: "I am Cornelia and we must lay this poor man down, as soon as possible please; as his leg is bleeding badly and he grows weaker every minute, can you lead the way?" Confused at the woman's words, Hannah looked at Christian for confirmation; and he spoke without delay and said: "Hannah, I will explain all the details later; but right now we have to do all we can to save Henry." Wasting no time, Hannah said: "Yes, please come this way, we will put him by the pot-bellied stove, but let me find some set curtains to make him a bed first."

When they finally settled Henry in the large ticket office by the pot-bellied stove, Hannah sucked in a breath, when she noticed the deep knife wound in Henry's thigh. Cornelia called out instructions for Hannah to bring water and material for bandages, and any alcohol the theatre might have and Hannah taking no offense, moved quickly to provide what Cornelia needed to help her friend. After she had given Cornelia the materials she required, Hannah watched the capable woman remove the blood saturated tourniquet and clean and dress Henry's wound. Hannah then turned to Christian and said: "Now tell me what happened?" Christian tried his best to fill Hannah in on the details, and when he had finished, they both turned to Cornelia and Henry and couldn't help but see the deep connection between the two, as their friend responded to Cornelia's ministrations. When she finished dressing the wound, Cornelia turned to the young couple and said: "We will need to watch him round the clock, because Henry's wound is deep and he has a high risk of fever and infection." "Would you mind young woman, watching him for now; because I would like to go and find my children?" Hannah introduced herself and readily agreed, and directed Christian to take Cornelia to her children. When they reached the actor's dressing room, Christian opened the door and Cornelia entered the room, smiling broadly. She opened her arms wide, and Helga and Olaf squealing "Mama, Mama" ran to hug their mother.

That night, Henry thrashed back and forth on the makeshift bed, burning up with fever. Although the bleeding had stopped, he hung tenuously between life and death, and Cornelia never left his side. The woman had an iron will and refused to leave Henry's sick bed after she had spent time with her children. Hannah tried to listen to her gifting and desperately searched for some way to help her friend. Yet the gifting remained quiet, and the hours wore on. Hannah couldn't help but admire the older woman's dogged determination and soon came to realise that this bond that was developing between Henry and Cornelia was somehow part of the greater plan.

The next morning, James arrived back at the Savoy Theatre with food provisions and the children squealed with delight when he gave them peppermint candy for a treat. Hannah and Christian thanked him for the provisions and filled him in on Henry's condition. James responded: "What a terrible thing to happen to the poor man, do you think he will survive?" Hannah choked up at his words and tears rolled down her cheeks; and Christian tried to comfort her by putting his arm around her shoulders. He then looked directly at James and said solemnly: "Cornelia said he has the makings of gangrene in his wound; because the knife he was stabbed with was likely dirty, so his chances are not good." James looked at him with disbelief and Hannah whispered to Christian, "I must have time alone to seek direction. I don't believe it is Henry's time to die," she declared, and quickly walked out of the room.

Cornelia kept watch over Henry and stared down compassionately at his face. It seemed his dear features were now a part of her, and she ached to see him suffering. She had lost too many to sickness in the last few years, the worst losses of her life, being her husband and four year old daughter, Sadie. She could not allow another person to die whilst in her care, especially this special man. While both women sat at Henry's bedside, Hannah had told her about Henry. She told Cornelia of his kind and compassionate nature, and about how he made her family laugh with his jokes and stories. She had also learned that apart from being an Episcopal priest, that Henry was a respected dignitary, and had been used by the President and the U.S. Army, as an emissary to the indians and had always been honest and fair with them, which made her drawn to him even more

Hannah paced back and forth on the balcony of the theatre, trying to think of what to do to help her dear friend, Henry. Christian and James had gone to send a telegram to Washington D.C. to explain the situation; and the children were sitting in one of the theatre dressing rooms with the night watchman, listening to his stories. At last, after about an hour, Hannah felt a stirring of her gifting. Yet the instructions given to her by her gifting seemed strange to her and she wasn't sure if Cornelia would take her seriously, when she shared them with her. Nevertheless, Hannah squared her shoulders and tried to release her doubts, and bolstering her courage; she made up her mind to go and speak to Cornelia about what they must do to save Henry.

When she entered the room, Hannah heard the laboured breathing of her friend, and she looked into Cornelia's brave face and said: "Cornelia, I know a way to heal Henry, but you must listen to everything I have to say, do you understand?" Cornelia's eyes widened; but there seemed to be no cynicism in her face, so Hannah pressed on. "Cornelia, I have a gift that has been used since I was a small child to help many people throughout the years." She hurried on and said: "The gifting has told me we must take Henry to a room that has windows, so he can get fresh air and also that then we must get onions, garlic, and peppers and we must boil them and then wrap them in a cloth in a sort of poultice for his wound. I have never done this sort of thing before; but my gifting has told me that this will draw the infection out of his leg," Hannah added, "will you help me?" Cornelia rose to her feet and walked across to Hannah and looked at her closely, and then taking her hands, she said; "Hannah, I would do anything to help Henry, let us start cooking the vegetables; and the men will be back soon and then we can get him moved." Hannah smiled at her new found friend, and felt the most hope she had in days for Henry's recovery, and knew deep within her heart that at last, Henry would survive this terrible ordeal.

Chapter 35

When Hannah went to find the night watchman to ask if there were any onions, garlic, or peppers in theatre, the old man chuckled at her request and said: "Missy, why do you think such things can be found in a theatre, most actors don't even eat here, much less cook here?" Just then, Hannah heard the men come in through the back door and she felt her gifting impart more instructions to her, which she was thankful for. Hannah responded and said: "Well thanks anyway. Sam, I will have to send the men to fetch these items, once we get Henry moved into another room to get him some fresh air." Sam looked at her incredulously and replied: "Miss Hannah with the flood waters everywhere in the city, it will be very hard to find fresh vegetables somewhere close; but if you have a mind to cook 'em, then I wish you luck and I will keep an eye on these little 'uns for you." Hannah thanked him again and went to find Christian and James.

The men had successfully sent the telegram to Washington D.C. delaying the meeting with President Lincoln for another few days; and were shrugging off their outer garments; when Hannah came to the cloak room to tell them the latest news. She blurted out her news in a rush, and said: "Christian my gifting has instructed me that we must move Henry to the main foyer where there are windows and let in some fresh air for him; and then we must cook onions, garlic, and peppers and place them in to a clean cloth to fashion a poultice to place on Henry's leg to draw out the infection. Can you boys please move him into the foyer and then Christian I will need you to go and get the vegetables; because there are none here in the theatre?" Christian listened intently to Hannah's description of the instructions she had been given, not once doubting anything she said; but James was amazed at the strange ideas, and looked at both Hannah and Christian in disbelief, saying: "Well I admire the fact you want to help your friend, you two; but where in the Sam Hill do you think you are going to find onions, garlic, and peppers after flood waters and looters have ravaged this city?"

Hannah looked past him, seeing and yet not seeing, as she stared vacantly ahead of her and then she said in a quiet voice: "My gifting has told me there is an old woman across the road, who has the items we need. She is very old and wise and lives in a wooden house, with a number three above the door," she added. James looked at them both dumbfounded with his mouth wide-open, and Christian ignoring the expression on his face, said: "Come on James, I will explain all this on the way; but right now, I have got a friend to save and I need your help." James closed his mouth and followed without comment, and Hannah smiled after them, thinking to herself it was not the first time she had received such a look, after she had exercised her gifting.

The men wasted no time in moving Henry to the foyer, and Cornelia fussed over her patient every step of the way. When he was finally settled, the men opened the foyer windows, and immediately, a fresh breeze blew in from the outside. Hannah entered the foyer, and was well satisfied that Henry was now in the right place, and she walked across to Christian and urged him to quickly leave to retrieve the vegetables. Christian agreed and walked out of the theatre, scanning the streets for any wooden houses across from it; but he did not immediately see any at all. Not to be deterred, he saw that there were large office buildings surrounding the Savoy, so he decided to go down several alleyways to see if it was somehow hidden from view... Several of the alleyways were blocked due to the flood waters; but as he walked in the early evening hours; Christian saw a light emanating from one alleyway, several streets ahead. The light drew him, and Christian made his way towards it, being mindful of both the crowds and the muddy waters which blocked him from his destination. At last, he reached the alleyway where the light was coming from, and was surprised to see that it was not an alleyway at all; but a narrow, cobbled street.

As if drawn like a moth to the flame, Christian turned into the narrow street and moved towards the light and saw a small wooden cottage with lights shining from the inside. He hastened his pace and hoped with all his heart that it was the right house, and within a short time he was approaching the cottage door. Christian was relieved to see the number three above the cottage door and before he could knock, the creaky door opened and a wizened, white haired old woman with a kindly face stood before him. He could tell the old woman could barely see and at first he doubted that she could help him at all; but when she opened her mouth, he was amazed at her words, when she said: "Welcome Dearie, what took you so long, I have been waiting for you?" In what seemed to be a Jamaican accent, the small black woman added: "I can barely see you man in the evening light, so you best come in; because my gifting told me to be expecting your company." Christian dutifully followed the old woman in, and she kept speaking, saying: "Now, I have gathered the things you need from my garden out back, the onions, garlic, and peppers, some herbs and I have added a few eggs for the little ones from my chicken pen in the bargain. Will you need a pot to cook these delicacies in? Well speak up, young man, does the cat now have your tongue?" the old woman asked. Although he felt like he was in a dream, Christian forced himself to answer her, and said: "Yes madam, these things are most welcome and a pot would be mighty useful I think too. I can have the night watchman at the Savoy drop it back to you, when we are done with it, if you like?" The old woman smiled with a toothless grin, and replied: "Yes, that would be nice, I get a bit lonely in here sometimes and I would be glad of his company." Feeling very grateful for the woman's generosity, Christian thanked the old woman and kissed her on the hand, saying: "Thanks for your obedience, madam, you like my fiancé, have made great sacrifices for your gift; but your rewards will be great one day."

The old woman blushed and said: "Now we will have none of that young man, just be on your way; your friends are waiting for you." Christian grinned and walked out of the cottage with the precious articles and moved at a swift pace down the cobbled street to the main road; but when he looked back to view the cottage, one more time; it was simply not there. Christian couldn't believe his eyes and rubbed them several times, looking again down the cobbled street; but there was simply no trace of the old woman or her cottage anywhere. Feeling frightened and somewhat weak after the supernatural experience, Christian beat a path back to the theatre running as fast as he could. He hoped that maybe Hannah could make some sense of what had just happened; and he quickly slotted the key in to the back door when he reached the theatre, and closed it securely behind him. Hearing his arrival, Hannah ran to greet him, and asked: "Did you get everything we needed?" Christian looked like he had seen a ghost, and Hannah showing concern inquired: "Are you alright Chris?" "You don't look so good."

Christian getting control of himself, replied kissing her on the forehead: "It is a long story, Hannah, and we don't have much time at the moment; so I will tell you everything later, don't worry I am fine. Here is everything you need," he added, and handed her his parcel and the pot. Hannah smiled and said: "Well done, Chris, we make a good team, you and I," and off she went to start cooking the lifesaving vegetables for Henry's poultice.

When Hannah had prepared the poultice, she quickly brought it to the main foyer where Henry lay on a bed made of set curtains in a weakened state. She handed it to Cornelia to place on his wound, and he groaned in pain when it was applied. Cornelia, however; whispered tender words of encouragement in his ear, which seemed to soothe him. It was a long and tedious wait after the poultice was applied; and the sick man seemed to go into a very, deep sleep while his breathing slowed down considerably, after the first hour it was used. Hannah was still worried, but knew she had followed her gifting's instructions completely; and so now they must wait to let it do its' work. Hour after hour passed through the dark night, and Hannah relieved Cornelia several times, so that she could eat and see to her children, nevertheless; she didn't stay away for long and for the most part maintained her place, as the main carer for the sick man.

Finally, morning broke along with Henry's fever and his eyes fluttered open. He looked at Cornelia, and her back was turned, because she was rinsing out a cool cloth for his head. She turned to place the cloth back on his forehead and met his gaze and a huge smile crossed her face. Henry broke the silence and asked in a quiet voice: "Sweet lady was it your beautiful voice I heard in my dreams, as I could feel you calling me back to the land of the living?" Tears pricked Cornelia's eyes and she said emotionally with her voice breaking: "Yes you silly man and why wouldn't I want such a handsome gentleman as yourself, to come back to life, I ask you?"

Just then, Hannah entered the foyer and clapped her hands when she saw Henry and Cornelia talking. She could see his colour had returned and that he looked strengthened and approached his bed saying: "Henry, it is so good to have you back, how are you feeling?" Henry took on a comical expression and said; "Hungry enough to eat a horse, do you have anything other than onions, garlic, and peppers about; because I feel like I have been smelling that stuff for hours?" Both women laughed and Cornelia replied: "Yes, that little concoction has made you a lot better, I think; but let me check your wound, before you start eating any horses." Hannah walked up behind her and watched as the poultice was removed and both women gasped; as no trace of the stab wound could be found on Henry's thigh. "Bless the Holy Virgin, it is a miracle," Cornelia exclaimed, "It is like he never had a wound at all." She then looked at Hannah with reverence and declared: "Your gifting is powerful, Hannah, and you can be proud, because with it, you saved this good man's life this day." Hannah felt both humbled and grateful at her words, and was too choked up to reply to her words, but nodded her head in thanks…

"Here stay with him, Hannah, I must go and tell everyone of this wonderful miracle," Cornelia exclaimed, and she dashed out the door. Hannah took Henry's hand and squeezed it, saying: "So, old friend, are you ready to get back to Washington D.C. to save the Lakotas? Because, you have spent far too much time being lazy in bed." she declared. Henry chuckled at her joke, and quipped: "Well, it has been well worth it; because I have been cared for by the lovely hands of the beautiful Cornelia." "Yes, I can see you two have hit it off, and I am happy for you, Henry," Hannah said. It wasn't long before the other inhabitants of the theatre came stampeding into the foyer, to view the miraculous healing of Henry's leg for themselves; and all were suitably impressed when they saw that his leg was completely devoid of any signs of injury. Shock and wonder showed on all of their faces, and Henry took their gawking in good grace; but finally broke the spell and said: "Now, if you lot are done with your entertainment for today, I need to have a wash and shave and I am dying for something to eat."

Cornelia smiled and said: "Your wish is my command, kind Sir, I will get you some water and towels and Hannah can you bring our restored patient some bread and cheese please?"

The next two days, Henry regained his strength and Hannah and Christian knew they could not delay their trip to Washington D.C., any longer. The young couple and Henry met together on the evening of the second day of the miraculous healing, to discuss their plans; and Hannah began the discussion, saying: "Sadly, we have had a great many things happen to us, which have delayed our meeting with President Lincoln; is he still agreeable to meet with us?" Christian answered and said, "Yes, his secretary said the President has been investigating the planned capture of the three hundred Lakota Sioux braves in the Dakota Territory; and wishes to speak to us, urgently about it."

Listening to his friends, Henry spoke and said: "Of course we must go; but we now have the responsibility of ensuring that Cornelia and the children are safe, and I will not leave them behind." Half expecting this response, because anyone with eyes could see how Cornelia and Henry felt about each other, Hannah was careful with her next words and said: "What are your intentions towards Cornelia and her children, Henry; because that will have bearing on how we help them?" Both Hannah and Christian looked expectantly at Henry, and noticed how their friend's face turned red, when he was put on the spot. Finally, after a few minutes he spoke and said: "It is as if I have always known her and she is the most beautiful woman, I have ever seen; so my young friends, I intend to offer her marriage, if she will have me." "That is wonderful news, Henry; I suppose we can delay our trip to Washington D.C. one more day until you speak to her; but we will need to get some sort of carriage with horses if our number is to double," Christian said practically. "Yes, you get cracking on rounding up the carriage and horses and a few provisions and I will do my part," Henry assured them. Hannah kissed Henry on the cheek and said: "Good luck Henry; but I am pretty sure from the look in her eyes, that she will say yes." "Well, let's see if she wants to take this old codger on," he quipped and then with a determined look on his face, said: "I suppose there is no time like the present," and strode from the room with Hannah and Christian smiling after him.

Henry knew he didn't look his best, but he went to the actor's dressing room and tried to find a shirt and breeches that would spruce him up a bit; and used scissors to trim his scruffy, russet beard. He looked at his short muscular frame once dressed and coiffed; and thought to himself, he didn't look too bad for a man of thirty nine; and he bolstered his courage to go a meet the beautiful Cornelia. He found her reading to her children in the ticket office, with both of the small tykes, sitting on either of her legs. She looked beautiful and serene and Henry knew she was the woman he wanted to spend the rest of his life with; but the task ahead would be to convince her, he was the man for her too. He had thought out his reasons why she should accept him and gave her a serious look when he entered the room. Cornelia looked up and was immediately glad to see him and said; "You look nice. Is there something you need Henry, because I would be happy to fetch it for you, if you like?" she asked. Cornelia was perplexed by his serious expression, but trying to lighten his mood, she joked: "You have a powerful serious expression on your face, Henry, for someone who has just been a product of a miracle."

Half smiling at her light hearted attempt at humour, he replied: "Yes, I am grateful for that miracle, my dear; but I wondered if I might steal a moment of your time to speak to you, alone?" Curious to hear what Henry had to say, Cornelia looked down at her children and said: "Helga, Olaf, go and find Mr. Sam and stay with him for a while, Henry and I have something to talk about." Helga kissed her mama on the cheek and agreed; but the younger child, Olaf, didn't want to go, and Helga pulled on Olaf's hand saying, "Come on Olaf, Mama wants to talk about grown up things with Henry," and the children finally left the office hand in hand. Pulling up a chair beside Cornelia, Henry took in her lovely face, and green eyes, and her alabaster skin and red hair, and she took his breath away. Faltering for words, Henry just looked at her for a time and didn't say anything. Amused at his loss for words, Cornelia spoke up and said: "Well Sir, this is one for the books, are you expectin' me to read your mind?"

Regaining his composure, Henry garnered his courage and forged ahead, saying: "Cornelia, as you know we will soon all of us have to leave this theatre, and I wondered if you had thought about what you are going to do?" "Henry, my parents died soon after arriving with me to New York; and I am all alone, so there is a convent on Mercy Street that takes in families; and I thought I might head there until I find another job," she explained. Henry admired her spirit and said: "Well, I would like to offer you another solution if you will consider it. I am a man of some means and well paid by the U.S. government, as an Indian emissary and also I receive support as an Episcopal minister in the Dakota Territory,"

Henry continued and said. "And I know I am about twelve or thirteen years older than you; but you will find me an honest and fair man," he added. Cornelia said nothing; and just smiled at him. Unable to read her expression, Henry continued on, fearing that he might lose his confidence, and said: "Cornelia, I am quite taken with your beauty, your resourcefulness and strength, and would be honoured if you would marry me, if you don't mind taking on such an old man, as myself." he ventured. Cornelia continued to look at him contemplatively and finally after several minutes, asked: "Henry, are you sure you want to take on a penniless widow from Dublin and two orphaned Norwegian waifs, this is no small thing you are proposing?" Henry looked her in the eye and said firmly: "Cornelia, I have never been so sure of anything in my entire life." The normally strong Irish woman then began to cry and hugged him close. Confused, Henry said: "Cornelia, Cornelia, I didn't mean to make you cry, you don't have to marry me if you don't want to." Cornelia looked up through her tears and said to him simply: "You silly man, I have never been so sure of anything in my entire life," and the couple hugged each other for several minutes, laughing at each other's joke and gratefully let the reality of their future together sink in. When Cornelia stopped crying, Henry tipped her chin up to look at him and said softly: "Cornelia my love, we will have a good life together, a happy life; so dry your tears and let us go and tell the children." Cornelia, soon back to her old self, answered him and said: "Not before my husband to be, seals his offer with a kiss," and Henry leaned down and gave her a heartfelt kiss to do just that.

The rest of the evening was a joyful one, and the newly formed couple announced their big news to both Helga and Olaf, and the other inhabitants of the theatre and all of them happily received the news. Early the next day, Christian and James went out to secure a carriage, horses and provisions for the trip to Washington D.C. It was not easy for the men; because the hurricane had wiped out many of the stableyards in the city; but through James's contacts; they were finally able to secure two horses and a makeshift stock wagon to meet their needs. James was sorry to see them go, but was happy his efforts had met with such a happy ending for them all.

As they drove the wagon to the theatre, the women filed out with Henry and the children and congratulated the men on finding such a sturdy conveyance so quickly. They climbed into the back of the wagon with their belongings; and James stood with Sam, looking up at the lively group and wished them a good trip.

Hannah climbed out of the wagon and she and Christian walked over to James and Sam, and Hannah hugged them both. "I don't know how we can ever thank you both, for all you have done for us," she said. James looked at Hannah, feeling emotional at the parting; but tried hard not to show it. He finally responded and said: "Miss Hannah, you are an inspiration to us all; and I am very proud to know you." Christian followed Hannah and shook James's hand and also thanked him. Then Hannah moved to Sam and quipped: "I am going to miss your stories, Sam; life will be a lot duller without you around." The night watchman laughed and replied: "You and the children have brightened up my days too, little lady, may Lady Luck always smile upon you." With the goodbyes said and with tears in their eyes, Hannah, Christian and the others climbed into the wagon and set their sights on travelling to Washington D.C. at last, to try to save their friends, the Lakota Indians.

Chapter 36

Abraham Lincoln was by all accounts, a wise man with high morals and was winning the war by garnering the deep rooted convictions and backing of the citizens of the Northern States of America. He knew he had liberal views, especially in regards to the indians; and these views were not popular in most political camps these days. The President was also well aware, that although the Civil War was nearly over, that the task of rebuilding a deeply wounded nation, would be a precarious one at best. So quite honestly, Abe's only confidante he could turn to with trust, was his wife of 20 years, Mary Todd Lincoln. Mary's life with her husband had not been easy, he knew; for she was a genteel woman who had been raised by rich Kentucky plantation owners, and was used to the finer things in life. She had also battled with numerous health issues throughout the years, and suffered from terrible migraines and various women's complaints. Yet, Abe knew she loved him, and that her moral fibre and wish to extend kindness to others was strong and unbending, which was an admirable thing in his eyes. In fact, her compassion had been clear to him a short time after he had met her, when she had described to him the horror she felt, when her stepmother cruelly ordered a black housemaid to be whipped to the point of death, after soiling a pair of her favourite gloves.

So on this occasion, Abe sought out his wife for her advice about the plight of the Lakota Sioux Indians. He had always been opposed to the indians being forced onto reservations and starved to death; and he was painfully aware of the longstanding broken promises of government agents to the indians and the injustices they suffered whilst the white man stole more and more of their lands. Abe had also been told of the retaliation of the indians, and the violence which erupted on both sides and was convinced that this time things had gone too far.

Reports he had heard recently, were the worst to date, and they concerned him greatly. It had been reported to him, that three hundred Lakota Indian braves were being rounded up by army soldiers on and off the reservations; and that these braves were being tried for crimes committed against the white settlers in the Dakota Territory. Abe had done his research, and sent men he trusted to find out the nature of the court proceedings; and found that all of the three hundred Indian braves were being tried with the purpose of condemning them to die by the hangman's noose. It seemed the evidence was being based on the testimony of one man, a black farmer named Josiah Smith. The President's intelligence agents also reported that Smith was being paid off by prominent white men in the territory, to testify that he had witnessed all of these indians, raping white women and burning down white settler's farms. Yet, how can I prove that such a claim is ridiculous, Abe thought, and bring justice to such corrupt court proceedings. For this, he knew he needed his wife's council and time to think.

Mary welcomed her husband into her sitting room, and put down her embroidery; smoothing out her skirts, and patted the cushion for him to sit down beside her. She knew better than to quiz him about what was wrong; because Mary was aware that her husband had many worries that had built up throughout the controversial years of the Civil War. She listened to him patiently, whilst Abe described the plight of the indians in the Dakota Territory, and saw the stress etched in lines across her husband's face. "The thing is, Mary, there are all these people baying for the blood of the indians and they want all of them, every man, woman and child wiped out completely, and I cannot in good conscience, allow three hundred men to die; be it Indian or white man; based on the testimony of one man. One man who has claimed to have single-handedly seen all of these Indian braves commit some heinous crime. The idea is ridiculous to the extreme," Abe declared angrily.

Mary looked at Abe sympathetically, and answered him, saying: "My husband, you must act as you always do, follow your heart, and do what you feel is right and stick to your belief that all men are created equal." Abe looked at her tenderly, and said: "I have my old friend, Henry, and some young people who are coming to meet with me tomorrow; and I hope to come to some decision, then." Mary looked at him, and replied in a motherly tone, saying: "Now Abe, you have enough burdens on your shoulders, let this issue settle in your mind for now; at least until Henry and the others come. Once you have a chance to speak with them, you will know what to do, mark my words," Mary added convincingly. "Yes, you are right my dear," he said, patting her on the knee, "I will heed your words for now and have a little rest, you are always so sensible," Abe replied kindly.

During the time Hannah and the men had been absent from the Dakota Territory, much had transpired across the region. Due to the capture of Little Crow and the subsequent rounding up by the US army of hundreds of male indian boys and men across the territory, renegade Indians began burning farms and killing and capturing settlers far and wide. In addition, after the indian renegades started down this path, the movement gained momentum and escalated tensions to the extent that it became an embittered life and death struggle between the opposing sides. One of the worst incidents occurred in a place called Red Ferry, where the indian renegades over-ran the soldiers, killing twenty four men. From that point onwards, the violence escalated to epic proportions and the roving bands of Sioux renegades initiated an all-out assault; and smelling victory began destroying whole townships for the next several weeks; plundering and killing masses of white settlers, in a desperate attempt to eradicate the white man from their lands. During this violent and bloody struggle, several appeals had been dispatched to President Lincoln, pleading for his intervention; but coincidentally his attention had been diverted to the second battle at Bull Run, one of the most important battles in the Civil War. The Rebels of the South, who were led by General. Robert E. Lee; had invaded the state of Maryland; with the reinforcements of Rebel General, George B. McClellan. The battle ensued with major losses of life from both The Union and Rebel armies; however; in the end, the overcautious battle tactics of General McClellan caused the downfall of the Rebel armies, causing one of the bloodiest days of the Civil War.

Finally, after a month, President Lincoln responded to the pleas coming out of the Dakota Territory, by assigning General John Pope, who needed a change of scene after the battle of Battle Run, and the glory seeking military man embraced the task of ending the indian uprising, with enthusiasm. President Lincoln knew the man's agenda and was ambivalent about sending the merciless man to take control of the desperate struggle between the Indian and white man; but he was pressured by political adversaries in Congress, and he hesitantly came in line with the decision.

General Pope was a pompous and self-righteous man, and made the statement shortly after being assigned to the Dakota Territory that his purpose was to utterly destroy and exterminate the Sioux Indians. Dismayed by the man's single-minded prejudice against the Sioux Indians, President Lincoln recognised his grave mistake in succumbing to political pressure. He had in fact, removed General Pope from the forefront of the Civil War, replacing him with someone far more competent, a man named General Meade; but in the process, he had succeeded in making the plight of the Sioux Indians infinitely worse.

Within a matter of weeks, an almighty battle ensued in a place called Wood Lake in which both US Army soldiers and Indian forces suffered heavy losses; however, in the end, the indians were subdued. Soon after the victory, General Pope ordered the continuance of the rounding up of indian boys and men across the territory, many of whom had nothing to do with any violence that had been committed against the white settlers. The Sioux Indians who had surrendered to such capture were promised safety; but instead were arrested and tried by a five man military commission, based on the corrupt testimony of Josiah Smith. General Pope's intent in his ambitious mind was to orchestrate mass executions to show the white settlers he had subdued the Sioux Indians, once and for all.

Chapter 37

President Lincoln knew of the reputation of both Henry Whipple and Hannah Nelson and was aware that many people had branded them as "Indian Lovers." But he had also known Henry for many years and believed him to be an honest and just man. Regarding Hannah, his intelligence agents had told him the stories of her powers and her unique relationship with Little Crow and the Lakota Sioux Indians; and he was intrigued by her. His firm desire was that these people could somehow help him to make a very tough decision that would satisfy his conscience as well as the inhabitants of the Dakota Territory; and he fervently hoped their meeting would live up to his expectations.

Hannah, Christian and the rest of the weary travellers were relieved to finally reach Washington D.C. after a day's travel. The journey had been much slower due to the necessity of stopping for rest and respite for the women and children. Once inside the busy city, Hannah could see streetlamps lighting up the government buildings and was fascinated to see the grand avenues of the metropolis. Henry had told her about President Lincoln's building plans for the capital, which included the building of the U.S. Capitol building; which would be overlooking the Potomac River, when it was completed. She, and the men, would be meeting with President Lincoln at the White House, his official residence and principal workplace, and they felt a great sense of awe about visiting the famous place; as it has been the residence of every U.S. president since John Adams in 1800. The group finally arrived at the boarding house suggested by President Lincoln's secretary; and were humbled to find that the President had generously paid for their stay. The Fairfax Inn was a homely place with thick carpets and a roaring fire in the guest sitting room off the main foyer; and the men and women of the party were pleased to find that their bedrooms were of an equally high standard.

Henry and Cornelia planned to marry as soon as possible; however, the matters of meeting with the President and buying Cornelia a wedding trousseau; had to be attended to first, for now. In the meanwhile, the party would take three rooms to allow Hannah and Cornelia to bed with the children. Hannah's clothes had been stored at the other boarding house they had stayed at, before her kidnapping; and Christian went to retrieve them for her, soon after they arrived. Hannah was pleased after she had taken a luxurious bath; to be able to wear her own clothes again; because she felt like her old self at last, which was a comfort.

Henry went out to buy a paper and was incensed to read the events that had transpired in the Dakota Territory, since their absence. He returned to the boarding house angry beyond words, and knocked loudly at Christian's and the women's doors, saying: "Hannah, Christian please meet me downstairs in the sitting room, because we have important subjects to discuss before we meet with the President tomorrow." The doors opened to both rooms and Christian readily agreed to his suggestion; however, Cornelia opened the other door and not wishing to exclude her, Henry politely said when he saw her quizzical expression: "My dear you are also welcome to come, but if you would rather stay with the children, I can fill you in later." Cornelia smiled and said: "Thank you Henry, you three go ahead; I know you must prepare for your important meeting tomorrow." Kissing her hand, Henry left to go downstairs with Christian following; and Hannah soon joined them in the sitting room. Each of them ordered cream tea and scones, and Henry looked at them with a thunderous expression and said: "The President has sent that incompetent clown, General Pope, to put down the Indian uprising in the Dakota Territory; and the Sioux have gone mad since he enforced the order to start rounding up hundreds of indian boys and men. The renegades are burning down whole townships in revenge," he added, incredulously. Hannah's throat constricted and she felt like the wind had been knocked out of her, when she heard the news.

Christian looked across at Hannah and squeezed her hand, knowing how devastating this news must be to her. She finally found her voice and asked: "What does General Pope plan to do with these indians once he has captured them all?" Henry looked at her, not wishing to distress her further, but decided he had to be honest with her and said: "Pope plans to stage a mass execution of the three hundred Indian prisoners, to show his supremacy over the region; but we need to find out from the President, if he has a legal leg to stand on, even if it is the Dakota Territory."

From her visions, Hannah had been forewarned of the terrible event, but the reality that it was actually happening, was almost too much to bear. "But what about Little Crow and Wowinapa?" she asked, feebly. Henry looked at her compassionately and replied: "Hannah, I really don't know, but I pray they are all right." "We will get to the bottom of this tomorrow," Hannah declared, "surely the President will want to right this wrong. I have heard he is a just man?" Christian agreed and said: "Yes, I have, as well." Henry nodded and said: "That is true, I have never known Abe to act unjustly, and I am sure he will do the right thing; but remember he is under tremendous pressure at the moment, because he has two wars on his hands right now, not just one,"

During her time away from the Dakota Territory, Hannah had worried incessantly about Little Crow and his family and she was plagued with dreams of white soldiers attacking her friends in various settings. Henry had also read in the newspaper, that Little Crow had broken out of the fort stockade, after some Lakota braves had created a diversion; but that he was soon apprehended again, after he rode back into the fort with his braves a few nights later, to break into the fort's stores to provide food for his people. He pointed out through an interpreter at the time that this food was meant for the indians on the reservations anyway; but instead of distributing it, Pope's men had been ordered to, in Pope's words: "let the stinkin' indians starve and eat grass." Comments like this, angered the indians greatly and even though the scales were not tipped in their favour, they continued to retaliate against the white man's callous treatment. One of the first victims of the Indian uprising, after such comments were made about 'Indians eating grass' was a man named, Andrew Murick. Murick had been one of the men that had professed such sentiments, and he was scalped with his mouth stuffed with grass, in revenge for his words.

The next day Hannah, Christian and Henry rose early to prepare for their fortuitous meeting between the President and themselves. Much rested on the outcome of this meeting and the pit of Hannah's stomach tightened with nerves, when she thought of how much the Lakota Sioux were depending on her. Henry had informed her there were hundred and thirty two rooms, thirty five bathrooms, twenty eight fireplaces, and eight staircases, in the White House; and she was very excited when the President's carriage came to collect them at 9:00 am. When they were driven through the White House's iron gates and ushered into the Oval Office to meet the President, Henry led the way; making it obvious he had attended these meetings many times in the past.

When the three entered the Oval office, President Lincoln had his back turned and was looking out the window. Henry strode forward smiling and called out "Abe, how are you, my friend? It has been too long, since we saw each other last." The President turned and smiled back, shaking Henry's hand, and replied in a slow drawl: "Well Henry, you old badger, I see you have endured the wilds of the Dakota Territory." Both men laughed and Henry introduced both Hannah and Christian, and said: "And Hannah here has a special interest in the welfare of the Lakota tribe; but I will let her tell you for herself, her reasons for it. I am sorry we have had to delay this meeting Abe, so many times, we have had a few mishaps along the way, which held us up," he added. The President looked inquisitively at the young people and replied: "Well, I understand that things can happen, Henry, the main thing is that you are here right now; please all of you sit down," motioning to the chairs behind them. The group sat down in the leather chairs across from the President's desk, and waited expectantly for him to speak again.

"I have heard that things are going very badly in the Dakota Territory," President Lincoln said haltingly, "Pope has reinforced an order to round up hundreds of Indian braves and it has caused major upheaval there and countless deaths." Feeling frustrated, Henry spoke up and said: "I mean no disrespect, Abe; but why the hell did you send that buffoon out there to start with? He was a pretty poor specimen on the battlefield in these parts?" he added. Hannah sucked in a breath when she heard these words, and quickly looked across at the President to see how he had re-acted to Henry's words. She briefly looked across at Christian as well, and could see he couldn't believe Henry's words either and they both waited, wondering what would happen next. The President's shoulders sagged and an apologetic look crossed his face, and he replied tersely: "Well Hell Henry, Pope has a lot of supporters in this here government and I needed to get him out of this conflict betwixt the Rebs and us; because his decisions were costing us lives." Henry fired back: "Well now he is cost-ing lives in the Dakota Territory; and you know that idiot is a law unto himself, all ego and no brains. You've got to do some-thing, Abe; there are two sides to the story out there, and many of these Sioux Indians are peace lovin' souls who have been treat-ed very badly by the white soldiers and agents alike."

The President was silent for a time and then said: "Now sim-mer down Henry, I would like to know more about these peace lovin' Indians. Miss Hannah, can you tell me about your deal-ings with them please?" Startled by the shift in the conversa-tion and the direct question from the President, Hannah cleared her throat and replied politely: "Yes Sir, I would consider most of them to be honourable people with families and hopes and dreams just like we have, and Chief Little Crow saved my mama when she was kidnapped by a very bad man." Hannah contin-ued to describe her interactions with Little Crow, and his family and tribe over the past year; and when Christian was questioned by the President next; he backed her up with his own positive observations concerning the indians, as well. The President and Henry stayed quiet, while the young people recounted their experiences, and the President studied their faces, and decided that they were both credible and of good character.

When at last, Hannah and Christian finished telling of their experiences, they both sat quietly and looked uncertainly at the President and Henry. "Well Henry, from what these young'uns are saying, I will need to intervene with an executive order to veto any court decisions being made at the present time out there. As we speak, three hundred Indians are being tried corruptly in court; and being convicted and prepared for a mass hanging," the President stated. "And unbelievably, the evidence for these convictions is being based on the testimony of one man, who claims he has been an eye witness to crimes committed by every single one of them, which in my book, is humanly impossible and does not sit well with me," he announced. Hannah broke in with emotion and said: "They could die, Mr. President, if we don't move quickly; please Sir, don't let this happen." President Lincoln looked at her young and innocent face and could see what the Sioux tribe meant to her and replied compassionately: "I will do what I can for them, Miss Hannah; but I suggest you go back to the Dakota Territory and use that gifting of yours to lend them all the support you can right now." "You know about my gifting?" Hannah asked. "Yes, and I don't claim to be an expert on that type of thing; but you have a heart to help those indians and that will go a very long way, I believe," the President responded.

Henry stood up and moved forward, putting his hand out to shake the President's hand and said: "I knew you wouldn't let us down, Abe, thank you; we will be headin' back to the territory, very soon." The President stood up and shook Henry's hand, and replied: "Henry, thank you for your honesty, I value your point of view; and I will act as my conscience dictates, I can assure you." He then turned to Hannah and Christian and concluded the meeting by saying: "I wish you both a good journey back, and remember to always be led by an equal measure of compassion and common sense and most of the time, you will see yourselves right."

Chapter 38

The trio left The White House, encouraged that the President was sympathetic to their cause; but were unsure how far his political arm would reach and wondered if he would act in time to save the three hundred Sioux braves. Hannah and Christian had been awed by the experience; but at the same time, felt an urgency to get back to the Dakota Territory before it was too late. Henry had Cornelia and the children to consider, and wanted to marry his newfound love before they embarked on the journey back to the Dakota Territory; but Christian and Hannah were certain time was running out; and made the decision to leave the next morning on their own. Hannah could feel the stirring of her gifting calling her back to her frontier home and so the two awoke early the next day and left at sunrise on fast horses to embark on the long journey home.

That same morning, the President had received a telegram from his government agents in the Dakota Territory that the court commission were halfway through their court trials and had already condemned one hundred and fifty Indian braves to die at the gallows; and Chief little Crow was among them. Angered at the audacity of Pope and his court puppets, President Lincoln sent a direct telegram to General Pope using strong language and warned him: "If the court proceedings and executions are not halted immediately, until I, the President of the United States, can study the matter more in depth: I will hold you, General Pope, personably responsible and thus you will be in line for an immediate court martial." This definitely gained General Pope's full attention and he gave orders for the court commission to stand down for the time being, leaving the captured Indian braves to languish in captivity; not knowing what would happen to them next.

President Lincoln was a trained lawyer and knew U.S. law backwards and forwards, and was shocked to find out, that the accused Indians of the Dakota Territory had been refused representation by counsel. In thinking about this basic human right being denied to them, coupled with the indians being trapped behind cultural and language barriers, the President knew that their chances for survival were very low indeed. Also, the speed of the trials alone, prevented a full and fair analysis of the events; which had happened between the white settlers and the indians in the past year. In addition, President Lincoln was savvy enough to consider how the rest of the world would view the execution of three hundred Indians. Clearly, if the mass hangings went ahead, it could affect the outcome of the Civil War. In fact, even now Great Britain was considering recognising the Confederacy as an independent nation, which would be a major blow to the Union cause.

Little Crow knew the other braves in captivity watched his every move, and although he was desperately worried, he dared not show any weakness in front of them. The Great Chief was determined to keep a clear head and to remain an example to his men to keep their morale up. The white soldiers were starving them and only managed to feed them watered down porridge once, every two or three days; and provided very few buckets of water in the stockade for the Indians; which didn't stretch to give everyone the fluids they needed. Even worse, the stockade was only built to house fifty men at full capacity; and the soldiers had jammed one hundred and fifty men inside it. Also, slop buckets were brimming over and were only cleared at nightfall, which added to the general misery of the place.

During his brief bout of freedom, after his tribesman broke him out of the fort stockade; one month earlier by using a diversion, Little Crow had gone to check on his wife and infant son and had found happily, that Wowinapa was taking care of his mother and younger brother, as he had somehow escaped Fort Webster in the early days of his capture; and that they were safely hidden in some nearby caves. Yet, he feared daily that Wowinapa would be caught by the white soldiers again; because the young brave held a deep anger and resentment towards the white man, and Little Crow was convinced his son's prejudiced attitude would land him back into captivity; leaving his mother and infant brother to fend for themselves. Little Crow; knew the scars on his eldest son's heart ran deep, and would not be wiped away easily.

Hannah and Christian had been travelling ten days on the trail, sleeping together at night and riding side by side every day. The closeness between the young couple was evident to all who came in contact with them and many passers-by thought the pair were husband and wife. Christian did kiss and caress Hannah in the night hours; but he did not make love to her, as it was her wish to stay pure until they married. Hannah hated to refuse Christian, because she felt a hunger for his touch like none she had ever known; but she knew she must keep herself pure for her gifting to remain intact; and explained this as tactfully as she could, in hopes he would understand.

Reluctantly, he agreed to her decision; but on the condition that she would marry him once the Indians had been rescued. Hannah wholeheartedly agreed, kissing him on the cheek. "It won't be long, Christian, in just a little over a week and we will be in the Dakota Territory, can you believe it?" she asked. "I hope that President Lincoln has used his powers to stop these terrible trials from going forward, and that we can get there in time," she added. "But Hannah, what can we do when we get there, because we don't have the power to stop anything, if he hasn't managed it?" Christian asked. "I don't exactly know just now, Chris; but my gifting has told me that we must get there as quickly as we can, because we still have a part to play in all of this," she answered vaguely. Christian stared at the faraway look in Hannah's eyes and knew better than to question her further and smiled at her indulgently, saying: "Well then my girl, we best break camp and get back on the trail, there is no time to lose."

President Lincoln spent a week pouring over the terrible injustices being carried out against the Sioux Indian braves, in captivity. And even though he had given orders for the court trials and planned executions against the Indian braves to be temporarily halted; he was convinced that with the blood thirsty prejudice and hatred that existed between both sides; that more violence would soon inevitably erupt, if he didn't act soon. In the end, it was President Lincoln's compassion and great pity for both sides that motivated him to make a decision he believed was fair to all concerned; however, because it was an unprecedented decision, it could not be sent by telegram. As a result, President Lincoln signed and sealed the official letter with his decision inside, addressing it to General Pope, and made arrangements to have it personally delivered by the Dakota Territory's first delegate, J.B.S. Todd, a cousin to his wife.

The question was, would Todd be able to get the President's letter to Pope before either side took matters into their own hands? President Lincoln honestly didn't know, but hoped that justice would prevail; and for now he had to focus his attention back on the war between the North and South, and so he traded one problem for another, moving on to solve an endless barrage of issues, as was his lot in life.

Each night on the trail, as Hannah and Christian drew nearer and nearer to Fort Webster, Hannah dreamed of dark gallows and hangman's nooses and heard the desperate cries of the Lakota people. She tossed and turned, feeling terrified by the pictures in her head, and snuggled up to Christian during these times, trying to block out the memories of the dreams. She also worried for her parents and siblings; and hoped that they had not been targeted because of her association with the Lakota Indians; and said as much to Christian. He hugged her close to him and responded: "Hannah, your Papa is an able man and can protect his family, and remember the Lakotas are indebted to you, because of all you have done for them, they will protect your family." She nodded and said sleepily: "Yes, you are right Chris, I am being silly, I must stop worrying so much."

The night before they arrived at the fort, Hannah's gifting stirred within her, just before she fell asleep, and although she dreamed of dark gallows and hangman's nooses again, she also dreamed of a great whirlwind that blew them all away." The dream startled her and she woke up, sitting upright, and shook Christian's sleeping form beside her, saying: "Christian, wake up, I need to tell you about my dream." Patiently turning over, Christian looked at her startled face and dishevelled hair, and asked: "What is it, Hannah, are you alright?" Hannah's eyes had that faraway look again, and he worried that maybe the strain of all that had happened to her in the last few months, was now taking its toll.

Hannah then spoke in a halting voice and said: "Chris, my gifting has told me that although the President has made the right decision, it will not come in time, to stop the killings of the Indians and so a mighty whirlwind will be sent, to delay the evil men; until the President's messenger arrives." "What do you mean a mighty whirlwind, Hannah, and what is your part in it?" Christian demanded. "I will not let you come to harm, even if is to save those precious indians." Christian said with conviction. As if seeing him for the first time, Hannah looked at Christian tenderly and said: "Chris, my gifting has told me that I must let Little Crow and his braves, and the white soldiers know that the winds of justice are coming, but I don't know exactly how just yet." Christian looked at her incredulously and said: "That will put you at grave risk, Hannah, and you might even be arrested, and you won't be able to help the Lakotas if you are behind bars." Hannah focussed on Christian and thought he looked like a small boy, with his yellow hair tousled from sleep and wearing his long handled underwear; but she could hear the honest concern in his voice and said: "Chris, surely you must know by now, I won't disobey my gifting, even if I must sacrifice myself in the process." "Well then, I will stand with you, Hannah, because your Papa entrusted you to my care, and I will keep my promise to him," Christian said stubbornly. "Yes, Chris that will be fine, it will help me to have the courage I need to do this thing, for I am frightened right down to my toes," she admitted.

Henry and Cornelia had found a minister to marry them in Washington D.C. and had married the day after Henry's meeting with the President. Before she left, Hannah had helped Cornelia choose a beautiful lilac dress made of the finest linen material and having no other frills, Cornelia was happy to walk down the aisle with Henry and say her vows. Henry had been generous and paid for more dresses, chemises and petticoats and another pair of boots for Cornelia; because with the flooding, and his illness, there had been little time to retrieve her own clothes in New York City, before they had left. He also bought clothes for Helga and Olaf and the children squealed with delight at their purchases, when he paid for them. The next day, still having the stock wagon, the couple prepared themselves to leave for the Dakota Territory, putting the excited children in the back of the wagon. Cornelia warned them to be quiet and behave, and then climbed up beside her new husband on the buckboard and smiled at his dear face. Henry winked at her and said: "Well what's that smile about, Love? If I didn't know any better, I would think you were happy to be here with me?" he added cheekily. Cornelia grinned broader and said: "You silly man, you are more than a bargain for me, and I am happy to be startin' a new life with you," and then kissed him boldly on the lips. Henry grinned and quipped: "I am blessed because you are a passionate woman, Cornelia, I just hope to God I can keep up with you." Cornelia shot back good-naturedly: "Life with me will never be boring, Henry, of that you can be sure." With that, Henry laughed and snapped the reins and clicked to the horses to begin moving, and the newly formed family began their way to their new home in the Dakota Territory.

Chapter 39

Hannah and Christian rode into Fort Webster, weary from the long trip. They had made good time, however; and the journey had only taken them three weeks. Christian looked at Hannah and could see the strain on her face. She had taken to piling her hair on top of her head, which was a habit she had acquired whilst under the influence of Cornelia. He thought to himself, she had really grown up in the last year; and looked every inch a young woman rather than a little girl. He was proud of her intelligence and heart to help people; and in his eyes she was beautiful to look at. Yet he worried that this time her gifting had taken her a step too far, and Christian stayed close to her to make sure she was protected at all times.

The young people both dismounted and led their horses over to a central watering trough to give them a drink. They then loosened the saddle girths on their horses and tied the animals to a hitching post. At that point, Hannah and Christian decided they needed to eat and drink themselves, before anything further could be done; and went to the company store, buying enough to slake their immense hunger and thirst. After eating, Christian nervously asked her, "What do we do now, Hannah, do you have any direction?" She answered, saying: "No, my gifting has only said, that I have to find the gallows we have heard so much about for now." Christian agreed and followed Hannah dutifully, around the back of the main buildings of the fort and they both saw an imposing structure directly across from the army stockade, which was equipped with ten gallows that had been prepared for the hanging of twenty condemned prisoners at a time.

Hannah stifled a cry, putting her hand over her mouth, when she saw the hideous structure, and coincidentally she looked across at the barred window of the stockade, and noticed that several Indian prisoners were watching them. Hannah had been told by her gifting, that she must inform Little Crow and the army soldiers about the winds of justice coming soon; and she walked to the outer perimeter of the stockade, and stood on her tip toes to see in. The unwashed bodies of the indian men, was the first thing that assaulted her nostrils when Hannah looked inside the prison; but she kept her resolve and continued to search for anyone she knew.

At last, her persistence paid off, and she saw Little Crow, sitting upright in a corner of the stockade, with his arms folded across his chest. Hannah called to Christian to help her and he came up behind her lifting her small frame higher, so that she could see the Chief and she spoke loudly to Little Crow, saying: "Great Chief, it is Hannah, come and speak to me by the window please?" Startled to hear her voice, Little Crow looked in her direction and upon recognising her, stiffly rose to his feet and walked to the window of the stockade.

Hannah was horrified to see how much weight the Chief had lost, and could clearly count the ribs on his gaunt frame, and tears sprang to her eyes. Little Crow looked at her solemnly and nodded when he met her eyes; but his grateful expression showed how glad he was to see her. Hannah impatiently wiped the tears from her eyes, and said to him, gently, "Great Chief, it is good to see you. We spoke to President Lincoln in Washington D.C. and I believe he is going to help you and your people; but it may take some time." Staying calm, Little Crow spoke quietly to her and replied: "White Buffalo Woman, time is not something we have on our side right now, as you can see," he said motioning to the gallows, "the white man's only wish is to kill us." Hannah undaunted by his discouraged tone responded and said: "Yes, I know you and your people have suffered much at the hands of these evil men; but take heart Great Chief, a miracle is going to happen very soon and will delay these hangings until the President's help arrives. Watch from your window each day; and you will see it with your own eyes," she instructed. Little Crow's eyes widened with amazement when he heard her words; but he had great faith in her gifting and he bowed his head in thanks, saying: "You have honoured us again with your obedience to your calling White Buffalo Woman, I will wait by the window and watch as you have asked."

Just then, Christian broke in and said: "Hannah, we must go now, the army guard is coming!" The Chief shrank back from the prison window to avoid being seen; and Hannah and Christian quickly darted around the other side of the stockade to stay hidden, as well; and then walked across the compound to the market stalls, to appear as normal as possible. Hannah whispered To Christian: "That was too close for comfort, Chris. Did you see how badly The Great Chief has suffered?" Not daring to look at her, Christian replied, "Yes, but he is strong in here, Hannah," pointing to his heart, "and that will keep him alive. I shall have the horses ready to ride; when you decide to call in the winds of justice, for sure, so try to find out the timings of this thing, will you?" he added.

As midday approached, Hannah felt her gifting stir in a different direction and said to Christian: "I must take some time by myself because my gifting has more instructions to impart. Please wait for me here and I will be back within the hour," she added. Looking confused, Christian knew better than to question Hannah when she was under the power of her gifting and patiently responded: "Stay inside the fort, Hannah, perhaps you can go to where the livestock are being kept, there are less people there to distract you." Hannah nodded, grateful for his understanding and replied: "Thanks Chris, I will do that, let us meet back at the market stalls soon," and then turned and walked away without a backward glance. Christian watched her go, wishing with all his heart he could take her burdens away from her; but he knew the gifting she carried was hers and hers alone, so he was resolved to support her anyway he could. Christian knew the fierce protectiveness he felt towards Hannah, was borne from the deep love he felt for her and he was determined to make her life easier in the days ahead.

Christian waited nervously by the market stalls in the allotted time Hannah had given him, and he was relieved to finally see her walking towards him with a contemplative look on her face, an hour later. He glanced at her curiously and said: "Well that took a while, what now Hannah? Did you get the direction you needed?" he inquired. Hannah looked up as if broken from a spell, and met his eyes saying quietly: "Come, walk with me, I must tell you the new instructions I have been given, and it will not be easy for you to hear." Christian feeling concerned, did as she asked and when they were out of ear shot of the soldiers and market stall vendors, Hannah began speaking, saying: "Christian the winds of justice will not be coming today. I have been told by my gifting I must speak to the Fort Commander, General Hart and tell him that unless he puts a stop to the inhumane treatment of Little Crow and the Indian captives, that a mighty wind will be sent to destroy the fort in three days' time." Christian gasped and said more loudly then he intended: "You can't go in there and tell General Hart that, he will either laugh you out of his office or put you in chains." Hannah shushed him, and said: "Christian be quiet, people will hear you." She then looked at his worried face with stubborn conviction and declared: "Surely, you must know by now, I cannot disobey my gifting, whatever the cost." Christian admired her pluckiness, but was still gravely concerned and responded: "Hannah, this isn't some kind of game you are playing, this is your life you are putting in jeopardy, these indians that you love so much, are hated in these parts and are destined for the hangman's noose." Keeping her stance, Hannah retorted: "Not if I have anything to say about it, right will prevail, you will see." Christian then realised he was fighting a losing battle, and drew her behind the fort barracks, and put his arms around her and gave Hannah a long hug. He whispered against her hair and said, "Be careful my love, I can't lose you, even if it is the right thing to do." Hannah looked up at him contritely and kissed him on the cheek, saying: "It will be alright Chris, you will see, right will prevail."

Chapter 40

By late afternoon, Hannah was able to ramp up her courage and walked to General Hart's office to give him her message. She walked towards the military office and looked uncertainly at the two guards stationed at the door, saying: "Begging your pardon, Sirs; but I must see General Hart, to give him a message." The younger guard looked at the petite girl and smiled indulgently: "Miss, the general is a very busy man, so if you have baked him a pie or need to give him a message from your parents, we will make sure he gets it." Frustrated at his attitude, Hannah held her ground and said: "No, I must deliver the message myself; and I only need five minutes of his time, if you please?" The older of the two guards, looked at Hannah's determined face and finally said: "Okay Miss, if it is that important, what is your name and I will announce you to the General?" Smiling sweetly at the older man, Hannah replied: "My name is Hannah Nelson, Sir, and thank you." The guard went inside the office and returned shortly, saying: "The General will see you now, young Hannah; but please be quick about it, because he does not like to be kept waiting." She straightened her shoulders, tilting her chin upwards and nodded agreeably, whilst walking quickly through the office door. Upon entering the office, Hannah saw a thin, middle-aged man with spectacles and silver grey hair with a severe look on his face. She stood uncomfortably before him, waiting for him to speak, and when he finally did, he said impatiently: "Well what is it, young woman, I haven't much time, I have a stack of invoices that I need to get through before sundown." Hannah swallowed a few times and cleared her throat, not wishing to appear nervous before him, even though she was petrified. She then spoke in a high, shrill voice, saying: "Sir, I have a God given gift, which I have been honoured with since I was a child and it has spoken to me to give you a message." Hannah saw the exasperated look on General Hart's face; but remained undeterred by his cynicism and rushed on saying: "My gifting has told me that if you do not stop your inhumane practices against Little Crow and the Indian captives, the winds of justice will be sent to destroy Fort Webster within three days." Taken aback by her words, the beleaguered General scratched his head, saying: "Young woman I am far too busy for this claptrap, kindly remove yourself from my office," and then waved her out of his office, callously dismissing her.

Hannah walked out of the military office with her head held high, and hid the sting of tears that threatened to flow down her cheeks. Christian was not far away and she went to find him and seek comfort, after her words had been totally ignored by the General. Christian looked at her woebegone face and asked: "What did the General say? Did he take you seriously?" Hannah could only shake her head as her throat was closed with emotion. Christian squeezed her hand and said encouragingly: "We knew your words would not be easy for him to hear, Hannah. You showed great courage today by following through with your gifting's instruction," he added, "so what happens next my love?" Hannah finally found her voice and said woodenly: "Christian, my gifting has said that I must go and warn General Hart two more times, tomorrow and the next day; and then if he does not stop his mistreatment of Chief Little Crow and the indian captives, then Fort Webster will be destroyed."

Henry and Cornelia had made good time on the trail, travelling in the covered wagon with their two children. The middle-aged couple had fallen deeply in love, and were excited to be spending their lives together and talked endlessly of their plans for the future. After the fourth week, the family were camping along the Lakota River, and Henry was savvy enough to keep his eyes open for renegade Indians. But the truth was, Henry had been made aware before leaving Washington D.C. that over three hundred Sioux Indian braves were being rounded up by army soldiers; and in his mind the back of the Sioux nation had been severely fractured, so the threat was probably minimal. Henry's heart grieved for the wild and proud Sioux people. he had come to love and respect during his years on the frontier; yet he knew that between President Lincoln's sense of fairness and the enormous gifting and courage of his extraordinary friend, Hannah Nelson, that somehow right would prevail. "There can be no other outcome," he thought and so he lived in hope that when he and his family arrived to Fort Webster, that peace and order would be restored.

Hannah and Christian camped that night inside the fort, because even though they both longed to see their families, Hannah was duty bound to carry out the rest of the instruction from her gifting. She felt sick with fear at the thought of having to face General Hart again; but was careful not to voice her fears to Christian, because she knew his protectiveness might be a barrier in the days ahead. The next morning, they both woke to the military bugle at dawn, and Hannah quickly washed her face with the water in her canteen and pinned up her hair. Christian gave her a steaming cup of coffee, having already been awake for a half an hour and he looked tenderly at her sleepy face. "Are you ready for today my love?" he ventured cautiously. She raised her eyes and met his with a determined look and replied: "Yes, Chris, I must not falter, for the lives of Little Crow and his tribe are at stake." He grinned at her encouragingly: "I know, I haven't exactly agreed with these doom and gloom announcements you are making to General Hart; but Hannah, I have seen the wonders of your gifting too many times, to doubt you now; and I have a feeling this will somehow all come right." Hannah still solemn and somewhat frightened by the daunting task which lay ahead of her; looked at him gratefully saying: "Chris, thank you, your words mean a lot to me right now. I may as well get this deed over with right after breakfast, please wait for me by the market stalls again and I will try to meet you there when I am finished," she added. After a quick meal of bread and buffalo jerky, and another cup of steaming coffee; Hannah hugged Christian and walked again towards General Hart's office halting before the two army guards which stood at the door.

The older guard gave Hannah a friendly grin and said: "Well hello there, little lady, have you come to have a chat with General Hart again today? I'll warn you now, he wasn't too happy after your visit yesterday," he declared. Hannah folded her hands in front of her and tried to keep a dignified expression on her face, and looked him directly in the eye, saying: "Well Sir, I am very sorry to hear that; however, he is a hard man and doesn't take to new ideas easily, so yes; I will need to present my declaration to him once again today, if you please?" The younger guard looked at her and then at the older man beside him and retorted: "Surely you are not going to let her in again to see the General, Cecil? He gave us a fair ole' tongue lashing for letting her in there the last time," he added irritably. "Ahh, settle down Mike," the older soldier said, chuckling; "I kinda like seeing the old man riled up, it makes for a very entertainin' day." "OK then, but it is on your head if he starts barkin' at us again Cecil, do you hear me?" the young soldier replied angrily. The older soldier still grinning, with an evil gleam in his eye, winked at Hannah and said: "Miss, wait here so I can announce you and then you may go in straight away." Hannah nodded, amazed that the soldier was being so agreeable, and waited patiently, while he slipped inside the General's office. Upon his return, he stepped out of the office with a mischievous grin on his face and announced: "The General is a bit flustered Missy, but he will see you now. Go easy on him do you hear, for all our sakes." he added, chuckling. The younger guard rolled his eyes, shaking his head and declared: "Cecil, your silly brand of entertainment is going to land us in the stockade one of these days, you wait and see." He refused to meet Hannah's eyes, ignoring her completely; and the guard called Cecil, motioned for her to go inside the General's office. Reluctantly, Hannah forced herself to step through the door and she rallied her courage for yet another confrontation with the taciturn military man. General Hart was again working at his desk with an irritable expression on his face and he impatiently looked up at Hannah and asked scornfully: "Alright, what is it this time, young woman, is a lightning bolt from heaven about to strike me down?" Hannah felt angry at the man's ridicule and hit back saying: "General, you are welcome to think what you like; but regardless, I have been sent here with a message by my gifting, which I believe has been imparted to me by God." The General blinked and looked at her as if she had grown two heads and replied scathingly: "Well then, out with it young woman, so I can get on with my day."

Hannah drew herself up to her full height and said as forcefully as she could: "You have not heeded the first warning, so I am here to give you a second edict and say that if you do not desist from mistreating Little Crow and the indian captives; then the fort will be utterly destroyed by the winds of justice in a terrible catastrophe." General Hart's eyes widened in amazement and his face hardened at her words. He then muttered in a low growl, saying: "Young woman, my patience with you is wearing very thin and if you persist in wasting military time with these rantings; and if you ever come again in to this office for this purpose again, I will be forced to place you under arrest." Hannah sucked in a breath and not knowing how to respond, she quickly turned away and walked quickly out the door. The guard named Cecil saw her strained young face, and he asked kindly: "Are you alright Miss, you look flustered? What did the General say to you?" Hannah still shaken by the experience, looked at him blankly and said: "Thank you Sir, I will be fine, the General just thinks I am taking up too much of his time." He spoke again and said: "Don't take any offence Miss; he is like that with everyone." Hannah nodded her thanks and left to find Christian, feeling shaken, but satisfied she had carried out the second part of her instruction successfully. When she caught sight of him by the market stalls, she could see he was haggling with a market stall vendor over some food provisions and she walked up beside him listening patiently, whilst he negotiated a fair price for some salt pork and beans for their supper.

When he finally turned to her, Christian could see that Hannah's visit to the General had taken its' toll. She had been up half the night worrying about the fated meeting, and he was sure the interaction with the straight laced military man could not have been easy. Christian tenderly took her hand and said: "How are you my sweet, did you manage to deliver your message?" Hannah tiredly looked up at Christian and said: "Let us walk this way and then I can speak to you in private," and she pulled him in the direction of the gallows. Once arriving in front of the hideous gallows, she said bluntly: "The General is not listening and I feel very strongly that a catastrophe is about to take place, because of his stubbornness." "What do you mean Hannah; please tell me now; because I must protect you?" Christian asked anxiously. Hannah tiredly responded, saying: "Christian, my gifting has shown me that a great whirlwind is coming to destroy the fort, like none that has ever been seen before in this land; yet it will not touch me or you or Little Crow or the indian captives." Christian gave a low whistle and looked at Hannah with a shocked expression, saying: "This is grave news indeed, what must we do now, before this calamity takes place Hannah, and when will it happen?" She gave him a troubled glance and replied: "I must go once more to warn the General and then we wait." "But surely he will arrest you, if you go back there a third time, and we can't take that chance Hannah, we must leave this place," Christian said in a worried voice. She looked and spoke to him as if to a small child and said: "Chris, I have no choice. I must see this thing through until the end. We can make ready our horses and provisions and leave tomorrow to go to my family's homestead, as soon as the third warning is given to General Hart," she added, comfortingly. "But when will it hit, has your gifting given you any sense of timing at all? And what about Little Crow and the other Indian captives, won't they be locked up in the stockade and be in the direct path of the storm?" Christian asked urgently. Hannah looked at him feeling helpless and said: "My sense is that it will be very soon after I give the third warning to General Hart tomorrow and all I really know is that Little Crow, the indian captives and you and I will survive this terrible storm."

General Pope rode into Fort Webster that afternoon having completed his tour around the Dakota Territory with his regiment of military soldiers. He had successfully rounded up the remaining one hundred and fifty Sioux braves to be tried and sent to death in the remaining weeks. He knew that President Lincoln was focussed on winning the Civil War and so in his eyes he had total carte blanche to purge the Dakota Territory of the indian savages, even though the President had threatened him with a court martial. In his opinion, the indians were a savage scourge which blighted the land and needed to be gotten rid of as soon as possible. He had shackled the proud braves and joined their chains together in an attempt to break their spirits and cause them to be more manageable; yet they still held fast to their dignity and fixed their eyes on him with arrogant and angry stares.

General Pope dismounted his horse, tying it close to the military command office; for he was intent on speaking to General Hart. A heavy man with greying hair and a full beard, General Pope's stomach rumbled as he smacked his lips eager to eat his evening meal. He entered the office and spoke loudly to the tense, and in his mind annoying, General Hart; and said: "Hart, have you managed to hang some of those indians in the stockade; because I have brought more of the savages in, and we need to make room for them in the stockade?" To General Pope, General Hart looked like a beady eyed bird and the smaller man jumped when he heard his commanding officer's voice. Hart knew that even though they were the same rank, Lincoln had clearly appointed General Pope as the ultimate commander of the Dakota Territory; so he did his best to meet the ever increasing demands of his colleague, as best he could.

"Well no Sir, I have had a lot of work on, so I thought I would start the executions by the end of the week," Hart responded weakly. "What," Pope roared, "get some balls, man; these murderers need to be exterminated as soon as possible. I want you to start hanging those Injun dogs starting tomorrow, do you hear me?" he shouted angrily. "As it is, my men have to forego a much needed rest to guard these savages we have outside, overnight; until there is room in the stockade," he bellowed. General Hart looked at his superior officer glumly, and said: "Yes Sir, whatever you say, Sir." Satisfied, Pope then left the office in search of something to eat,

John Blair Smith Todd, the first delegate to the Dakota Territory in the U.S. House of Representatives; had ridden his mount hard to try to reach Fort Webster in a shorter amount of time. Todd was trusted by the President, because of his common sense and had fought bravely as a General in the Union Army during the first part of the Civil War. Being a muscular and fit man, he had managed to cut the normally six week journey down to four weeks, and he expected to be arriving at the fort in the next few days, by his estimation. The President had taken him into his confidence, prior to his leaving the White House; and Todd knew the direction he must take when he delivered the President's letter. Todd had never been an admirer of General Pope. In fact, he considered him to be the biggest fool he had ever met, and he looked forward to taking him down a peg or two, when he arrived. He had every intention of restoring peace and order, as much as possible, to the Dakota Territory; and he was very aware that as the senior government official, that it would be his responsibility to take over the reins of territorial control from the military leaders, as soon as possible, and that is what he intended to do.

Hannah and Christian ate dinner that evening in virtual silence, both feeling the pressure of what was about to happen to the fort. Hannah particularly felt the strain of the impending disaster; because she knew she must go and warn General Hart one more time and she desperately hoped he would listen to her words the next day. But she didn't hold out much hope that this would be the case, because he was a stiff necked man and had not believed her warnings in the slightest.

Chapter 41

The next morning, Christian hovered around Hannah and wouldn't let her out of his sight for several hours. Hannah was grateful for his comforting presence and busied herself packing their things for the journey to her family's homestead, and also talked with Christian about her family. Around mid-morning, she decided it was time to go and see General Hart and felt the nerves tighten in the pit of her stomach. She kissed Christian on the cheek and said quietly: "I must go now Chris, and speak to General Hart. Don't worry, I will be back before you know it, just wait by this hitching post; and we can ride out of this wretched fort before the storm hits," she added, squeezing his hand. Christian looked at her anxiously and advised: "Just say what you have to say to that stubborn man, and get back here as soon as possible; because we need to be long gone before that storm hits, Hannah." She nodded and walked across the compound to the military command office. As usual, the guards, Cecil and Mike were stood outside the General's office and Cecil greeted her warmly and said: "Hello Little Miss, are you here for a third round with the General; because I think you will find there are two in there today, General Hart and General Pope." "Oh, that is surprising," Hannah exclaimed, "but I still need to go in there and say my piece, is that alright?" Cecil said good naturedly: "Well I'm game if you are, Missy, you just wait here and let Ole' Cecil work his magic." Without waiting for her to respond, he slipped inside the office to announce her, and she could hear raised voices inside. After a few minutes, the older guard stepped back outside and declared with humour: "Little Lady, I am not sure what exactly you have said; but you have General Hart tied up in knots. To be honest, he didn't want me to let you in his office; but General Pope overruled him, so good luck Miss, this should be interesting," he chuckled. The other guard stayed quiet, not wishing to get involved; but continued to roll his eyes at his fellow guard's antics. Hannah steeled her nerves and took a deep breath meekly entering the office. General Hart was not sitting at his desk, as usual; but had given his normal seat to his superior, General Pope; and sat awkwardly at a side desk not far away. Hannah looked at General Hart and then uncertainly at General Pope and she was distressed to see the cruel curl of the man's lip and his hard stare. General Pope's thick jowls literally hung from his face and his bushy beard seemed to add to his sinister appearance. "Well, what is it girl? I hear you have been coming in here spouting off about those injun devils and distracting General Hart with your nonsense?" he declared sharply.

Hannah felt a great indignation grip her heart and her gifting rose up within her with every fibre of her being and she said angrily: "You Sir, are an evil man and I have heard much about your unjust dealings with the Sioux Indians across this land. "What gives you the right to arrange the mass murders of these people," she asked forcefully. "And be warned in two hours' time, if you do not stop this grave maltreatment of Little Crow and the indian captives; then the winds of justice will utterly destroy Fort Webster," she declared. General Pope's fury was evident on his face and his eyes nearly popped out of his head, while an ugly blue vein pulsated on his right temple. To complete the look, his face had turned an ugly beet red colour. "Get out, you little witch, or I will clap you in irons, even if you are a woman," he shouted. "How dare you defend those savages, when they have raped and killed countless decent white men and women in these parts," he declared vehemently.

Hannah hastily left the office with her head held high, and didn't bother to speak to the guards as she hurried to find Christian. He was waiting with their horses and both young people mounted them and quickly rode out of the fort; not wishing to witness the imminent destruction of the wooden fortress. Christian looked back at Hannah as he guided his horse outside the fort gates, and said: "How did General Hart react, Hannah?" She spoke up and said: "His commanding officer, General Pope, was also there, and he is a very rude and infuriating man; and neither one is taking me seriously, Chris, which is no surprise to me." "Well we can talk about this later, let's get as far away from this place as possible, because the skies are already turning black," he declared.

In an hour's time, funnel clouds started appearing in the sky and fierce winds blew furiously across the land. The winds were blowing at speeds of up to three hundred miles per hour; and huge numbers of people and animals were feeling the effects of the hostile weather. Inside Fort Webster, Generals' Pope and Hart shouted in vain at the soldiers under their command, to secure the livestock and ordered them to remain at their stations. Panic was palatable amongst the inhabitants of the fort, when a huge and dark funnel cloud was seen headed directly towards the fortress; and many frightened soldiers and civilians alike, ran out of the gates screaming, when the twister was spotted, in an effort to escape its' deadly force.

Suddenly, a deathly quiet occurred for a few brief minutes; and then the thunderous noise of the twister could be heard as it ploughed into the walls of the fort and the wooden gallows. Horses, cattle, wagons and shards of wood were shot through the air like missiles, as the F5 tornado found its' mark, leaving death and destruction in its' wake. The imprisoned indians shouted in desperation in the stockade; fearing for their lives; yet oddly, as the twister touched down and went back up into the sky; it destroyed everything around them leaving the stockade and the camp of Pope's captured indians entirely alone. Little Crow watched with fear and trepidation, when he saw the death and destruction happening all around him; and he was awed at the power and strength of his friend Hannah's gifting, and gave thanks to the gods that he and his brothers had been spared from this terrible calamity.

The aftermath of the Fort Webster tornado, was dire indeed and the loss of life was a dramatic blow to the Dakota Territory. Dead carcasses of oxen, cattle, and horses were strewn across the landscape, along with over one hundred and twenty deceased men, women and children; who had lived and worked in and around the fort. Hannah and Christian had reached the safe distance of five miles away from the fort, before the twister hit; however, they had still felt the daunting effects of the high winds. Fortunately, the pair found a cave to take refuge in, until the furious storm passed, and Hannah feeling hugely distressed over the deadly storm; cried real tears of pity for the senseless loss of life due to the evil works of a few men. She also feared for Little Crow and the indian captives, and even though her gifting had told her they would live; she still said to Christian: "Once the storm stops, I want to check for myself that they have survived." Christian shook his head and bluntly said; "No, Hannah, you must wait for the news to come to you. I will not allow you to be further distressed by the sight of dead bodies," he said. "You did all you could, to warn those stiff necked men; and you are not to blame for what has happened," he added firmly. Hannah curled up against him and said: "Thank you for taking care of me, Chris, this is the hardest thing I have ever had to go through and this terrible storm has frightened me to no end."

Cecil walked along the well-worn path away from what was left of Fort Webster; and was not sure exactly how he had managed to live through the terrible twister which had torn its' way through the wooden fort, in the past few hours. He also didn't know where he was going, but was happy to be alive, for the only ones still alive back at the fort, were the Indians and a much diminished General Pope, who was half out of his mind. But he was not one to shirk his duties, and Cecil had decided he would seek out help from some farmers who perhaps had weathered the storm safely, and had set out determinedly to achieve that purpose. Cecil remembered vaguely how General Pope had ordered him to guard the indian captives that the General and his men had brought in, earlier in the day; and then suddenly their entire world had been turned upside down by the deadly carnage caused by the twister in the next few moments. Somehow Pope had ended up with the Indian captives too and the eerie twister had destroyed out buildings and structures all around the perimeters of the indian captives and the stockade; and he and Pope had watched countless people and animals being swept up by the tornado and killed right before their eyes.

Cecil didn't know how long he had walked, but as the afternoon started reaching the evening hours, he began to despair that he would not find anyone alive at all; as it seemed all signs of life had been consumed by the ghastly storm. At last, he heard the whinny of a horse and started walking towards the sound; and as he approached the clearing past a grove of trees, he noticed two horses grazing by a large cave. Cecil could smell food cooking on a fire, and he cautiously approached the cave in hopes that whoever was in there would be friendly. He then walked through the mouth of the cave and tried to refocus his eyes, so he could see in the darkness and a huge grin spread across his face when he saw Hannah and Christian sitting by the fire. "Well I'll be, Little Miss, you are a sight for sore eyes you are; how did you manage to escape that terrible twister that hit the fort?" he asked. Hannah was startled to see Cecil, but was very relieved at the sight of him; and jumped to her feet and ran across to the older man giving him a hug. "Cecil, you are alive, I am so happy to see you," she exclaimed. "You were so nice to me, when I had to go and speak to the General, and for that I am grateful," she added. Christian came up behind her and shook Cecil's hand, introducing himself, and said; "We left before the storm hit; but can you tell us what happened back there?" Cecil replied: "Yes, I will do that; but could I trouble you for a bit of food and water, I have been walking for hours and feel dead on my feet?" Hannah said: "Sorry Cecil, where are our manners? Please sit down you must be exhausted," she added and with that Hannah set about getting him some food and handed him a steaming cup of coffee for good measure.

Finally, when he had ravenously consumed his meal and had drunk a second cup of coffee, Cecil began recounting the gruesome details of the deadly storm. "It was the strangest thing I have ever seen," he declared, "that twister touched down and destroyed the offices, the outbuildings, the gallows, and the walls of the

fort; yet went straight up into the sky and did not touch the indian captives or the military stockade where the others were being held. Generals Pope and Hart were shouting at us soldiers to
stay at our stations; but men, women, and children were screaming and crying and being swept up into the mouth of that twister
and disappeared right before our eyes. General Pope ran across
and joined me in the Indian encampment; but I never saw General Hart again, but he could have been dropped by that twister
two fields away, for all I know," he added.

Tears were streaming down Hannah's face as the details of
the story unfolded, and she said emotionally: "Thank you Cecil for telling us what happened; I know it could not have been
easy for you." Cecil gave her a kindly look and feeling curious,
he asked: "What was your part in this Miss, did you know this
storm was coming? Of course, I have heard the rumours about
your powers; but I never believed them until now," he commented. Christian intervened and said: "Let us stop while we are
ahead, Sir; this has all been very hard on Hannah; and I would
prefer for her not to be distressed any more today." Giving Christian an understanding look, Cecil replied: "I understand young
man; however, I will need for someone to go back with me to
the fort, to give help to the living and bury the dead; can you
lend a hand in helping me to round up a few farmers, as soon
as possible?" "Yes, it is another five miles, Cecil, to Hannah's
family homestead and mine is a mere eight miles away," Christian responded. "Let me get Hannah safely to her family; then I
will bring some men back with me to help at the fort, as soon as
possible," he explained. Cecil thanked him and saw that it was
getting late and accepted the young couple's invitation to spend
the night with them in the cave. He then set out at first light, to
head back to the fort.

Christian and Hannah went the opposite direction to the Nelson homestead that morning; and both young people felt they
had been gone for a lifetime. At last, after two hours of travelling, they reached the Nelson homestead and although Hannah's
father Eric was already out in the fields; she was delighted to see

her mama and little sister, Maggie, hanging out laundry on a clothes line her father had erected at the side of the house. Hannah was amazed at the changes in little Maggie and jumped off her horse to hug her mama calling: "Mama, Mama, I am home at last." Anya's face lit up at the sight of Hannah; and Maggie, who was naturally a lively and animated child, chortled beside her mama to get her share of the attention. After kissing Anya on the cheek, Hannah exclaimed: "Mama you look healthy and happy," and leaning down to tweak the four month old child's chin, she added, smiling; "And you my little sister are pretty, as a picture." "Oh Hannah, I was so frightened for you both, I am so happy you are back safe and sound," Anya said in a heartfelt way. Christian also greeted Anya and Maggie, giving them both a kiss on the cheek and asked: "Are both Eric and Peter out in the fields, I need to speak to them, as soon as possible?" "Yes, they are in the fields, but they will be in for the noon day meal soon, please come in and refresh yourselves and they will be joining us shortly," Anya said, and they all went into the cosy homestead to catch up on much missed conversation and news

The next hour the men joined them, and Hannah and Christian recounted the events of the past few months. Eric's eyebrows furrowed with worry when he heard some of the details of the ordeal they had gone through. Hannah held nothing back and broke down in tears during some parts of her story; but persevered, intent on telling everything as clearly as she could. When she completed her tale, and had told her family everything, except for the storm hitting Fort Webster; Christian picked up the story, telling them about Cecil and what had happened as a result of the twister hitting the fort. He went on to tell them about Cecil's request for help back at the fort and waited for their response. Eric replied solemnly and said: "Yes, it is the right thing to do and we must do what we can to relieve the suffering of the living and bury the dead. Daughter, you say this General Pope would not listen to your warnings; but that he is still alive?" Eric asked. Peter then chipped in and said: "That twister must have been a sight to behold; I have never heard of anything so terrible in my life." Anya looked at her husband and son, terribly worried and blurted out: "But isn't there a chance it could come back? I don't want you two taking any chances," she exclaimed.

"Don't worry, Anya, that mighty storm was sent for a reason and has already done its' terrible work; and we will be safe enough," Eric said kindly. The men agreed to leave in the next hour in hopes they would reach the fort by nightfall. Hannah drew Christian aside and said: "Please do all you can to help Little Crow, even if you must bring him here for a time. He looked very ill to me, when I saw him last." The couple embraced and Christian agreed to help the Great Chief to the best of his ability, and then kissed her tenderly saying, "Now you just rest and get over this ordeal. You have been very strong and brave; but now it is time for you to restore yourself my sweet Hannah," he added; and giving her one more hug, left with the men to go and help Cecil and the indians.

Chapter 42

J.B.S Todd looked towards the horizon and couldn't believe his eyes when he saw instead of a large military fort; what looked to be a pile of rubble. He urged his horse forwards, wondering with a sense of dread, what had happened there; and as he rode closer he saw white men and indians alike, digging graves for the dead. He then quickly trotted his horse to where the men were digging and asked loudly: "What has happened here, Sirs?" A tall army soldier walked across to the newly arrived General and saluted him, saying: "Sir, we were struck by a fearsome twister and it has totally destroyed the fort, killing over a one hundred and twenty people or more and nearly all the livestock." General Todd pushed his hat back on his head and looked at the man in disbelief, and responded: "How long ago did this happen Corporal and is General Pope still among the living?" Cecil looked directly at the newly arrived military man and said: "Sir, it happened only yesterday, and although General Hart is among the missing, General Pope is very much alive; but if you excuse me for saying so, Sir, he is not himself at all."

Just then, Christian walked up to join the two and asked: "Sir, have you come recently from Washington D.C.; because we have been waiting for help from President Lincoln concerning the indian captives?" General Todd dismounted his horse and said: "Yes, I am here as the First Delegate for the Dakota Territory and I mean to put to rights the terrible injustices that have been happening in these parts. Corporal, if you can kindly take my horse and give him a drink; he has been a faithful beast during my travels," and he handed Cecil the reins. Cecil agreeably took responsibility for the horse; and General Todd turned to Christian and asked: "What is your name young man and can you tell me what has been happening here prior to the storm?"

Christian introduced himself and gave the short version of how he and Hannah, along with Henry Whipple had visited President Lincoln on behalf of the indians. He further explained about Hannah's gifting and how she had warned the Generals Hart and Pope about the twister before it came; and that neither man had taken her seriously. General Todd listened patiently to the words of the young man and didn't pass judgement and then asked: "And Pope, where is he now?" Christian responded: "We have released the indians from the stockade and placed him in there instead; because he seems to have truly lost his mind since the storm hit, Sir." General Todd's eyes widened and he said: "Well Christian, President Lincoln has given a reprieve to Little Crow and his three hundred Sioux braves, and only fifteen renegades are to be rounded up and hanged for their murderous crimes against the white settlers. With your help and the help of the white settlers, we will restore order here and I believe we can develop a civilised community that we can be proud of; but for now let us bury the dead." Christian shook his hand and said: "Sir, with your permission, I will be returning Little Crow to his people tomorrow; as his health has suffered greatly because of the poor conditions he has had to endure, during his extended captivity in the Fort Webster stockade." "Yes, Christian, do as you must; but I would like to meet the Great Chief before he makes his journey home," General Todd requested.

Eight weeks later, music could be heard playing merrily at a celebration at the Nelson homestead. Hannah stayed inside the cabin, while her mama and Cornelia fussed over her dress and hair, and she was terrified that she would not remember all the words during the wedding ceremony. But at last, after all they had been through; she was going to marry the man she loved, Christian. Cornelia and Henry had returned to the Dakota Territory three days after the twister had annihilated Fort Webster, and were like second parents to both she and Christian, and she was very glad to have them back. Hannah tapped her foot to the beat of Henry's fiddle, as he played a lively tune, and she was honoured that he had agreed to marry them. "Well it's about time," he had said chuckling at them, when he had been asked. Christian had kept his promise and brought Little Crow to meet General Todd before helping the weakened Chief return to his people and General Todd had formally apologised to the beleaguered Sioux leader at the time; and had promised that things would be different and better for the indians and the Dakota Territory in the future. Of course, Little Crow had heard it all before, but he was grateful to be alive and free; so he decided to nod amiably without comment. He was anxious to return to his people and to see his wife and sons, and didn't want any more trouble.

White settlers had come from all over the Dakota Territory to attend the couple's nuptials; because Hannah's fame had spread across the land like wildfire after the tornado destroyed Fort Webster. Eric was dressed in a black suit and tie; and waited eagerly to escort Hannah during the wedding march down the aisle and marry her. Another nearby farmer had agreed to play the fiddle, whilst Henry officiated at the ceremony, and the women had been cooking for days for the wedding celebration. Christian was over the moon that at last he would be married to his brave and beautiful Hannah; and he couldn't wait to start a new life with her. Eric was worried that the couple's fame would be very tough on the pair during the wedding; and in the future, but was resigned to the fact that there was very little he could do to change things. But he did feel that Christian had proven he was the right man to protect his daughter and was satisfied with her choice.

General Todd was even in attendance and added an air of dignity to the affair; and had proven in the last two months, to be true to his word in bringing peace and order to the Dakota Territory. Although most white settlers and Indians were still uncomfortable with each other, the old animosity had died down significantly since the catastrophe at Fort Webster. Hundreds of Sioux Indian braves had been set free in the aftermath of the twister; and only twenty renegade Indians, as promised by Todd, had been hung in the end, for crimes against the white man.

Little Maggie cried out in jealousy, when her mother put her down on a blanket to play, not far from where Hannah sat, clearly not understanding why her big sister was getting all the attention. Cornelia laughed and picked the young baby up, holding her close and said to her in a jolly voice: "Come now you little beauty, we can't have you getting tear stains all over your dress, you are going to be the prettiest baby at your big sister's wedding," and then she kissed Maggie on the cheek and held her affectionately on her lap. The raven haired child looked at Cornelia with her cherubic face and smiled back, not really understanding what she was saying; but she clearly was enjoying the attention. "Oh Mama, I hope everything goes well, I want everything to be perfect," Hannah declared. "It will, you will see," Anya assured her. "People have been cooking for days and there will be dancing and celebrating for the rest of the evening," she added, "which will be most welcome after all that has happened in the last six months or more in these parts." "Now Anya, there will be no talk of hard times on today of all days, because your lovely daughter is getting married to the man of her dreams; and our men are dressed up for a change," Cornelia declared, jokingly. "That is enough to smile about right there," she quipped.

Just then, Eric cracked the door open to peek inside the homestead and said: "Hannah, I know you are getting ready for your big day; but there is someone out here that wants to see you and I think you had better come." Hannah hadn't seen Little Crow since before the twister hit Fort Webster; but she had thought about him and the Lakota people every single day for two months. Christian had taken the weakened Little Crow back to his family and tribe after the Fort Webster catastrophe; and he had forbade Hannah to go to see the Chief and Lakota people because he rationalised that the Great Chief was a proud man and needed time alone to heal and to be with his people to plan what they would do next. Hannah could understand what Christian was saying, and agreed to give Little Crow time and space; but still had worried about him continually; and wondered if maybe her visitor was him. She eagerly put on her shoes and looked at Cornelia and Anya, saying: "I won't be long, I promise and I can put on my wedding dress when I get back." Both women looked at

Hannah with an exasperated expression and before they could put up an argument, she slipped out the front door with her papa. Eric then took her to the back of the cabin; because he claimed: "It is bad luck for Christian to see the bride before the wedding." Then suddenly, Hannah put her hand to her mouth and her eyes welled up with emotion, when she saw Little Crow and his braves standing before her with a pure white buffalo calf in the centre of a small circle. Little Crow nodded to her solemnly; and gave her a warm and welcoming look, and said: "White Buffalo Woman, I have come to wish you good fortune and many happy years ahead with your new husband. I also bring to you the most precious gift the Lakota people can offer, a white buffalo calf; which is a symbol that all living beings are linked together and despite the hard times we have endured, we have proven together, you and your family and the Lakota people, can be as one, and that as long as people learn to protect and value each other, that all men can live in peace and harmony throughout life." He continued and said: "The white buffalo calf brings the message 'that all people watched over by it,' will not only survive; but that their lives will have great value in this world. You, White Buffalo Woman, will always be honoured by our people; because you have watched over our people like a mother has looked after a child," he added. "May you have much happiness in your life and continue to use your gifting as a light and safe place for all men," he concluded.

Extremely overwhelmed at Little Crow's speech, Hannah was at a loss for words at first and then she quickly shook herself and replied: "It has been a great honour for me to help you and your people Great Chief and I will gladly take the white buffalo calf and treasure him always." She then looked at Little Crow more closely and found with relief that he looked like he had gained weight, and aside from a few more lines on his face, he seemed fit and healthy again. "Can you and your braves stay as special guests at my wedding?" Hannah asked. "I would be most honoured if you could," she added. Little Crow sadly shook his head and responded: "It would not be wise with so many white settlers here to honour you, White Buffalo Woman, and I do not wish to disturb the fragile peace that we have all worked so hard to ensure," he said honestly. Although disappointed, Hannah understood his line of thinking; and asked: "But where will you and your people go now, Great Chief; and will I ever see you again?" Little Crow answered, saying: "The elders have finally agreed with me, that my people should be moving on to Canada; so that we can begin a brand new life," he informed her gently. "We will meet again as the gods see fit, my dear friend; and please remember always; that if you call to the wind; we will hear you; because you are a part of us and we are a part of you, and the Lakota people will always keep you close to their hearts." The Chief then spoke a command in the Lakota language and motioned for the brave holding the calf with a rope around its' neck; to lead the lumbering animal to Eric. He handed the rope to Eric and without delay, Little Crow said: "I wish you well, White Buffalo Woman," and turned to go, with his braves following closely behind him.

Watching them go, Hannah's tears started flowing in earnest; and she walked into Eric's arms and said: "Oh Papa, what will I ever do without them?" Eric held her close for a time, and patted her back and finally said: "When one door closes another door opens; my daughter; you have many adventures just around the corner, and your gifting will carry you from strength to strength; as you obediently follow its' direction. "Now dry your eyes; because we have a wedding to attend and we better get back to the homestead quick, before your Mama and Cornelia, send out a search party for us," he added comically, kissing her on the cheek.

Later that day, Hannah and Christian joined their lives together, as man and wife; in a joyous wedding ceremony; in which there was much laughter during Henry's best man speech and good food and dancing was enjoyed by all. Hannah was dressed in a deep purple muslin dress with a beautiful brocade neckline, cut down from one of Cornelia's best dresses and refashioned to fit her perfectly. Christian was dressed in a white cotton shirt and a purple and grey vest to match Hannah's dress. During the evening hours of the dance, Christian took Hannah's hand and led her to the dance floor and said romantically, in her ear: "I am married to the most beautiful girl in the world and even though, at times, I will have to share you; because of your great gifting, there will always be a part of you that is totally and completely mine." Hannah looked at her new husband lovingly and said, with humour: "I am so proud to be your wife, and remember, it is not every day that a man can boast he is married to a White Buffalo Woman." Christian drew her to him and kissed her full on the mouth and said: "I would say you are more of an Angel, my love, than a White Buffalo Woman, and your loving-kindness towards those in need, is an inspiration to us all."

The author

Leisa Ebere, was originally born in San Francisco,
California in the USA; and now resides in Graves-
end in the UK. She is married has three children
and one grandchild. She works as a Medical
Practice Manager and when she's not doing that,
she writes for an online newspaper. Leisa has been
writing poems and stories since the age of twelve
and was inspired to write Crows and Angels,
her debut novel, by the stories her grandmother
told her, of her ancestors settling in the Dakota
Territory. Leisa is 1/16 Sioux Indian by birth and has
a special place in her heart for Native Americans.
Her aim is to tell their side of the story through her
writing.